ANDREW GRAYSON (WITH CUTTER SIMMONS AND THE SAMARITANS)

The Christmas Meeting

This novel is entirely a work of fiction. The events portrayed in it are the work of the author's imagination; however, the author has tried to accurately represent the backgrounds and views of the historical figures featured in this novel.

First edition

ISBN: 979-8-218-36353-6

Editing by Adana Gardner Marfield

This book was professionally typeset on Reedsy.
Find out more at reedsy.com

To my lovely wife who endured listening to me read my chapters aloud, and to my children who offered generous encouragement and technical support.

"The thing about conspiracy theories is that they create the illusion that if something could happen, it did happen.

The other thing is—sometimes, it really did."

PETER HUBBARD, MENTOR,
EDUCATOR, AND FRIEND

Contents

Prologue: Oxford, Mississippi (1922)

He strode across the campus where he had dropped out—for the second time the year before—towards the post office that was his latest workplace after retreating back to the South from his dead-end job at a Greenwich Village bookstore. The young man unlocked the back door and walked into a processing room where every available surface was covered in *un*processed mail. He laid down the leather satchel and paper sack that he had carried with him from his off-campus apartment with the express purpose of *getting to work.*

He hazarded a glance at the closest pile of accumulated letters, magazines, and fliers; however, the dapper twenty-four-year-old in his summer seersucker suit quickly lost interest and deposited the annoying detritus in a trash can by the back door. As he whistled the opening bars of Fanny Brice's "Second Hand Rose," he checked his pocket watch, reclaimed his satchel and sack, and exited out the front door of the post office past a surprised group of arriving customers, pausing only to flip over the sign reading *Temporarily Closed.*

Strolling into the center of town, he soon arrived at a two-story red brick building festooned with a lacy wrought-iron railing. The young man climbed the stairs to a second-floor apartment and quietly let himself in. After preparing a breakfast tray in the kitchen, he drew back the curtains in the adjacent darkened bedroom and placed the tray on the bed beside his grandfather who was just waking up. As always, on the nightstand lay the stacked, well-worn copies of Mark Twain's *Life on the Mississippi*, Jules Verne's *Twenty Thousand Leagues Under the Sea*, and Herman Melville's *Moby Dick*. *An odd obsession with the sea*, mused the young man, *for someone who has spent almost his whole life in land-locked Oxford*. The old man squinted as he looked out the French doors that overlooked Courthouse Square to the bank where he had served as president for over a decade.

"I picked up the coffee beans at Café du Monde last week," the young man began. "I wish I could have brought you some beignets, but I didn't figure they would travel too well."

"What were you doing in New Orleans?" his grandfather asked.

"A literary magazine, the *Double Dealer*, is publishing a poem of mine. It'll be the first piece of my writing I've ever seen in print. I rode the train down to preview the galley proofs." He reached into his leather satchel and discreetly—but proudly— laid a copy of the proof beside his grandfather's tray.

"Congratulations, Billy," the old man said, "I'm sure this is just the first of many." He shakily lifted the cup to his lips and breathed in the chicory through his bushy white mustache. "Have I ever told you about my first trip to the Big Easy?"

The young man's eyes betrayed a hint of worry as he looked down at his grandfather. "Yes, you have, Grandpa, but you ought to share your story with everyone else. It's a humdinger. If I got a stenographer to come up here, would you tell her the story so she could write it down?"

"I could give it a shot, Billy. I suppose with the way my memory is fading, if I'm going to do it... it probably *can't wait*. Actually, I've never told anyone *all* of my story..."

He paused for a beat as his milky eyes with their long-ignored cataracts flickered over to his nightstand. "But who knows? Maybe it will turn out you're not the only writer in this family."

"What about your father—the Old Colonel?" the young man asked, knowing what his grandfather's reaction would be.

The old man coughed up a dismissive *humph* before mumbling the epithet "hack" that he typically pinned to his late father's dubious writing career. He gazed down at the thin paper beside the tray. Taking his bifocals from the nightstand, he adjusted them on his veined, now-crinkling nose and held up the proof—rotating the print to face his grandson. "Billy, they misspelled our last name. They've put a *u* in there."

"I know, Grandpa, but when I saw it *that way* for the first time," rationalized the young man, "it just looked right." He stood ramrod straight in his suit, puffing up his five-foot, five-inch frame as he theatrically cleared his throat.

"'Portrait,'" he recited the title block from the proof that his grandfather held before him like an orchestra conductor's score, "a poem by William Faulkner."

PART ONE: Ripley to New Orleans (December 1860-January 1861)

Chapter 1

On Christmas Day in 1862, the greatest meeting of minds in the history of the world took place—in secret—at an inn in Nantucket, Massachusetts. I know because I was there. As I begin dictating my story to Miss Betty, the stenographer that Billy has hired, I am reminded of what Benjamin Franklin wrote in his *Poor Richard's Almanack*: "Three may keep a secret, if two of them are dead."

I have kept the secret of the Christmas Meeting for half a century, and now—with my dear friend Joseph's recent passing—I am the only one still living who knows the whole truth. I've heard from my grandson that the story of my journey from Ripley, Mississippi to New Orleans, and ultimately to Nantucket, is a *humdinger*, but that's only *part* of the story. Now—before my memory recedes like the ebbing tide—maybe the rest should be told.

My nonheroic (and non-Homeric) odyssey began two years before this climactic meeting when I was a twelve-year-old runaway, banished from home after a combustible Christmas morning in 1860, exactly seven weeks after Abraham Lincoln had been elected sixteenth President of the *then* United States of America.

I was born John Wesley Thompson Falkner in Ripley in 1848, a year after my father—the "Old Colonel"—returned from fighting in the Mexican War. My mother died when I was less than a year old, so I don't have any memories of her, other than a gnawing sense of something missing from my life. The Old Colonel remarried when I was two, and our house began filling up with subsequent children. My stepmother made no pretense of caring to raise *me*, however, so those responsibilities often fell to one of the five Black slaves that my father struggled to afford.

When we gathered that morning in 1860 around the Christmas tree, a pitiful specimen of a cypress that the children had chopped down from behind the house, my father—and the presents he was responsible for procuring— were nowhere to be found. As the oldest child, I was soon surrounded by my four crying half-siblings. "John," my stepmother commanded, "light the candles on the tree. I'm sure *your* father will see fit to show up *sometime*." I enlisted the kids to help me with this (after surreptitiously doling out peppermint sticks that had been hung on the tree), and soon their tears had lessened, but their expectations had grown.

An hour later, the Old Colonel staggered into the room with nothing in his hands but an almost-empty bottle of his ever-present Macallan Scotch whisky. "William?" his wife cautiously asked. "Where are the presents for the children?"

"They're gonna hafta wait a li'l," he slurred as he sunk down into an armchair.

"What do you mean *wait*?" she probed. "Today is Christmas. I know you had the money to buy the presents when you went into Ripley yesterday."

"Lost it," he muttered.

"What do you mean you *lost it?*" she asked, inching further into dangerous territory. "You mean it fell out of your pocket, and now you can't find it?"

"N'side straight," he grumbled. "...Know 'e cheated. Cards up sleeve..." My father drifted into a noisy, snoring sleep.

I had suffered years of abject neglect and hostility from this scoundrel. *Does he see my late mother when he looks at me— which is not that often?* From the daguerreotype of my mother which used to sit on our fireplace mantel (before being put away by my stepmother), I could see that I share her dark hair, heavy brows, and almond-shaped eyes. *Does he blame me for her death?* Finally, I had had all I could take. I strode over to his chair and kicked his muddy boots that were stretched across an ottoman. "What kind of father loses his kids' Christmas presents in a poker game?!" I yelled at him.

He stirred enough from his drunken stupor to heave the Macallan bottle at me. I saw it coming and ducked to the side. The flying bottle sailed by my head and toppled the spindly Christmas tree, knocking it to the ground. The remaining whisky in the bottle leaked out and spread to the still-lit candles lying on the floor. The brittle, dry tree flamed up, igniting the drapes of the nearby windows. A sweet, whisky- and-peppermint-infused black smoke filled the house. As the children screamed, my stepmother ran out into the front yard pleading loudly for help. The five slaves soon ran into the living room with buckets of water—and oddly I noticed—a pot of salt that quickly doused the fire; regardless, our Christmas had gone up in smoke.

When my father was conscious enough to realize what he had done, he looked around the room and saw me glaring, backed by the slaves' fearful eyes. "Yer not welcome in this house anymore," he declaimed as he aimed a crooked finger at me. I glanced beseechingly to my stepmother for some semblance of support—or sympathy—but she looked away and gathered *her* children at her feet. "If yer gonna stay here," my father continued, "you can live with *them*." He pointed to the slaves as if they were just random, anonymous objects.

In fact, they were a family. Their names were Simon and Mary (the parents), Henry and Lucy (their teenage children), and their grandfather George. I did not delude myself in thinking that their care for me was anything other than what they were obliged to do as property of my father; nevertheless, they always treated me kindly and fairly.

[*"Miss Betty," the old man said as he interrupted his narrative. "Looking back at my youth with the clarity of hindsight, I would like to think that I reciprocated this kindness, but I don't know." He sighed heavily and resumed.*]

"We can lay out a pallet for you on the floor tonight, John," Mary said as I blindly followed them through the field behind the house in the darkness of that Christmas night. As we neared their cabin at the rear of the property, she added, "But I don't think you want to do that for long."

"Thank you, Mary," I replied. "I'm not going to impose on you beyond tonight. I can't wait to get away from this awful place where I am no longer welcome." *I just don't know how.*

An unexpected opportunity presented itself the next morning when a friend of George's named Jim pulled up in a loaded timber wagon on the dusty dirt road in front of their cabin. "George!" Jim called, bringing all the family out to the ramshackle porch. "I've got this load of pine to take to the river launch at Norfolk. Care to keep me company for a couple of days?"

"I've got a garden full of spinach and mustard greens that I need to pick," replied George, "but I got a young man here who might take my place on your wagon."

* * *

"So, you're running away from home?" Jim asked me as he gently, but confidently, held the reins leading back from the huge dray horse pulling the timber wagon. Jim was old—like his friend George—with deep creases in his brown face, his eyes cloaked in the shadow cast by the wide brim circling his leather hat.

"I don't have much of a choice," I answered.

"You think I've *ever* had a choice?" Jim returned. His sad eyes hid in the shadows.

I don't know what to say. He must just see me as a spoiled, whiny white boy who's never had to work a day in his life. "I guess not. I'm sorry," I said weakly.

"Not your fault, kid. We each have to play the cards we're dealt."

The cards I was holding included only the clothes on my back. *I have nothing else.* We didn't talk very much as we rode slowly westward on the dark, treacherous logging roads that eventually would lead us to the Mississippi River. After two days, we reached a crossroads where a wider, more traveled road ran south towards the town of Hernando. Paralleling this road were the gleaming new rails of the railroad tracks running between Memphis and New Orleans.

"You got a choice to make *here*, kid," Jim said as he pulled the wagon to a stop by the tracks. "Road, rails, or river? Each one will take you to N'Awlins."

"Which one would you choose?" I asked.

"The road would be the most dangerous. Mississippi militiamen are always patrollin' just lookin' for a fight. The rail'd be the fastest, but you gotta hope a train is goin' to stop at the right time so you can climb on, and you gotta hope you don't get tossed off a movin' train by the s'curity folks. The river'd be the slowest, but you stand the least chance of gettin' caught. You just gotta be patient and choose the right boat to hop aboard."

"You're going to the river with this load of logs?"

"Yep. To Norfolk Landing where the loadin' dock is."

"If it's all right with you, I'll stick with you and try the river."

We arrived at the landing late in the afternoon. A cold breeze was blowing down the Mississippi River spurring the men waiting to unload goods to start fires in the discarded wooden barrels that were scattered along the riverbank. As I stood by one warming my hands, Jim approached an imposing white man standing on the sloping porch of a dilapidated building. The man looked at our wagon and asked, "Evenin', Jim, whatcha got for me today?"

"Loblolly pines, Mr. Jones. Straight, m'ture trees. Make some good rafters."

Jones ran his hand along the skinned logs, nodding his head. "They're throwing up houses like anthills in Memphis right now before the war starts, so this will bring some decent money." He reached into the worn leather apron he wore around his ample waistline and pulled out a wad of bills. He counted out seven dollars that he handed to Jim. "Keep 'em coming, Jim, while there's still a market. Your master's lucky to have someone like you he can trust."

Jim looked down at his feet and mumbled inaudibly. After

the timber was off-loaded, he grabbed a bag out from under the box seat of the wagon and tied the reins to a hitching post. He took a small sack of feed out of the bag and placed it at our horse's feet before pulling out another sack containing his dinner. We walked down the river away from the other people and sat down beside a glowing barrel as darkness descended on the Mississippi.

"I can't offer you much," Jim said, "but you can have half of what I got." *The same thing he says at each meal.* He opened a tattered bundle of cheesecloth and spun it towards me.

Even though I had only known Jim for the few days that we had ridden together on the wagon, as we shared a wedge of hardtack, I could tell that something was weighing on his mind.

I don't know if that weight had been there all the time we had been traveling, or if it had just begun surfacing—like a dead body—when we got to the river.

"You're choosin' to run away from your family," he began as I felt him trying to unburden himself of that weight.

"My father said I wasn't *welcome* anymore."

"Your father is a hard man, and it's not easy to be around him, but at least the Old Colonel has kept George's family together."

"Do you have family?" I asked tentatively.

"Got a daughter. My wife died years ago. After she passed, my master sold my little girl—figured I couldn't take care of her anymore—and I've felt like a part of me was missing ever since."

I know that feeling. "Do you know where she is?" I continued.

"She was sold to an old Frenchman that owns a plantation near the river at Natchez. I think she was thirteen when they took her away."

We looked down at the bank of the river, and in the flickering light of the barrel fire, we could see where some shorter logs that had rolled off a timber barge were being trapped behind a rock outcropping in a slight bend of the river. I don't know when the idea sprung into Jim's head, but he got up from where we were sitting and purposefully strode over to the wagon to retrieve a long piece of rope.

He climbed down the steep bank of the river and began pulling the trapped logs onto shore. "Help me lash these together, kid," he called up to me from the dark.

After we had joined three logs, it hit me what we were doing. "Are we making a…?"

"Yep. A raft. I'm going down the river with you. To Natchez."

* * *

I wish I could say this is where the humdinger of a story begins, but the truth is that Jim's and my journey together down the Mississippi on our raft was sort of humdrum.

[*"Miss Betty," the old man explained, "it would be another twenty years before another writer's pen brought that story to life."*]

We tended to float our raft in the secrecy of the night while spending the daylight hours hidden on the banks where we hunted for food or slept. On the fourth night, we began seeing the lights of Natchez up ahead, and we pulled our raft over to a sandy shoal.

Again, I wish I could say that Jim and I had a grand farewell, but—in fact—we parted undramatically, each of us simply going our separate way. I retreated into the dark safety of the woods, while Jim headed to the lights of the city.

[*"Now, Miss Betty,"* *the old man confessed, "I choose to cling to* *the belief that Jim reunited with his long-lost daughter and that* *they found a way to live together for the rest of his days."*]

I woke up in the woods beside the river the next morning—all alone—and began walking along a narrow dirt road towards the rising sun. This southeasterly path would seemingly point me towards New Orleans. I had walked several hours without encountering another soul on the road when I heard the clatter of a wagon rapidly approaching behind me. I stepped over to the side just as the wagon turned a bend in the road and came into view. It was a covered wagon, with curlicue script reading "Professor Moore's Minstrel and Medicine Show" on the canvas cover. The driver was a Black man who was madly swatting at his own face, which was engulfed in a pulsing, buzzing cloud. This swatting caused the confused dray horse to weave erratically back and forth, so I jumped out of the way onto the banks of a shallow creek that ran beside the road.

"Ahhh!" screamed the driver as he veered off the road right beside me, jumped off the seat, and dove headfirst into the murky creek. It was only then that I could see that the cloud was a swarm of bees that dispersed when he went underwater.

"Are you okay, mister?" I asked the man. He pulled his head out of the water and frantically looked around.

"Are they gone?"

"Yeah, they flew away." Looking closer at the face of the Black man, I didn't know what to think. Welts were rising all across his cheeks, but they were not the normal dark-brown color I was expecting; instead, his face was a purplish-black that unevenly spread up from the pink neck that protruded out of the dark-stained collar of his shirt.

"Thank God. I thought they were going to kill me." He stood up, wiped his very white hands on his trousers, and extended a hand out to me. "Pleased to meet you, kid. My name is Bob O'Malley."

After our conversation began, another dark face appeared from out of the covered wagon. "Is the coast clear, O'Malley?" whispered the man who donned a tattered velvet top hat when he saw that his partner was not alone. He climbed down from the wagon and asked with a lilting voice, "And whom might this young man be?"

I could not think of a reason to be evasive. "I'm John Wesley Thompson Falkner. I'm on my way to New Orleans."

"As are we," replied the man in the top hat. "Let me introduce myself." He lifted his also-white hand to the script on the wagon and proudly declared, "I'm the purveyor of this comic commodity: *Professor Moore*." He bowed slightly as he placed his other hand across the front of the frayed, black wool vest that strained across his prominent belly.

I must not have been able to disguise my skepticism because he quickly followed up, "You're confused by our appearance, young Falkner. I can assure you that we are Caucasian men just like yourself."

When my eyes narrowed (mostly from confusion about what a *Kaw-kay-shun* was), O'Malley elucidated, "We are minstrel performers. What our audience seems to want now is white men in blackface singing Stephen Foster songs." He began singing in a falsetto voice:

To smile upon earth and sky!
Why should the beautiful ever weep?
Why should the beautiful die?

"So, we had one more show to do tonight in Natchez before heading to N'Awlins, but we ran out of our stage makeup. Professor Mor-on, here…"

"O'Malley!"

"Sorry. The *genius* professor here decided that it would be a good idea to create our own blackface makeup by mashing blackberries into a paste that we could spread on our faces."

"The bushes were covered in them at our campsite!" interjected Professor Moore in defense of his scheme. "And they seemed to sparkle like ebony jewels."

"*Anyway*," continued O'Malley, "after we slathered our faces in this stuff, the bees got a whiff of us and attacked. I tried wiping it off, but it's like it's permanently dyed our skin this god-awful color. We were trying to outrun those devil bees when we came upon you by the creek." He stopped talking as he tenderly probed the coalescing welts on his face with his finger.

"You are welcome to accompany us to N'Awlins, if you so desire, John Wesley Thompson Falkner," invited the Professor. "That's a lot of names for a fellow to carry around on his own. We would enjoy the company, and maybe you can be of service along our journey."

"Thanks, Professor. I'll accept," *and I can't wait to find out what that service might be.*

I didn't have long to wait.

Chapter 2

O'Malley drove the dray horse hard all the rest of that day, as he and the Professor seemed anxious to put as many miles as possible between them and Natchez. Also—for some reason—they removed the *Professor Moore* sign from the side of the covered wagon.

As it was beginning to get dark, we arrived on the outskirts of Liberty, a small town in southern Mississippi, where we heard the excited voices of men punctuated by sporadic gunfire. As we turned onto the main street, an old woman approached our wagon with waving arms. The Professor, O'Malley, and I sat three abreast across the driver's box. "It's your business," she said, "but if I were you, I would turn this wagon around and go the long way around Liberty."

"Thanks for the warning, ma'am," said the Professor as he courteously doffed his top hat to the elderly woman. "What's all the excitement about?"

"Word just arrived by telegram that the State of Mississippi has seceded from the Union," the woman answered. "We're all on our own now. God help us." As she looked closer through the darkness at the Professor and O'Malley, she added, "God especially needs to help *your kind*. I'm afraid it's going to get ugly *real* quick."

The Professor began to protest, but O'Malley jabbed him with a sharp elbow. "Hush! There's no way you can explain our damned faces to her."

With the old lady's cryptic warning, they climbed into the back, out of view, and O'Malley whispered instructions as I took the reins. I turned the wagon around, and we circumnavigated Liberty until we were again headed southward, guided by the gleaming new steel of the moonlit railroad tracks. The two men joined me again on the driver's seat. "I'm not sure what this secession means," O'Malley said, "but I'm worried this new country of Mississippi might not welcome us as citizens. We need to get to Louisiana as fast as we can."

We stopped for the night on the edge of a meadow bordered by a creek running with clean water. After starting a small fire and refilling several canteens with boiled water, the Professor and O'Malley prepared their bedrolls in the back of the wagon. "Sorry, kid," O'Malley said, "but there's only room for two. You're going to have to sleep by the fire. You're welcome to this blanket and a piece of bread. Thanks for your help in getting around the town."

It was only after I had settled in by the fire that I felt the pangs of hunger in my belly. I savored each crumb of bread as I ate under the cold January stars, serenaded by the duet of snores coming from the back of the wagon. The only canteen I could find was full of cold, strong coffee, but I quaffed all its contents hungrily.

It seemed as if I had just closed my eyes when I heard the rustle of footsteps in the dry leaves behind me. Before I could sit up, two hands locked themselves like a vise around my neck. "If you want to live," whispered a voice, "don't make a sound." Three shadowy shapes appeared in the faint glow of the campfire's embers and converged at the back of the wagon.

Dark, nebulous arms reached in and snatched the Professor and O'Malley and roughly dumped them by the fire. The man who had throttled my neck let go and added wood to the fire. As it sparked and burned brighter, I looked into the terrified eyes of my two traveling companions.

"In the Free State of Mississippi," said the obvious leader of the group, the man who had held me, "we don't take too kindly to runaway slaves. Especially ones that steal money from helpless old women like y'all did in Natchez."

"We ain't slaves…" protested O'Malley before the leader slapped him in the face.

"And we didn't steal any money!" said the Professor in a panicked voice. "We sold them medicine…" His comments too were met with the sharp *clap* of a hand across his cheek.

"If you ain't slaves, then show us your emancipation papers," said one of the other men. "Like the woman and boy had that we ran across yesterday."

"It's just makeup!" O'Malley pleaded in vain. "We're as white as y'all are." This defense was met with a solid punch to O'Malley's gut, dropping him to his knees.

"What kind of idiots do you take us for?" asked the leader as he rubbed the sore knuckles of his hand. "That's the lamest excuse I've ever heard."

"You gotta help us, kid!" beseeched the Professor. "Tell 'em about the blackberries!"

But before I could be *of service*, the shadowy men hauled up O'Malley and the Professor and tied them face down across the back of a horse. "By the power vested in us as the *Militiamen of Mississippi*," declared the leader, "we hereby take you runaways into custody so that we can fulfill our God-given duty to return all of *your kind* to your rightful masters."

"Yeah, *God-given* duty is fine," laughed one of the men, "but don't forget about the rewards!" All but one of the gang mounted their horses and took off with my companions.

"You know, kid," said the leader as he came back to me, "I could string you up right now for helping slaves to escape, but—lucky for you—I'm just going to teach you a lesson instead."

With his vise-like hands now gripping my arms, he led me in the dark down to the banks of the creek. He struck a match on the side of his boot and used the light to guide me to the base of a huge cedar. "Sit down behind the tree and wrap your arms and legs around it." He lit a long, hand-rolled cigarette and began tying my wrists and ankles together with a piece of leather strapping that he pulled from his pocket. As he tightened the strap, I began to cry. "Shut up, kid. I could kill you if I wanted to, but at least I'm giving you a chance." As I continued to whimper, he pulled a bandana from around his neck and wrapped it around my head, gagging my mouth.

"You just better pray that it don't rain any time soon so that creek don't rise."

* * *

Even though I grew up in a household where the only time I heard the Lord's name was when it was uttered *in vain*, I followed my tormentor's advice and prayed all night long. I prayed for it not to rain, for me not to die alone tied to this tree, for someone—anyone—to come along to my rescue. What I didn't think to pray for was for the crawdads not to crawl out of the creek and burrow inside my pants. That started at daylight after I spent the night drifting in and out of hazy stages of delirium.

My wrists were circled in blood from my efforts to squirm free from the leather strap binding my hands and feet, but I had not been able to loosen it at all. Now I bucked up and down to try and shake the crawdads out of my pants. Their claws at first tickled but then turned to pain as they got skin between their pinchers. I tried to hold my water, but all the effort caused me to lose control. I flooded my pants, and—lo and behold—the crawdads scurried out of my wet breeches like rats out of a house fire, repelled by the bitter coffee odor of my urine.

Saved from this potential catastrophe, I relaxed and laid my cheek against the thick, soft bark of the cedar tree. I don't know how long I slept, but the sun was high in the sky when I was woken by a soft lapping coming from the creek. A red fox in its full winter coat was dipping its delicate, fleshy tongue into a stagnant pool, oblivious to my condition. A murder of crows sat in the top of a dead elm tree casting an ominous shadow across my feet. Their noisy, incessant *caws* sounded like the chatter that bandied among the women who would gather in the courthouse square in Ripley to swap rumors and baked goods. I drifted off again…

The next time I awoke, I felt like I was surfacing from the bottom of the creek. There was darkness, and then the light grew brighter and brighter as I ascended. When I was fully conscious, I felt a strange calm suffuse my tired, crumpled body. I realized that I was resigned to dying there, tied to the tree like a helpless domestic animal. *Would anyone miss me?* I had been gone from home for less than a week. I doubted that my father or stepmother gave much of a thought to their missing son. *Will I be able to recognize my mother if I see her in heaven?* I hoped—even prayed again—that I would know her when that vacant piece within me that I had always felt no longer ached. *Do runaway boys even get a chance at heaven, or am I doomed to an eternity down below?*

It was at this moment, when I had hit rock bottom, that I heard the voices. At first, I thought I was just humanizing the *caw-caw-caws* of the crows overhead. But no, I held my breath and listened closely, and I could discern actual words and names: "Joseph… gather… firewood… cooking started." It was a woman's voice. She spoke again in a louder, more urgent tone as if the target of her words was moving away. "And go down into that creek before it gets too dark and catch all the crawdads you can. The bigger the better."

With this mention of the creek, I began to moan through the bandana stretched across my mouth. My dry throat burned as I tried to be heard. The voices were coming from the meadow on the other side of the creek. I was shielded from that side by the trunk of the cedar, so the only thing visible to someone approaching from that direction would be my forearms and lower legs. *Would they even see me?* I had to make myself heard, but I sounded like a desperate, feral animal. *What if I scare them off with my cries for help?*

I quieted myself and listened as I peered around the tree as much as my bonds allowed. I heard a different sound. It was a bird but not a crow. No, it wasn't a bird. Whoever was walking towards me was whistling. I recognized the tune. *It's "Camptown Races!" Did the minstrels somehow escape and come back to find me?* But no, as the figure appeared above the opposite bank of the creek, the backlit form was not a man.

It was a boy like me.

He appeared on the crest in black-and-white relief, his features obscured by the contrast of the setting sun behind him. He was tall and thin, his spindly frame topped by wispy black hair that I could see through like a dandelion puff held up to the sky before a scattering blow.

[*"Looking back at this episode early in my life," the old man told the stenographer, "I can only figure that it was my fleeting embrace of death that caused the image of this boy to be so etched into my retina—like the silvery daguerreotypes by Matthew Brady that I would later see in Northern newspapers during the war."*]

As the boy descended the bank down to the creek, he continued to whistle—the chorus *Do Dah, Do Dah* warbled out of his lips like the cooing of a dove. The steady song was how I knew that he had not seen me yet. I moaned as loud as I could without making it sound like a threatening growl. The boy reached the level of the creek and began gathering firewood. As he turned his back away from me, I moaned louder—it was truly more of a pathetic whimper—but the whistling stopped. He spun and looked warily about him.

Now that he was out of the direct sun, I saw that his skin was a deep, reddish brown—the color of the flame-licked mat of cedar sprays lining the creek bank that crunched under his feet. His large, round eyes darted back and forth as he searched for the source of the strange noises. I bucked up as much as I could, rustling the leaves at my feet. He stopped and quietly laid down the wood he had gathered, leaving only one club-like piece gripped fiercely in his right hand. He raised his weapon midway above his head and took a furtive step in my direction. I again bucked and shook my hands and feet as much as I could. I saw blood dripping onto the wet leaves under me from my bound wrists as a searing pain licked my forearms like a flame.

"Who's there?" the boy hissed. I moaned again, and he saw me.

He made a wide circle behind me so that I could not see him as he approached.

"You're white," he said with surprise in his voice. "I thought they just did this stuff to *us*."

* * *

My Good Samaritan untied my hands and feet and helped me to stand. "I don't think my legs are going to work," I said as I stumbled, trying an unaided step. My feet were asleep, and all I felt were pins and needles. He slid his arm around my back and under one of my arms. I tentatively took a step… and another… and gradually the feeling came back.

"I'm Joseph," he said as he looked at my bloody wrists. "I'm going to run get Mamma."

"So, that was your mother's voice I heard?"

"We're traveling with a tinker named Mr. Hallahan to New Or-lins."

Even though we were way off to ourselves, I whispered, "Are y'all runaways?"

"No!" he objected. "We got our papers. My daddy bought our freedom."

"I'm *so* sorry," I apologized. "It was wrong for me to have assumed that." I thought back to something one of the bad men said last night: *Like the woman and boy that we ran across yesterday.* "Were y'all stopped by militiamen a couple of days ago?"

"Yeah. I was really scared. They had so much hate in their eyes."

"I'm pretty sure they're the ones that did this to me."

"Joseph?" We both heard his mother calling out to him.

"We need to get you back so Mamma can tend to your wounds," Joseph said.

"Coming, Mamma!" he called back.

"I heard your mother telling you to get firewood and crawdads before it got dark. It's almost dark now. If you wait any longer, you're not going to be able to see. Let me help."

"Are you sure you can?" asked Joseph.

"My legs are feeling okay now. But if you don't mind, I'll get the firewood if you'll get the crawdads." He looked at me quizzically. "It's a long story," I replied with a weak smile.

It was pitch-black dark as we made our way back to the tinker's wagon. An oil lantern marked our destination as I struggled with an armful of wood. "Mamma?" Joseph called out as we approached. "I found a boy down by the creek."

His mother stepped into the pool of light cast by the lantern. "Is he dead?" she asked. As I stepped into the pool, Joseph's mother flinched: "You're not what I was expecting. I thought Joseph found someone hanging from a tree."

"No, ma'am. I was tied to the bottom of one. I'd have died if Joseph hadn't found me."

"You're bleeding," she said as she took my wrists in her hands. "Joseph, bring me the poultice out of my bag." When he returned, she wrapped wet rags that smelled like rotten eggs around each of my wounds. Despite the sickly smell, the pain began to ease immediately. She saw my face slacken and said, "Unfortunately, I have a lot of experience treating wounds like this." I thought of the public whipping of slaves that I had witnessed at the square in Ripley.

"What's your name?" she asked cautiously.

"John Wesley Thompson Falkner. I ran away from home in Ripley, and I'm headed to New Orleans."

"Are your people out looking for you?" she continued. I shook my head.

Joseph looked at his mother. "Mamma, he could travel with us to New Or-lins." He turned to me and explained, "We're taking a ship from there to Massachusetts."

His mother turned to the round white man who had joined us in the pool of light. "What do you think, Mr. Hallahan? Is it safe for us—*for you*—to have him along?"

The tinker looked down into the shadows on the ground cast by Joseph and me as if the answer lay somewhere in the darkness. He finally spoke up: "I don't see any trouble with him joining us. Maybe he can be of some help along the way." His words sounded like an eerie echo of the Professor's pronouncement about me being *of service*.

Mr. Hallahan had taken his dray horse into a nearby town to buy food for that night.

"With war on everyone's mind," Mr. Hallahan addressed Joseph's mother, "people are starting to hoard supplies. I got what I could. I hope it's enough for you to conjure up a meal from." He pulled a sack off the back of the horse and unloaded the contents one by one. "Meat-wise, all they had was a handful of salted pork. I also got some dried apples, red beans, flour, cornmeal, and sugar." With a gleam in his eye, he continued, "I have a lady friend at a farm on the outskirts of town, and I was able to trade something for these." He pulled a basket off the other side of the horse and proudly displayed a slab of butter, three eggs, and a sweating tin pitcher of milk."

"You've outdone yourself," Joseph's mother said to the tinker. "I can promise you that none of that will go to waste. Joseph, I'm going to be cooking on the ship that will take us to Nantucket, and you're going to need to be my extra two hands."

"John," Joseph's mother asked, "do you know how to start a good cooking fire?"

"No, ma'am," I answered. *I need to start pulling my weight.* "But I *can't wait* to learn!"

"Miss Estelle," the tinker said, "help yourself to any of the pots and pans you need."

While Joseph and his mother rummaged through the back of the tinker's wagon for the right cooking utensils, Mr. Hallahan showed me how to construct a proper cooking fire. "You want to end up with embers that burn hot and steady—not flame up which makes your food char." We built a pyramid of kindling and then stuffed it with dry grass. As the flames grew, he showed me how to add in logs on the perimeter to create a cooking surface for pots and pans.

"Mr. Hallahan! Is this a Dutch oven?" Joseph's mother called as she pulled out a dented, covered pot that resembled a cannonball more than a cooking tool.

"Maybe it once was," he answered, "but I'm not sure it's still useable."

"Oh, it is," she said as her eyes sparkled. "Joseph, it's time you learned how to cook."

Chapter 3

As she nestled the Dutch oven down into the glowing red coals of the campfire, "Miss Estelle" began teaching her son: "Joseph, scoop out a spoonful of butter into the skillet and place it on those rocks right above the flame. After the butter melts, break a couple of those eggs into the skillet."

"What are we making?" Joseph asked.

"Cornbread. I'm going to mix together some flour, corn-meal, salt, sugar, and my secret ingredient." She pulled a tiny glass jar out of the same bag that had held the poultices.

"What is that?" I asked. *It looks like sand. The jar reminds me of the hourglass our teacher had on her desk at our one-room schoolhouse in Ripley. An hour ago, I thought the last grains of my life were trickling out.*

"This is yeast. I need it to make the cornbread rise. I've heard that in big cities cooks are starting to use 'baking powder' instead of yeast, but I've never had the chance to try it."

As I watched by the light of the fire and the lantern above, Joseph's mother mixed her "dry" ingredients together in a big pot and then poured the melted butter and eggs like lava into the center of the victual volcano's crater. I pictured the illustration of Mt. Vesuvius hurling its fiery death to Pompeii below in the *Mitchell's Primary Geography* text that we studied at school.

She handed her son a large spoon and instructed, "Joseph, stir that until it's just one big creamy mix, and then we'll pour it back into the skillet." His mother added a dollop of butter with a backhanded flick of her wrist. After Joseph gave the mix one last stir, he used both his hands to nestle the heavy black pan into the smoldering embers.

Mr. Hallahan, Miss Estelle, Joseph, and I feasted on cornbread that we dipped into the crawfish gumbo that she made in another large pot, followed by dried apple cobbler that she cooked in the Dutch oven. After we scrubbed the pots, pans, and plates, we sat by the fire as Mr. Hallahan filled the bowl of his pipe with a rich, redolent tobacco that evoked home. As the flaming leaves lit his ruddy, red-bearded face, he explained his plan for the remainder of our journey to New Orleans.

"If we keep a good pace, we can make N'Awlins in a week. I'm going to skirt east of Baton Rouge because I think it would be best to avoid cities. We will come in on the southwest side of Lake Pontchartrain and stay between the lake and the Mississippi River until we get to Metairie. The marshland along this route gives us plenty of places to hide if things get dicey."

"What does *dicey* mean?" I asked Mr. Hallahan, whose face was now hidden behind a bulbous cloud of smoke.

"I don't want to scare you boys, but I mean if things get dangerous. Louisiana is liable to secede at any moment now, and chaos may break out. Luckily the Cajuns in the area we'll be passing through are a pretty independent bunch of people, and some of them are willing to help Blacks and Indians because they know what it's like to get singled out and treated badly."

"How's *that?*" Joseph's mother asked with a hint of skepticism in her voice.

"The Cajuns are French Acadians," he explained, "who were forced out of their part of Canada about a hundred years ago in what was called 'The Great Expulsion.' They ended up exiled in southern Louisiana sort of like the Indian tribes that were forced to march to Oklahoma on the Trail of Tears. It seems like people never run out of ways to be god-awful to each other."

This explanation seemed to exhaust the tinker who yawned loudly. "I think I need to get the sleeping set-up ready," he said. "After that delicious dinner, I can't keep my eyes open. John, how about giving me a hand?" He pulled a wide canvas tarp out of the back of the wagon that we stretched across the wagon bed and staked the ends into the ground with metal spikes, creating a lean-to on each side of the wagon.

"Miss Estelle, you take your usual side, and I'll take the other," Mr. Hallahan dictated. "The two boys can keep each other company by the fire." He tossed two rolled blankets to us. After what had happened as I slept by the fire the night before, I was relieved to see that Mr. Hallahan pulled a shotgun from under the seat of the wagon and laid it inside his lean-to.

As we lay by the fading campfire, Joseph began to tell me the story of how he and his mother came to be on the road with Mr. Hallahan.

"My mamma, daddy, and I were the property of Mr. Thomas Rossiter, a horse trader who owns the *Raw Cedar Plantation*, like his father did, and his father before him. I've always been told that the plantation had gotten its name from slaves messing up the owner's family name. His two thousand acres run as far as the eye can see with fields of rice, corn, and tobacco. It's near Jackson between the Pearl River and the hills to the southeast. I know this because of what Father Matthew has taught me. Our master's mansion stands on high ground in the center of the plantation surrounded by a bunch of cedar trees. My family lived with the other eighty-five slaves at the rear forty of the property in a 'village' of falling-down shacks where we sweated in the summer and froze in the winter."

"Who is Father Matthew?" I asked.

"Father Matthew helped bring me into the world at the Church of the Cross that's just north of Jackson. My mother tells me that I was born impatient, like I just couldn't wait to start causing trouble. She gave birth to me—*way too early* she says—in the basement of the church. Father Matthew has been my teacher, doctor, and minister. I've been able to keep track of our progress on the tinker's wagon because the father taught me to read and the basics of math. I would never call our master a *kind* man, but he did allow Father Matthew to teach some of us children on his plantation to read and write."

* * *

"What's your father like?" I asked. *I don't want to have to tell Joseph about mine.*

"I'm eleven years old, and I'm already nearly as tall as Daddy. Although he says I just look as tall because of my hair. Most people have told me that I have my mamma's face and my daddy's build, but I don't know, because the only mirror in our 'home' was a cracked piece of a chiff-a-robe mirror that hung on a pantry door, too high for me to really see myself."

"As much as I can tell by firelight, you *do* look like your mother," I offered.

"Yeah, my mamma and I share the same hair and the same brown eyes. Even though the law calls my daddy an 'African American,' his skin is a burnt-red color, giving away that he's part Choctaw. His mother's father—my great-granddaddy—was a Choctaw, and he traded and owned slaves in Mississippi until he and the rest of his tribe were shipped out West by Andrew Jackson. He sold his baby grandson—my daddy—to Rossiter for two hundred dollars and a broken-down mule before marching on the Trail of Tears to Oklahoma."

"So, your father grew up on the plantation where you just left?"

"Yeah, but not my mother. She was born in New Or-lins and sold to Mr. Rossiter when she was a little girl."

"Why does Mr. Hallahan call your mother 'Miss Estelle'? She's married to your father."

"I think it's just his way of showing her respect. Back at the plantation, all the white people called her by just her first name, like she was a child. What is your mother like?"

"She died when I was a baby. I have a stepmother, but she couldn't care less about me."

"I'm sorry. What's your father like?" Joseph asked me innocently.

"The old drunk kicked me out of the only home I've ever known. 'Nuff said…" I answered sounding more bitter than I meant to. "I'd rather hear more about *your* father."

"Uh, okay… My father has these intense eyes that glitter like bits of coal," Joseph continued, "and strong fingers like strands of cable that are always moving when he talks, and that makes me and Mamma laugh. He is the best jockey in the county, and he tends to the horses on our master's farm. Mamma says Daddy has a 'natural way with animals.' He has all these scars on his back that he told me had come from being a jockey. I'm not sure he's telling me the whole truth. Even though he's taught me everything he knows about horses and riding, he always swore to Mamma that my life would be different. He was telling the truth about that."

"On the day after Christmas last month, Mamma and I were led into the fancy library in Mr. Rossiter's mansion. It's got this wall of shelves that are full of dusty books that I bet have never been read. We stood in front of his huge desk where our owner sat looking down at a bunch of numbers in a book. I felt like that's how he saw us—numbers on a page. I held my mother's hand, and I thought about our lives on the plantation, where each day of long, hard work was just followed by another… and another. But as Mr. Rossiter began to speak in what Mamma says is his 'Scottish-Southern drawl,' our lives really were about to change."

"I hate to lose you two," the old man said. "Estelle, you're the best cook I've ever had. I'll never be able to replace you with anyone nearly as good. But a deal is a deal. I told your husband if he could come up with the money, he could buy your freedom. I don't know how he did it—I better not find out he's been throwing races he's been jockeying—but as of today, you and your son are free people. You're welcome to stay here and work, but I can't pay you anything with war on the horizon. After Lincoln's election, we've got no choice but to fight."

"So, a week later Mamma and I got ready to leave the Raw Cedar Plantation on the back of the tinker's wagon, heading south to New Or-lins and then on a ship to Massachusetts, while my father stayed behind—still a slave."

Even though the fire was almost burned out, I could see the wetness in his eyes. "I'm sorry, Joseph," I whispered. "I'm sure y'all will be together again."

Joseph sat up and held out his wrist to me: "Daddy gave me this leather and iron bracelet which was made from the bridle of the horse that he won my freedom with. While we loaded the few things we had on top of the pots and pans of the tinker's wagon, my daddy made us a promise in his quiet voice—and with his busy hands." A brief smile came to Joseph's face.

"'Don't worry,' my daddy said," Joseph continued, "'I'm on a hot streak with Mr. Rossiter's new stallion, and I'll soon have the money to buy my own freedom. Y'all just need to follow the plan. Catch the ship in New Or-lins to Nantucket, and before you know it, I promise I will be joining you.'"

"My mamma smiled when he said this—I'm sure mostly for my sake—and said, 'We know, honey,' and she gave my father a long, last hug. But as he disappeared into the distance when we rode away, I wondered if we would ever see him again."

"Why are y'all going to Nantucket?" I asked my new friend.

"My daddy met a man while he was at a horse race," Joseph answered, "who told him that he knew of a—What was the word Daddy used?—Oh yeah… a net-work. This network helps free Black people get jobs if they can get to Nantucket."

"How do you know you can trust what that man said?"

"Mamma said that Daddy trusted him, and she trusts my daddy."

"Your mother seems like a really strong person," I said.

"She is. When the militiamen that attacked you stopped us

the other day, they wouldn't take Mr. Hallahan's word that we had our papers. When they challenged us, Mamma looked at me with her calm brown eyes. We had to get down from the wagon and prove that we were the people described in our freedom papers. When she was quizzed about her name and date and place of birth, Mamma answered the men as she looked down at the ground: 'Yes, sir. I was born in New Or-lins in 1832.' She had to pull up the sleeve of her dress to show the cross-shaped scar on her right arm that was listed in her papers. I was so scared, but she got us through that."

We heard Miss Estelle's soft, motherly voice come from the shadows of the wagon: "I was scared, too, Joseph. Now y'all go to sleep. We have a long way to go tomorrow."

* * *

Over the next few days on the road, our roles became defined. Joseph and his mother cooked each night while I gathered wood and built the cooking fire, and Mr. Hallahan continued to find mysterious ways to scavenge food supplies. We all enjoyed the fruits of our labors each night by the campfire. Joseph especially embraced helping his mother and learning about cooking. He was constantly peppering her with questions as they worked.

"Does it matter if you salt food while it is cooking or after?"

"How do you know which parts of a squirrel taste good?"

"When do you know that beans have boiled long enough?" His mother patiently answered each of his questions, as she obviously enjoyed his growing interest.

We averaged about ten miles a day on the road to New Orleans. I knew this because Joseph taught me how to look

31

for the milestones placed along the new railroad tracks that still paralleled the road that we traveled. Joseph noted our progress in a diary that he had been given by Father Matthew when he heard that Joseph and his mother had been freed.

"I sincerely apologize," the priest had said, as Joseph recounted his conversation with Father Matthew, "but it's an 1860 diary, so you're going to have to change the date on each page. I want you to document the adventure you're about to begin. It seems appropriate—a new year and a new life."

"When he saw the puzzled look on my face," Joseph said, "Father Matthew explained, 'Today is January 1st. It's now 1861.'"

I looked over Joseph's shoulder as he recorded our day's mileage, and I saw that he had scratched out the *27* beside "Friday, January" and hand-written a *25* in its place. *So, today is Friday, January 25, 1861,* I thought to myself. *I have been on the road (and the river) for thirty-one days now—a month. It feels like years.*

Despite Mr. Hallahan's caution concerning our route, we had run into little trouble on our last stretch of road that ran between the Mississippi River and Lake Pontchartrain. This path was dotted with Cajun encampments, populated by strange people with even stranger accents. We were befriended by the Boudreaux family late one afternoon as we stopped by the river.

"You folks headin' to N'Awlins?" a man asked as he approached the tinker's wagon.

"We are," replied Mr. Hallahan with a hesitant tone.

"Mais, yeah!" returned the man in a boisterous voice. "I've had all de youngins out in de pee-rows." He pointed to the children of all colors who were pulling three flat-bottomed boats out of the river. "And we gotta mess a catfish if you be 'ungry. We're de Boudreaux's." He extended his hand out to each of us in turn.

That night we feasted with the Boudreaux family as Miss Estelle and Joseph fried the catfish and served it with collard greens and roasted yams. They were joined at the cooking fire by Mr. Boudreaux's wife, a small brown woman who did not seem to speak English.

"She's from *Gwad-a-loop*, down in the *Carry-bean Sea*," explained Boudreaux, "and she just talks French. But she makes a mean shrimp *e-tou-fay*."

We set up our regular camp around the wagon after a full night of Cajun cuisine and music. Mr. Boudreaux had played an accordion while his oldest son strummed on a washboard, playing what they called *zydeco* music. "Zydeco," said Boudreaux after he had settled down by the fire after the music, "is a lot like our Cajun community. It's a mix of lotta things. We be French, Creole, Indian, white, Black, you name it… we got it."

Mr. Hallahan asked, "What will y'all do if Louisiana secedes?"

"Well, as you might guess," Boudreaux said as he looked at the rainbow of faces circling the campfire, "we ain't too keen on fighting to keep slavery."

At daybreak, we were awoken by the rustle of horses and loud voices. Though they were coming from around the bend of the river, one aggressive voice carried clearly across the water: "Boudreaux! We're the 1st Louisiana Militia Infantry. It's reckoning day for you Cajuns. Secession is coming any day now. It's time for you to decide. Are you with us or against us?"

We still could not see any of the militiamen, but Mr. Hallahan got us all working on breaking camp and loading the wagon. Before we could finish, Boudreaux's oldest son came running out of the trees. He went to the tinker and whispered urgently, "I'll hide your wagon in the woods. Y'all need to climb under the boats!" He pointed down to the river's edge where the pee-row boats were flipped upside down on the shore. "If they find your wagon, they will think you ran off into the woods."

"Can we trust him?" asked Joseph's mother.

"I don't think we have a choice," answered Mr. Hallahan.

We ran down to the boats which were made from hollowed-out cypress logs. Joseph and I climbed under one, and Miss Estelle and Mr. Hallahan each climbed under a boat as the Boudreaux son lifted them up. Once we were entombed under them, it was impossible to hear anything clearly. Instead, we heard muffled shouting and footsteps as we held our breaths and prayed. We could feel the *thump* of the horses' hooves in the sand, but no one lifted the boats.

When the noise subsided, Joseph whispered, "When do you think we can come out?"

"Let's wait a little longer," I whispered back. "I think I smell smoke."

After a few moments, Mr. Hallahan lifted the boat enough for Joseph and me to roll out. We moved to the third boat and helped Joseph's mother out. After we found the wagon in the nearby woods, we rode over to the Boudreaux's camp. It had been burned to the ground, and there was no one left.

PART TWO: New Orleans
(January-February 1861)

Chapter 4

When we reached the ridge road overlooking the river in Metairie, we bid a tearful goodbye to Mr. Hallahan, and Joseph, his mother, and I walked the rest of the way by ourselves. We arrived in New Orleans on a Sunday morning—the streets of the French Quarter littered with the debris of the previous night's partying. We stepped around broken bottles and vestiges of vomit as we learned that that Saturday night's revelries had been especially rowdy. Louisiana had just joined Mississippi in seceding from the Union.

As we threaded our way through the narrow streets, Joseph explained where we were headed: "My father made both me and my mother memorize three things: *'Hawkins* at *Antoine's* on *St. Louis Street.'* He drilled this into us in the days before we left the plantation."

The second-floor wrought-iron balconies of Bourbon Street were festooned with white flags bearing a red star in the center and a big, white-winged bird. As Joseph and I walked beneath them, we spotted white ceramic tiles with blue letters reading "St. Louis St." set into the corner of a building at a quiet intersection. Joseph whispered to me that his mother was relying on us to navigate the street signs because she had never had the chance to learn to read and write. Just like the three things her husband had made her memorize, she carried all the recipes for her cooking around in her head.

We came upon an unpretentious sign reading "Antoine's Pension" mounted beside a heavy wooden door. The smell of coffee and bacon wafted from an open window. There was no one on the sidewalk to help us, so Joseph's mother timidly knocked on the door. After a moment, a thin, young white man cracked the door and asked in another strange accent, "May I 'elp you?"

"Is Mr. Hawkins here?" replied Joseph's mother. The thin man ducked back inside where he opened a ledger on top of a counter. He ran his index finger down the page, stopping midway.

"Oui, pardon me," he interrupted himself as he returned to the door with that same finger pointing up. "I mean, yes. E's in the room right above."

As if on cue, we heard a weary voice drift down from the balcony: "Can't a guy get any sleep around this dump?" We stepped back off the sidewalk into the street so that the man on the balcony could see us. "Who the hell are you?" he barked.

"I'm Estelle," Joseph's mother answered quietly. "Nathan's wife—from Raw Cedar in Jackson. This is our son, Joseph, and our... traveling companion, John Falkner."

"Yer the jockey's wife?" he asked, seemingly getting his wits collected.

"Yes, sir. Nathan said we should talk to you about..."

"Shhh!" Hawkins held a finger to his thin, pale lips that were framed by a black goatee. "Meet me in the alley behind this building..." We saw him lean into the open balcony door and speak to someone inside who giggled with girlish glee. "In an hour," he announced to us as he lecherously leered over the rail before ducking back inside with an emphatic *slam* of the door.

Once we met Mr. Hawkins at eye level in the alley behind Antoine's, we could see that he was the same height as Joseph, with the slight build of a jockey—like Joseph's father. He nervously passed several slips of paper back and forth in his small hands. He stood with his face hidden in the shadows as he explained how he would help Miss Estelle and Joseph sail north.

"Y'all are lucky. The ship to Nantucket leaves on Monday mornings every three weeks, and I bought two open tickets for y'all for whenever you arrived. So, tomorrow morning at six o'clock, y'all need to be at Wharf Nine at the end of Canal Street. This ain't a free ride though. Lady—you'll be cooking for a crew of twenty-two men. And, kid—you look just like your dad, though you're gonna be a foot taller than him— you'll be below decks tending to a load of beef cattle. Don't be late. With secession here, this may be your last chance out."

With her clear, confident eyes, Joseph's mother looked through the shadows at this white stranger who held her and her son's future in his nervous hands. Although I had only known her for a few days, I could tell that she was sizing him up—deciding if her husband had been right. She turned to smile at Joseph and said to Mr. Hawkins, "My husband said I could trust you, so we will be on that ship. Thank you for your help."

Hawkins nodded, handing her the tickets and slip of paper that he had been juggling. As he withdrew his hand, he explained, "This is the address of a place you can stay tonight, but you can't show up there until after dark. Y'all need to find a place to stay out of trouble until then."

She smiled again. "It's Sunday. I know just the place."

"When you see your husband—*if* you ever see him again," he sneered cruelly as he turned to leave, "you tell him that we're even. I don't owe him nuthin' anymore."

After he left, she handed Joseph the slip of paper, and he read it to her: "The corner of St. Peter Street and Cabildo Alley." She closed her eyes and nodded—as if searching her memory— as they again began walking. The streets of the French Quarter were coming alive as shop owners opened their doors and swept the sidewalks in front of their businesses. Oxford, Mississippi, was the only "big city" I had ever been to, but it was nothing like this. Horses, carriages, and wagons plodded along on the round paving stones as pedestrians tried to avoid getting run down. When we reached St. Peter Street, Miss Estelle led us to an alley beside the "Cabildo Coffee House" that squatted untidily on the corner.

"What is a *coffee house*?" I asked her.

"It doesn't make sense, but they don't serve coffee much here. It's more for people to drink alcohol." We continued down this alley until it turned left onto an even more dingy alley. She pointed up a rickety set of stairs to the attic above: "That is where we will stay tonight."

* * *

Does she also mean me? Mr. Hawkins had looked through me like I didn't even exist. As if she could read my mind, Miss Estelle assured me, "You are welcome to stay with us tonight, John. We will make room. You do not want to be on your own in *this* neighborhood."

"How do you know so much about this place?" Joseph asked.

"Like my freedom papers say," she answered patiently, "I was born here."

"You don't ever talk about it," Joseph said.

"Being here drags up a lot of bad memories I've tried to forget." She pointed across the alley: "This garden—St. Anthony's—behind this church was the slave market where me and my mother and father were sold on Christmas Day when I was nine years old. I never saw them again after that day." She took Joseph's hand and picked up her pace as if she were trying to leave her past behind. Miss Estelle's past seemed lurking around each corner that we turned that day.

[*The old man couldn't know it then, but his grandson Billy would one day write, "The past is never dead. It's not even past."*]

The alley opened up to a large park as we reached the end of an immense white cathedral. "This park was called *Place D'Armes* when I was a little girl, but it was for white folks only. It was the parade ground for soldiers to strut their stuff while they didn't have a war to fight in. One soldier hit my daddy in the head with his rifle butt because he didn't like the way my father was lookin' at him." We reversed course, again passing the stairs leading up to where we would stay that night.

[*The old man also couldn't know it then, that his grandson would write his first novel in the first-floor apartment of that building on Pirate's Alley.*]

"Where are we walking to now?" asked Joseph to his mother.

"A place of happy memories."

As we walked, Miss Estelle abruptly turned to address me, like she was seeing me for the first time. "John, I've put all my heart and mind into getting Joseph and me here. Now that we made it, I realize that there's lots of questions I should've already asked you. Like, now that *you're* here, what are you going to do? Do you know anybody here?"

"I think so… I hope so," I answered. "My father has always talked about a man he fought with in the Mexican War who he said had become a 'bigwig' in New Orleans. He implied that he had saved this man's life in the war and that he was owed 'big time.' He also hinted that this man might be a cousin of my mother's. She was born in Chalmette near New Orleans like this man was, and my father said she had 'French relatives.' I was hoping *he* could help me."

"What is his name?" she asked.

"Beau-re-gard," I answered, trying to get the pronunciation right. "It's a French name."

"Do you know where he lives, or where he works?"

"I figured if he was such a bigwig then I could just ask around and people would know," I said. As we continued up St. Peter Street, my heart raced as I suddenly realized how little real thought I had put into what I was doing in running away from the only home I had ever known. And now these two people who had helped me would be leaving… tomorrow morning.

We began hearing music. Maybe not so much hearing it as *feeling* it. The pulsating drums felt indistinguishable from my throbbing heartbeat. We passed through a line of huge oaks that shaded the crowded park beyond. I had never seen so many Black people gathered together; however, something else was new and different. It took a moment of looking around for it to register with me. These people were smiling… laughing.

"What is this place?" Joseph asked his mother in wonder.

"This is Congo Square."

"I used to come here when I was a little girl. I wasn't sure it would live up to my memories of it, but..." she smiled broadly, "it's even better than I remember."

The hundreds of Black people in the square were divided among several different groups—each defined by their unique clothing, language, music, and dancing. In one group, the women were wrapped in brightly colored fabrics of silk and muslin while men wearing nothing but colorful sashes danced to the rhythm of drums, flutes, and marimbas.

Joseph stood in awe—as I did—at the sights and sounds surrounding us. "What do the different groups mean?" he shouted to his mother over the din.

"It goes back to what tribe your people came from in Africa," Miss Estelle explained. "For some of these people, their grandparents may have been brought over. For others—like me—it may date back five generations."

I didn't know how to say this, but I asked, "How is everyone able to be here?" *My father certainly never gave Simon, Mary, Henry, Lucy, or George the day off.*

"In New Or-lins, they have a law called the *Code Noir*, which allows slaves to not have to work on Sunday," Miss Estelle answered. "Also, many of the Black people you see are now free—like Joseph and me."

On the periphery of these groups stood many white people who were equally enthralled with all the bustle in Congo Square. Some shopped in the open-air market for handmade goods and food. Some white musicians even joined the drumlines playing more traditional instruments like violins and banjos. In one corner of the square, however, no white people seemed to venture. Under dark tents, Black people in clothing of rich tapestries lit candles and chanted verses in strange, unknown tongues. "What is going on over there?" I asked.

"Oooh," grinned Miss Estelle. "That's *voodoo.*"

* * *

After spending the afternoon in Congo Square, where we were able to eat and drink enough to last us through the night, we walked back to Pirate's Alley. Miss Estelle held both Joseph and my hands tightly as she led us through the dark streets to our room above a noisy tavern reeking of stale beer. The floor shook with the sounds of musicians and drunken revelers singing "God Save the South" as the secession fervor continued for a second night. Each time the song ended with the chorus "Freedom or death!" it would begin again a little louder. We slept on old mattresses stuffed with peanut shells that crinkled with every movement. I imagined that Joseph dreamed of what lay ahead—at sea and beyond—while I pondered, *What am I going to do when I'm all alone?*

Joseph's mother woke us up the next morning while it was still dark. With her one bag of belongings slung over her shoulder that she had with her since I first saw her in the lantern light, we trudged down the stairs and began our walk to Wharf Nine at the end of Canal Street. *I say "our walk" like I am going to get on the boat with them. I'm not, and I know that, but where else do I really have to go?*

Our path followed the mighty Mississippi on our left which was dotted with the lights of the steamboats, fishing boats, and barges that were moving up and down the river. As we approached the wharf district, the sounds of wagons, railroad cars, and longshoremen emerged out of the dark. We had just passed a large cargo terminal when the ship came into view. Its profile was backlit by the wintry sun that was just now rising above the river. The *Helen Mar* was a massive sailing ship that I later learned had been regularly used as a whaling vessel out of New Bedford, Massachusetts. Its three masts towered above the wharf as men scurried up and down the riggings to prepare the sails for the upcoming voyage to Nantucket.

"How long will it take you to get there?" I asked Joseph's mother.

"A little over two weeks," she answered. "God willing."

Joseph jumped in: "Daddy told me that the Gulf Stream makes the voyage *there* much quicker than the one back. The currents are moving our way."

Despite the excitement that I knew they both had to be feeling, Joseph and his mother looked at me with regret. "I feel terrible just leaving you here on your own," Miss Estelle said, "but as Mr. Hawkins said, this may be our only chance out."

"What are you going to do?" Joseph asked me.

I told them the plan I had come up with overnight: "When we were first walking into town yesterday, I noticed the offices of the *Times-Picayune*, the newspaper here in New Orleans. I thought I would walk over there and see if they could tell me how to find Mr. Beauregard."

"That's a good idea, John," Miss Estelle said trying to reassure me. "If you don't have any luck there, you could always try to ask Mr. Hawkins. You know where to find him."

"I'll be fine," I said as I tried—in vain—to reassure myself. "I have y'all to thank for that." I felt tears welling in my eyes just as a piercing whistle blew.

"All aboard the *Helen Mar!*" a voice rang out from the gangway leading up to the ship.

Joseph, my friend, looked awkwardly at me. I thought about him describing the last, desperate hug that his mother had given his father as they left the plantation. Desperation was what I was feeling as I opened my arms to him and exchanged a wordless goodbye. Miss Estelle took her son's hand and began up the gangway. The man who had called out for all passengers to board took their tickets and pointed up at the ship. She looked back at me. "You know, John. You can always send a telegram to your father," she said. "He would come get you."

Even as I nodded my head, I thought, *I will never do that.* And then they were gone.

After they had reached the top of the gangway and boarded the *Helen Mar*, I stepped back and watched the busy process of preparing the ship to sail. There was a lower gangway where longshoremen were carrying supplies and leading livestock into the bowels of the ship. I thought about Mr. Hawkins telling Joseph that his job aboard the ship would be tending to the cattle. I hoped that he had inherited his father's "natural way" with animals. Even as I was thinking this, Joseph emerged from the cargo opening of the ship at the end of this lower gangway led by a red-headed white man who appeared to be barking orders to Joseph as they walked into the cargo terminal. A short time later, Joseph reappeared leading a cow up the gangway into the ship. He repeated this several times with cattle and then began carrying boxes of fruits and vegetables aboard. He came back out one more time followed closely by the red-headed man as the mooring ropes tying the ship to the wharf began being cast off.

"Last call!" the man sang out again. "All aboard that's coming aboard!" The passenger gangway was retracted back onto the wharf as the passengers crowded the deck of the ship to wave a final goodbye to their family and friends. I looked back down to the cargo gangway, but there was no sign of Joseph returning to the ship. A man in the cargo opening unfastened the gangway that began pivoting back towards the wharf.

The ship began to move away almost imperceptibly from the wharf. *Have I missed Joseph's final return to the ship?* I didn't think that was possible, but I began to panic. "Joseph!" I yelled as I ran down a set of stairs to the cargo areas where the gangway had been connected. I found the pen where the cattle had obviously been kept, but there was no one around. A wide overhead door was opened onto an alley where a covered delivery wagon was pulling away.

A tall, thin young man with dark curly hair and a bushy mustache approached me. "Kid," he said kindly, "you look like you've just lost your only friend."

Chapter 5

As I looked closer at this stranger who had approached me, I saw that he was wearing a uniform of sorts—a dark suit with a nametag on his lapel. "Are you a policeman?" I asked.

"God, no," he laughed. "We would know the world was really in trouble if they hired me as a cop. No, kid. I'm a riverboat pilot. My name's Samuel. I just got off the graveyard shift, and I heard you yell. Now, who might you be, who is Joseph, and why do you look so forlorn?"

I had no reason to trust this stranger, but I did. His twinkling eyes bore in on me like he did really want to hear what I had to say, so I answered, "Mr. Samuel, my name is John Wesley Thompson Falkner. I'm twelve years old, and I just ran away from my home in Ripley, Mississippi. Joseph is my friend who saved my life on the road to New Orleans, and I'm scared that he might be in big trouble."

"Well, it's nice to meet you, John. And please call me Sam. I'm not that much older than you. As far as Joseph, maybe I can help. But first, are you hungry?"

In my panic to find Joseph, I had ignored the gnawing hunger in my belly. The little that we ate in Congo Square yesterday seemed long ago. "Yes, sir," I answered. "I am."

Sam beckoned me forward, and I followed him to the first corner on Canal Street where we got on a "streetcar" which was like a single car of a train that ran on the road instead of on rails. The driver of the streetcar seemed to know Sam, as did several passengers. When we got to the corner of Canal and Bourbon Street, Sam stepped off the streetcar, and I dutifully followed him. After walking two blocks, we came to a simple white building with two wide and welcoming doors topped by semi-circular transom windows. "This is my favorite spot in N'Awlins, John. It's called Aleix Coffee House. They serve the best omelets in the city."

I was confused. "I thought coffee houses really just served alcohol," I said.

Sam smiled ruefully. "I have been known to partake of some *al-kee-hol* on these premises, but I also eat breakfast here most days. They actually serve a delicious cup of coffee."

After we had settled in and Sam ordered breakfast for both of us, he looked at me with a new seriousness in his eyes. "Now tell me about what you think happened to your friend."

I told him how I had been rescued by Joseph and his mother and the story of meeting Mr. Hawkins yesterday at Antoine's where he gave Miss Estelle and Joseph their tickets for the ship to Nantucket. "I watched both of them board this morning, but Joseph had to help bring cattle and food supplies into the ship. He was being bossed around by a white man with red hair. I saw Joseph come out of the ship one last time with that man, but I never saw him get back on!" The panic that I had felt as I ran down the stairs at the cargo terminal returned. "There was a wagon pulling away in the alley when I got down the stairs," I continued in anguish, "and I can't help but believe that Joseph was in that wagon."

Sam frowned at me, but he stayed silent as if he couldn't decide whether to tell me about what was making him frown. Finally, he spoke up. "There's been rumors around the city ever since I got here over a year ago about Black children disappearing off the streets, and I mean *free* Black children. I've been trying to get my friend at the *Times-Picayune* to investigate the rumors, but he keeps putting me off, saying, *Who cares about some missing Black kids?*"

Sam's mention of the newspaper reminded me of what was supposed to be my plan for the day. "Have you ever heard of a Mr. *Beau-re-gard* here in New Orleans?" I asked him.

"Major Beauregard?"

"I guess so. He fought with my father in the Mexican War."

"That would be him," Sam said. "Everybody knows him in N'Awlins."

"Do you know where I could get in touch with him?"

"Sorry, John, but you just missed him. He was appointed Superintendent of the U.S. Military Academy at West Point. The *Times-Picayune* had an article about his grand departure."

My heart sank with this news. My one connection to this city was gone, and evidently, the despair showed on my face. "Don't worry, John. I can help you. First thing, we need to get you a place to stay." He gestured to the black-bearded man behind the bar who immediately came over.

"Aleix," Sam said, "do you have that room in the attic available for a few days?"

"Sure, Mr. Sam," Aleix replied. "For you it is."

"Thanks, Aleix. I need it for my friend here, John. Are you still needing a dishwasher?"

"Sure, Mr. Sam. None of these bums around here stick with the job."

Sam turned his attention back to me. "John, I have to make a four-day trip up the river beginning tonight. You stay here with Aleix and work hard for him to pay for your lodging. When I get back, we will find out what happened to your friend Joseph. Can you do that?"

"Yes, sir," I answered, feeling a new spark of hope, though I was hesitant about the delay.

"Okay, good," Sam said in a settled way. He shifted his attention again: "John, you told me about how you met up with Joseph, but you haven't told me about why you left home."

I recounted the story of the burning Christmas tree and my subsequent trip on the timber wagon with Jim. When I got to the part about Jim and I floating down the river on a raft, Sam impulsively reached back and pulled a black leather journal out of the satchel hanging on the back of his chair. His brow furrowed as he opened the journal and began writing. The cover of the journal featured a gold embossed *M.T.* at the center.

"John, you just got *real* interesting. Do you mind if I take a few notes?" Sam asked.

"No," I answered quizzically, "but what does the *M.T.* stand for?"

"Oh," he answered. "That's for the pen name I write under: *Mark Twain.*"

* * *

I began working in the kitchen that night at the coffee house, and as Miss Estelle had said, this coffee house served very little coffee but lots of alcohol. My dishwashing duties that night consisted of washing scores of glasses that came to me with the foam of beers and ales still ringing the tops. As I worked, I couldn't stop thinking about both Joseph and his mother. *I can't imagine the fear that Miss Estelle felt when she realized Joseph was not on the ship. Does she think he has fallen overboard? Could I be entirely wrong about what I think I saw?*

For the second night in a row, I went to sleep to the sounds of drunken revelers thundering beneath me. I worked almost the entire following day in the kitchen. I felt like I had to show my boss, Mr. Aleix, that I was dependable and a worthwhile risk to occupy his extra room in the attic. He told me that Tuesday night, however, that I could have the Wednesday breakfast and lunch shifts off because he was closing the coffee house to attend a funeral.

Even though I had told Sam that we could look for Joseph when he got back, when I woke up early Wednesday morning I thought, *I can't wait.* I retraced the path I had taken with Joseph and his mother to Wharf Nine. There was a paddleboat steamship moored at the dock, taking on supplies for a trip up the Mississippi River. I bought myself a hot cup of coffee in the terminal, paying with coins that a waitress had given me the night before at the coffee house.

Using the coffee mug to keep my hands warm, I began my surveillance of the freight gangway below where I had last seen Joseph on Monday morning. For the next two hours, I watched as supplies were carried onto the riverboat, but there was no sign of the red-headed man. By nine o'clock, the passengers had arrived and boarded, and the boat set sail up the river. Sam—or Mr. Twain—had given me the name of the reporter at the *Times-Picayune* that he knew, so I decided to go talk to him to see if he could tell me any more about Major Beauregard.

"How old are you, kid?" Mr. Wilson, a chubby, bespectacled reporter, asked me.

"I'm twelve."

"And you're here in the city on your own?"

"Yes, sir. That's why I was hoping to find Major Beauregard. He fought with my father in the Mexican War."

"Who's your father?"

"His name is William Clark Falkner, but everyone calls him the 'Old Colonel.'"

"Never heard of him. Well, Sam was telling you right about Beauregard. He was appointed the Superintendent of the U.S. Military Academy at West Point last Wednesday, and he left for there by train immediately. But Louisiana seceding from the Union derailed his appointment—Sorry, kid, no pun intended—and we just got word over the telegraph that he has resigned his commission. Nobody has any idea about when he might be back in New Or-lins."

With this dead end, all I knew to do was stay put at Aleix's until Sam got back on Friday. As an afterthought, I asked Mr. Wilson about the rumors that Sam had mentioned concerning missing Black children. "Do you have any idea about what may be happening to them?"

"Jeez, kid, I don't know. It's my job to chase down stories that my readers might actually be interested in, and not even the police care about a bunch of young runaway slaves. There's bounty hunters crawling out of the woodwork down here to take care of that."

"But my friend Joseph was not a slave," I protested. "His father had just bought his and his mother's freedom, and he just disappeared from the ship that was taking him to Nantucket."

"I'm sorry about your friend, kid, but all I know is that there have been whispers about a 'Reverse Underground Railroad' trafficking in free Black children for years, but no one has ever found anything concrete about it. If it exists, you don't want to have anything to do with it."

"I've never heard of the 'Underground Railroad' or a reverse," I said. "What is it?"

I had obviously reached the end of Mr. Wilson's patience, as he stood up and beckoned me towards the door of his office: "What do I look like, kid—an encyclopedia? I've got *real* stories to work on."

I couldn't hold back a noisy, wet *sniff*, as this second dead end staggered me.

"Aw, jeez, kid—now you're going to start crying on me." He paused as a bit of humanity crept into his face. "Go down to the basement and turn right at the bottom of the stairs. Look for the 'Archives Room.' Mrs. Broder can help find some stories that we've written on the Underground Railroad. You can read, can't you?"

"Yes, sir," I said as another stifled sob escaped.

"Well, good luck then," Mr. Wilson said as he steered me from his office with a not-so-gentle push to my back.

Mrs. Broder in the Archives was a tiny, white-haired woman who was as sweet and patient as Mr. Wilson was gruff and curt. I felt immediately at ease with her, and she just gave me a wide-eyed smile when I asked her if she had "ever ridden on the Underground Railroad that Mr. Wilson had talked about."

"It's not an actual railroad with tracks and cars," she delicately explained.

"Is it underground?" I queried. I looked down at the floor

as if the cars might be passing beneath our feet even as we spoke.

"No, John," she answered. "*Underground* refers to it being secret and out of view. It's a network of people and 'stations' that help Black people escape the South and get to the North."

Joseph mentioned the word "network" to me. "Then what would a 'Reverse Underground Railroad' be?" I asked.

"Oh, my Lord, John. It would be just awful."

* * *

Mrs. Broder retrieved articles from the *Times-Picayune* that detailed possible escape routes that the Underground Railroad used in the New Orleans area. These included by ship to Northern cities and by foot through the swamps of southern Louisiana into Texas. As I understood it by these articles, the purpose of the Underground Railroad was to give runaway slaves a pathway to Northern cities where they would not be hunted down and returned to their owners in the South. The reverse of this would be a nefarious network that railroaded free Blacks to the South *into slavery*. I could only assume this meant kidnapping and taking people against their will. *Is this what happened to Joseph?*

After thanking Mrs. Broder for her help, I returned to the coffee house and worked the evening shift. Before leaving the kitchen that night, I asked Mr. Aleix if I could start the breakfast shift a little late the next morning. "I have a friend who may be in trouble," I explained.

"This is an easy city to find trouble in," he said. "You better worry about yourself."

"I will," I assured him, but little did I know of what I

was about to get into. I awoke early the next morning and again walked in the dark to the cargo terminal. Another paddleboat was loading as I arrived. I bought a cup of coffee—my breakfast for the morning—and kept my eyes glued to the gangway leading from the terminal up to the paddleboat.

As I watched, a crew member stood on the dock and lowered a line with a weight at the end into the river. He looked down at the colored knots tied into the line and called out, "By the mark twain!" *Mark Twain?* I looked around to see if Sam had come back early.

"What's he doing?" I asked the man at the food counter as I pointed at the crew member. "That's the leadsman," he answered. "He is measuring the depth of the river. It's low tide right now, and they want to be sure there's enough depth in the channel for the boat to get out."

"What does 'mark twain' mean?"

"*Twain* means *two*, so the depth there is two fathoms, or twelve feet."

The leadsman pulled the line out of the river, drying it with a handkerchief as the line pooled at his feet. He next coiled it around his elbow and placed it in a barrel on the dock by the gangway. After my coffee was gone, I waited in the cold for over an hour, getting up every few minutes to get blood flowing to my frozen feet. This time, however, my patience was rewarded. Just after eight o'clock, according to the large clock mounted on the wall above the food counter, I spotted the red-headed man on the gangway. He was again bossing a Black boy—about my age—who was carrying supplies aboard the paddleboat.

When I saw both enter the boat through a cargo door, I quietly crept down the stairs and wound my way into the area where the cattle had been kept previously. Though the pen was empty, the smell still permeated the terminal. Along one side wall, large wooden crates were stacked almost to the ceiling. I snuck behind this stack where I found a vantage point that allowed me to see both the door in front of the gangway and the overhead door where the wagon had left from three days before when Joseph disappeared. After a few minutes, the red-headed man and the Black boy re-entered the cargo area where I was hiding.

"Isaac, this is the last load to carry on," I heard the red-headed man say as he gestured to two boxes sitting on the floor, "and then you'll be done for the day. I'll have your pay ready for you when you come back."

"Yessir, Mr. Scott," the muscular boy said as he easily lifted the boxes into his arms and turned towards the gangway. When he had left, Mr. Scott walked to the open overhead door, took a red bandana out of his back pocket, and waved it at something down the alley. Just a few seconds later, the same wagon as before backed into the overhead door.

Another man wearing a wide-brimmed hat that obscured much of his face hopped down from the driver's seat and opened the hinged door on the rear of the boxed compartment of the wagon using only his right arm, as his left arm seemed to hang lifelessly at his side. He climbed through the door into the darkness of the wagon and whispered, "Ready!"

Isaac returned from the boat and looked at Mr. Scott expectantly. "They just delivered one more box," declared Mr. Scott and pointed to the open back door of the wagon. "It'll be worth an extra dollar for you to carry it onboard."

Isaac approached the back of the wagon warily and stopped before climbing up. When he paused, Mr. Scott rushed at him from behind with the red bandana wadded in his hand. A sickly sweet smell filled the room. He reached around the boy's face and clamped the bandana tightly over his mouth and used his other hand to shove the suddenly slack-legged Isaac roughly into the wagon.

Mr. Scott slammed the door and slid a bolt across to lock it. The man in the hat climbed out a hinged trapdoor in the roof of the compartment and pivoted into the driver's seat. Mr. Scott put the bandana back in his pocket as he climbed up beside the driver. With a flick of the whip that had been tucked under his lame left arm, the driver prompted the horse: "Let's go, boy!"

As soon as they were out in the alley, I checked both directions and emerged from my hiding place. I followed the wagon on foot until it took a right turn onto North Peters Street. Luckily, this was the main thoroughfare for wagons carrying cargo from the wharf area, so I was able to slide up onto the back of a flatbed wagon stacked with boxes labeled "Mazzola Seafood." When the wind shifted towards me from the north, the smell of fresh fish oozing from the boxes was almost overwhelming, but I was in a perfect location two wagons behind the red-headed man. *The chase was on!*

Chapter 6

I tailed them northward until we merged into the even more heavily trafficked Decatur Street that runs parallel to the river. This was the reverse of my walking path the two previous mornings, so I kept a map pictured in my mind. Soon we passed by the eastern side of what Miss Estelle had called the *Place d'Armes*—what I had since learned was now "Jackson Square." Dozens of haggard, gray-clad soldiers marched wearily in formation around the square.

The overpowering smell of fish was briefly blunted by the delicious aroma of coffee as we passed by the French Market, which marked the eastern boundary of the area I was familiar with in the city. After several blocks, the wagon I was riding in turned into an eatery at the corner of Elysian Fields Avenue, and I was again forced to chase after the other wagon on foot. I was lucky, however, because the other wagon also turned, and the heavy traffic on Elysian kept the red-headed man and his compatriot moving at a slow pace. I was able to dart back and forth behind other wagons and horses to stay within eyesight of them. The wagon turned onto the wide St. Claude Avenue where I was able to jump onto the back of a shiny, bright-red, horse-drawn streetcar running down the tracks in the center of the boulevard.

By staying low, hanging to the brass railing at the rear, I was able to hide from the driver and avoid having to pay for a ride that I had no money for anyway. We stopped every few blocks to take on or let off passengers, but no one gave me up to the driver. After we passed through the Poland Avenue intersection, the streetcar began to climb as we crossed a metal bridge spanning a finger of the river that snaked into the surrounding neighborhood. As I looked between my feet dangling in mid-air above the tracks, I could see a small boat loaded with flowers of blue, yellow, and red pass beneath the bridge. We began our descent and passed by a sign indicating that we were entering the "Lower Ninth Ward."

The houses were smaller in this district, though they still maintained some of the exquisite details of the French Quarter. There were still foreign and exotic-sounding street names like *Deslonde* and *Lizardi*, but as I spied the wagon with the red-headed man slowing down ahead, it was the ordinary-sounding *Flood Street* that turned out to be their destination.

They turned onto Flood Street and soon veered into an alley between two one-story shotgun houses decorated with gingerbread trim on their front porches. I knew what a "shotgun house" was from my one trip to Oxford with my father where he had pointed out the simple houses with a central hallway where one could fire a shotgun through the open front door, and the pellets would exit out the back door at the other end of the hallway. When the Old Colonel told me this, I half suspected that this was not just a hypothetical scenario to him.

I slipped behind a caustic cart collecting garbage in order to stay invisible until I saw the wagon pull off the alley into a gravel drive at the back of a lot next to a toolshed. The red-headed man hopped down from the driver's box and unlocked a padlock on the toolshed door. He directed the other man who backed the wagon up to the now-open door. In a flash, the driver scurried down through the trapdoor in the roof of the compartment and gave the unconscious Isaac a one-handed push out the back and through the toolshed door. Just as quickly, the driver was back in the box seat, pulling out of the driveway. The door slammed shut with the red-headed man and the young, helpless Black boy inside. From my hiding spot behind some dense shrubbery on the other side of the alley, I sat and watched, waiting for the red-headed man to exit. After what must have been an hour, I still sat and waited. I looked through the canopy of trees in the back to the elevated two-story house sitting proudly at the front of the lot. Another impatient half hour passed while I waited for some activity. *It makes no sense that two people would both stay in that tiny toolshed,* I thought to myself as my patience waned. *I can't wait much longer.*

A light came on through a window at the back of the house, and the silhouette of a man appeared for the blink of an eye. While I thought it looked like the red-headed man, that was impossible—he had not left the toolshed. After another few minutes, I had to try something.

I crept across the alley and into the noisy gravel leading up to the toolshed. I got down on my hands and knees as I approached the closed door. The walls of the shed were made of vertical pieces of siding that had the tiniest of gaps between them. When I pushed my face against the wall with my eye to the gap, I still could not see anything. I pressed my ear to the gap in hopes of hearing two sets of breaths escaping. *Nothing... Silence.*

I crawled to the other side of the door, noting that the padlock was missing, and the hasp was left unfastened. *The door is not locked!* I turned my body so that one foot pushed against the base of the wall while my other foot faced outward to the alley. I had seen the fast kids at school assume this pose when they were challenged to a race. With my weight on the balls of my feet, I took my right hand and pushed my thumb against the door jamb, and the point of my index finger settled silently on the hard edge of the door. I held my breath as I began to spread my thumb and forefinger apart. As the crack in the door widened a hair, I peered into the darkness.

That makes no sense, I thought. *This is impossible.*

I took the full thickness of the door in my hand and swung it open. The toolshed was empty! I once snuck into the county fair in Ripley with Henry and Lucy, my father's teenage slaves, and I will never forget the traveling magician who performed on a small stage behind his covered wagon, *that actually looked a lot like Professor Moore's*, now that I thought about it. The magician had made a small child disappear off the stage with a flick of his cape and some well-timed smoke. But the feat that the magician had performed was nothing compared to this.

Both the red-headed man and the boy have disappeared into thin air.

* * *

The toolshed—in fact—held no tools. There was nothing on the walls, and the floor was bare, though there were splattered dark-brown stains that could have been blood. I opened the door wider to bring in more light, but it was hopeless—there was nothing to find.

I ran my hand along the floor, but it was just planks of wood, tongue-and-grooved to fit tightly into each other. As I dragged my hand outward, however, I felt a joint in the floor. As my finger probed this slightest of gaps, it turned ninety degrees and ran almost to the wall. Again, it turned ninety degrees, and again, until I was back where I had started. The floor appeared to be one big trapdoor, but there were no visible hinges or handles to get it open. If I had a crowbar, I could have pried it open, but there were no tools. This shed had a more sinister purpose.

With this dead end, I pivoted to the other source of my curiosity: the silhouette in the window. I exited the toolshed, pushed the door closed, and walked back to the alley. As I looked back towards the house, I realized I was hidden from anyone in the house by the gnarled branches of the huge live oaks that filled the backyard. Hanging from the branches was Spanish moss that reminded me of the metallic garlands that my stepmother used to hang from the branches of the Christmas tree back when she gave a damn about the holidays.

As I sighted across the rear of the backyard parallel to the alley, I detected a peculiar, cleared lane under the live oaks that gave me a pathway across the yard. I bent over and moved stealthily across. After a few steps, however, I tripped across a tree root sticking out of the ground. As I examined it closer, I discovered it was not a root after all. It had a metallic hardness to it, and it was covered by a hood, like the cap of a large mushroom. Disguising the hood was a thatch of Spanish moss that had fallen from a tree. I continued for several yards only to trip over another hood. I made it to the side boundary of the yard where I slipped through a gap in a fence.

Creeping along the back side of the fence, I reached Flood Street where I looked both ways, and there did not seem to be anyone around. I walked on the hard-packed dirt that comprised the street until a hedge gave me cover to duck towards the house that I had only seen from the rear. From the front, it was remarkable.

The house sat perched high above the street, reachable by a broad set of stone stairs that led to a wraparound porch. At the end of the porch, a semi-circular "turret" anchored the corner of the house like a castle rook. The foundation of the house was built from stone that projected an image of solidity and permanence. *This house is going to be here forever.*

I was so enraptured with the front of the house that I almost missed the sound of footsteps approaching from the opposite direction. I ducked further into the hedge to keep this interloper from seeing me. As the person came into view, I could see through the dense branches that he wore a derby hat and a long black coat with the lapels turned up to hide his face. He paused at the base of the stairs and then began to climb. He was smallish in stature with short legs, requiring great effort to climb the stone steps. When he reached the porch, he disappeared into the shadows as I heard his knuckles rap on the front door. I adjusted my position in the hedge so that I could see up the stairs. When the door opened, I received my first shock: the bright red hair of the man from the wagon and the toolshed was clearly visible in the doorway, backlit by the sparkling tin ceiling tiles of the foyer behind him. As he stepped out and began talking to the visitor, the second shock hit me. After removing his hat and settling his lapels, I recognized the face of Mr. Hawkins, the man who had provided the tickets to Joseph and his mother.

After Hawkins entered the house, I turned and ran up Flood Street, all the way back to St. Claude Avenue. I could see the horse-drawn streetcar coming back from the opposite direction, but I knew better than to try my luck twice. I was doubly surprised then when the driver spoke to me as the streetcar neared: "Kid, you look like you've just seen a ghost." I mumbled something as I looked down at my feet like this might help me disappear, but the driver continued as the car came to a stop: "I know you hitched a free ride with me. If you need to get back where you came from, I can look the other way again." He made a comical attempt to turn his head and look innocently into the distance.

I couldn't help but laugh at this, which was the ticket that the driver was looking for. He shrugged his head towards the back and started the streetcar back on its route. I stepped onto the back and this time settled myself into a seat as I began trying to make sense of everything that I had just witnessed at the house on Flood Street. Mrs. Broder at the Archives had smiled when I asked her if the Underground Railroad was really underground; however, that was the only explanation for what happened to the boy in the toolshed and how the red-headed man ended up inside the house. *They must have gone underground.*

I felt so tired that I couldn't think clearly. I couldn't see through the fog of this mystery that had enveloped me. Instead, my focus shifted to the floor of the streetcar where a child had dropped candy near one of my shoes. I thought back to bribing my half-brothers and -sisters with peppermint sticks to stop them from crying about not getting Christmas presents. A trail of ants led from the sill of the window beside me, down the wall, and across to the candy. I couldn't see it yet, but the puzzle was starting to come into focus. *Ants... Ants dig tunnels... Tunnels!*

I hadn't had time to think about it at the time, but the "roots" that I tripped over suddenly made sense. In the schoolhouse in Ripley, we had made an ant farm last spring, building a box with a glass front. After filling it with sandy soil, a supply of food and water, and—of course—ants, our class watched as intricate tunnels grew horizontally and vertically. Our teacher took a pencil and poked it down through the tunnels to provide the third thing that the ants needed: *Air!*

* * *

I hopped off the streetcar at St. Louis Street and gave a wave of thanks to the driver. I practically ran to Aleix Coffee House, entering the kitchen through a back door off the alley, and donned an apron to begin washing dishes. As I did this mindless work, my imagination swirled like the draining water in the sink with images of tunnels, mushrooms, and trapdoors.

I was brought back to earth when Mr. Aleix entered and hoisted a barrel off a shelf in the storage area at the back of the kitchen. "If everyone keeps drinking like they are this afternoon," he said, "we're gonna run out of ale by dinnertime." He set the barrel upright on the floor and pulled a cork out of the top. Getting down on his knees, Mr. Aleix tried to peer down into the barrel with his head turned to one side and one eye closed. "It's too dark in here. I can't see a thing. I need to know how much is left in this barrel."

He stood and put his finger to his lips as he looked deep in thought. His hand moved around to the back of his neck, and he lifted a thin, silver chain up and over his head. When he saw me looking quizzically at him, Mr. Aleix explained, "This is my lucky Saint Christopher necklace. I've had it since I was your age." As I watched, he lowered the medal at the end of the chain down through the narrow, circular opening at the top of the barrel. He pinched a spot on the chain and withdrew the medal, checking it as it surfaced out of the barrel. "Still dry," he announced. He repeated the action, this time allowing the medal to drop deeper into the barrel. He again pinched the chain as he withdrew the medal that now sparkled with a sheen of foamy ale. "We should be fine," Mr. Aleix declared as he held the necklace out at arm's length, "if our precious patrons won't feel like they have to spend *another* night celebrating secession."

I worked hard in the kitchen that night. When bedtime came, I was tired, but I couldn't sleep. I didn't know what to do or who to trust. But early in the dark morning, I had a dream.

In my dream, I was chasing someone through the streets of New Orleans, but as I paused to look around me, the city unfolded itself—not horizontally as a flat city like New Orleans would do—but vertically with streets stacked on top of each other like… like an ant farm. People scurried through streets that shrunk and expanded like tunnels, according to their needs. When a tunnel reached an endpoint, the people would dig down and create a new thoroughfare.

At some point right before my waking, my view of this scene pulled back, and the people really were the size of ants. Mr. Aleix appeared—a colossus to this miniature colony— and lowered his silver necklace into the vertical city. The Saint Christopher medal began spinning and burrowed its way like an awesome awl through the tunnels, opening up vertical shafts of light and air. As he began to pull upward, I woke up—and I knew what I had to do.

As I had done every morning since I arrived in New Orleans with Joseph and his mother, I awoke in the dark. I climbed down the stairs from my attic room that emptied out into the dining—or drinking—room of the coffee house. I found a stack of preprinted cards that the waitresses used to take orders and wrote out a note of explanation and apology to Mr. Aleix. I told him—with any luck—I would be back for the dinner shift. I left the note on the bar under an ashtray and stuffed two pencils, some order cards, and the elastic band around them into my pocket.

I retraced my route in the dark to Wharf Nine at the end of Canal Street and found it quiet and empty for a change. Fridays, evidently, were a slack day on the river. The cargo terminal was starting to come to life, though there was no sign of the red-headed man. I quickly took care of the task that had brought me there. I went to the barrel by the gangway entrance and discreetly removed one of the coiled sounding lines from the top. It fit neatly into the side pocket of my jacket. I walked northwesterly on Canal Street—away from the now-rising sun—to North Rampart Street and boarded the same horse-drawn streetcar that I had ridden the day before.

"No free rides, kid," a new driver greeted me as I approached the car.

"I can pay," I said defensively as I scrounged for coins in my pocket. These had also come from the kind waitress at the coffee house as a "tip" for my extra efforts in the kitchen.

I settled in for a long ride, wishing that I had had enough

money for both this ride and a cup of coffee back at the wharf. After several blocks, we passed Congo Square which sat dark and deserted, though I felt the echo of the drums thrumming somewhere within me.

As the streetcar began a slow bend to the east and North Rampart transitioned into the more familiar St. Claude Avenue, we came to a stop, and an influx of passengers boarded the car. A white-haired priest in a black coat and clerical collar worked his way down the center aisle. "Is this seat taken?" he asked. I shook my head. He sat and began gently probing me with questions like "Where are you headed so early this morning?"

I thought of Joseph describing Father Matthew, his "teacher, doctor, and minister." What I needed more than anything right now was a *friend.* I would have liked to confess the things that I knew right now about Joseph and the house on Flood Street, but how could I know if this stranger was anyone that I could trust? I think he sensed my wariness and paused his gentle interrogation. "Are you hungry?" he asked instead. Before I could answer, he began unrolling a piece of bread from a sack that sat in his lap.

"Thank you, Father," I said as I hungrily broke off a piece of the bread and stuffed it in my mouth. I couldn't remember when my last real meal was. I guessed my breakfast with Sam, or Mark Twain, or whoever he was. The priest handed me a "business" card that read, "Father Andrew O'Mara: Minister of the Church of the Good Samaritan." When I looked up from the card, I glanced out the window and across the boulevard where I saw the wagon with the red-headed man and the driver pass us going in the opposite direction. *The coast is clear.*

Chapter 7

I jumped down from the streetcar at the stop before Flood Street because I didn't want to give away to Father Andrew where I was going. "If you ever need help, young man," he called to me as I walked away from the streetcar, "you know where to find me." He pointed to the card that I still clutched in my hand.

I continued down Egania Street to where it intersected with Burgundy Street. I turned left and walked three blocks to Flood Street. On this corner, a white church stood with a tall bell tower above the front entrance. At the top of the bell tower, there was a gap in the center where a clock hung. It was six forty-eight in the morning. Once I was on Flood Street, I paid closer attention to who was out, but it was still very quiet. I saw the house up ahead, and I moved over to the far side of the street into the shadows. When I passed the end of the fence that I had crept behind yesterday, I ducked inside the hedge. I peered through the branches at the house that looked dark and almost abandoned. I waited several minutes, but no one was stirring. I backtracked to the fence and used it as cover to get to the back of the lot, which was heavily shaded by the gnarled arms of the live oak trees and the still-low sun. After observing the back of the house for a few minutes, it was time to put my plan into action.

First, I checked the toolshed, and the padlock had been put back on the door. *There's no getting in that way*, I thought to myself. I got low to the ground and soon found the mushroom-shaped cap protruding from the ground and removed the Spanish moss that covered it. I uncoiled the sounding line and left the lead weight at the end poised by the opening in the ground. I took the order cards out of my pocket and removed the brownish band around them. I had never seen a rubber thing like this before, but I thought it might come in handy. I had been pondering my plan for a while now, but it was time to put my thoughts on paper.

"I am looking for Joseph," I wrote on the card with the pencil, *"a freed Black boy from Jackson. I think I can help whoever is down there, but I first need to know if Joseph is there. Please pull on this line three times if you get this. My name is John."*

I folded this note up around a pencil into the smallest piece possible and wrapped it around the lead weight with the "rubber band" holding it in place. I carefully put the weight inside the pipe under the metal cap and began lowering it. There were colored pieces of fabric marking the increasing depths of the line. A twig of blue passed through my fingers labeled "Half Fathom." I let the line, propelled by the heft of the weight, continue to slide. A red piece reading "One Fathom" went by. Just as the yellow marker "One and One-Half Fathoms" went into the pipe, the line stopped. I held the line gently, eager to feel a tug.

After a few minutes, the realization hit me that I might have a long wait. There was no way for me to know what lay nine feet below my feet. I thought about the times that Simon, my father's kind slave, and his son Henry would take me fishing with them at the pond in Ripley. Simon just had one cane pole, so he would cut off pieces of string line for Henry and me to use. Simon would attach a cork and hook at the end of each line that he would bait with moldy bread. Henry and I would sit with our backs against a log by the pond with the lines running between our toes so we could feel the smallest strike of a fish. *What I didn't realize at the time was that these fishing trips were not for fun like my friends at school talked about. Simon needed the fish he caught to help keep his family fed.*

I sat down a few feet from the pipe running down into the earth, wondering if I had the whole thing all wrong. Just as my self-doubts were beginning to fester, I felt a twitch in the line between my fingers. This was followed by three deliberate tugs.

I began bringing the weight up to the surface, not really knowing what to expect. What I found at the end of the line was a new note wrapped around the weight. When I unfolded it, I immediately recognized a page from the diary that Father Matthew had given Joseph. The *6* on the top left of the page indicating "February 6" had been scratched out and changed to a *4.*

"John, I don't know how you found me, but Thank God! You have to get us help. There are 14 of us down here, and they are going to sell us as slaves! They leave us alone in this tunnel—just give us food, water, and oil for a lantern. We are digging our way out at the far end.

Does Mamma know what happened to me?"

I looked all around me—through the backyard to the house, out the drive to the alley, and across the "lane" above the tunnel to the adjacent lot's fence—and I saw no one around. I took another card and began writing: *"I'm sorry, but I don't know what your mamma knows, other than you're not on the ship. Can you tell me where the end of your tunnel is?"* I lowered this note down and felt movement on the other end as soon as it hit the bottom at one and one-half fathoms. After a short time, there were again three tugs on the line, and I retrieved the new note.

"You are at the first air hole. There is another one about sixty feet away in this straight part of the tunnel. Many children before me have been digging upward just past the second air hole. We are running at a 45-degree angle to the right of the straight tunnel. We thought we were getting close to the top when we hit a wood wall. I think we've dug about sixty more feet, but it's hard to tell because we're going up at an angle. Please get help! I don't know when they're coming to get us!"

As I read this, I remembered Joseph telling me how Father Matthew had taught him the basics of mathematics. I hoped I knew enough to follow his directions. I wrote one last note and lowered it down into the pipe: *"Hang on, Joseph! I am going to get the police. We will get you out."* Even as I wrote this, I thought about Mr. Wilson's warning that the police didn't care.

* * *

I pulled the sounding line back up and coiled it into my pocket. I walked along the lane until I found the second air hole. It was right before the gap in the fence that marked the adjacent lot. I stood with my back to the line created by the two air holes and pictured a vertical line reaching into the sky. Placing my right shoulder against the fence, I reached my open hand out to the vertical line with the same gesture that I used playing

"Rock, Paper, Scissors" with my classmates. I pivoted to my right forty-five degrees—halfway around to the fence—and sighted along my extended arm and hand. *This should be the path of the escape tunnel they are digging.*

The line intersected with the rear left corner of the neighboring house—a shotgun house like those at the entrance to the alley. It appeared to have a brick foundation, but luckily there was an outside bulkhead with a door that might lead down into the basement. While I was *this* close, I had to at least look for the end of their tunnel before leaving to find the police. I crept through the backyard of this house with my eyes peeled on the rear windows. I could see no lights and no movement as I tiptoed up to the bulkhead to examine the door. Fortunately, it was not a door; instead, it was two pieces of hinged, repurposed sheet metal with no sign of any lock or latch. There were two stone steps down to the angled panels, and I almost tripped and fell right onto them. I regained my balance, however, and bent down to insert my finger under the bottom corner of the left panel. As I began to lift, a creaking from the rusted hinges rang out like a growling dog. I gently lowered that side back down and waited for any response to my commotion. After none appeared to be coming, I tried the other panel, and it lifted silently. I opened it all the way and rested the panel against the sides of the bulkhead because I would need the daylight inside the basement to look for evidence of the tunnel. I retrieved Joseph's note from my pocket and reread his message: "*...we were getting close to the top when we hit a wood wall.*"

I climbed down the steps into the low-ceilinged basement and began looking around. The floor was hard-packed dirt, and all the walls were whitewashed stacked stone under the outside brick. There was no sign of any wood walls as Joseph's note had said. I looked closer at the corner that I had sighted, but there were no variations in the stone walls. In the back left corner, there was a hoe and a shovel propped against the wall that the owner must have used to tend the vegetable garden I had passed in the back. I turned the hoe upside down and began prodding the dirt floor with the end of the handle, but I didn't feel anything but solid earth. I stomped around the entirety of the basement floor with similar results. *Dead end.*

I climbed back up the stairs and gently lowered the sheet metal panel back into place. I stepped back into the yard and tried to repeat my process of sighting a forty-five-degree line. By extending it through the corner of this house, I peered through a scraggly hedge to the adjacent property. The next point of intersection looked like it would be the side of the church with the bell tower that I had passed by earlier.

Boom! I heard the very recognizable sound of a screen door slamming shut. I ducked over behind the hedge to shield myself from the front of the house whose basement I had just "broken into." I heard a voice call out from the porch: "Good morning, Officer Craven! It's good to see you out patrollin' the streets."

Again, I couldn't believe my luck. While I wanted to go explore the side of the church, I realized it was much more critical for me to get the police involved, despite what Mr. Wilson had said. I eavesdropped on the conversation between the officer and the homeowner, which touched on both the weather and secession, until I heard the door slam again. I waited a beat for any more noise, and then I hurried along the church side of the hedge until I was back on Flood Street. I looked left, and there was the police officer walking in front of the church. I turned onto the street walking slowly because I wanted to keep my distance until I was clear of the house where Joseph was imprisoned. Once he crossed Burgundy Street, I sped up to catch up with him.

As I approached from behind, something about the officer and his gait seemed familiar. The stocky policeman stopped to read a piece of paper that was tacked to a tree beside the road. He snatched at the paper and ripped it down, just as he heard my approach from behind. He spun around and flinched like he wanted to draw the gun from the holster around his waist. However, he looked at the piece of paper in his right hand, looked at me, and then tucked the piece of paper under his lifeless left arm. I was staring up into the bloodshot eyes of the driver of the wagon that had taken Joseph away.

"Did you need something, kid?" the officer said as he fumbled at his belt for a flask that I assumed didn't contain water. The paper under his arm fell to the ground.

"Uh… uh," I stammered. I looked down at my feet and saw the paper that featured a drawing of a Black boy's face with a headline of *MISSING* above. *No wonder he pulled it down.*

"Speak up, kid. I don't have all day." He took a long swig from the flask.

"No, sir. I'm sorry, sir," I finally spat out. "I'm fine."

I walked hurriedly away. When I was out of his sight around the corner, I began running.

I ran until I reached St. Claude Avenue and caught up to the rear of the streetcar. As I jumped aboard, the driver from the first day leaned out the window and waved to me. I held onto the brass rail like it was my only remaining lifeline. *Who do I have left to trust?* I could count the number of people I knew in this city on one hand: Sam—who wouldn't be back until tomorrow; Aleix—who already had done me more favors than I deserved; Mr. Hawkins—who betrayed Joseph; Mr. Wilson—who couldn't get me out of his office fast enough. *And Mrs. Broder.*

* * *

By using the streetcar and hitching on various wagons, I made it back to the offices of the *Times-Picayune* just as workers were leaving for an early "liquid lunch," as Sam had described with his characteristic chuckle. After working a couple of lunches at Aleix Coffee House and seeing the lunch "diners" stagger out, I finally understood what he meant. I looked for Mr. Wilson, but he had already left. My only hope was Mrs. Broder. I went downstairs to the Archives and found her sitting at her desk behind the counter eating a sandwich with her glasses hanging on a chain from her neck.

"John?" she asked as she laid her lunch down and repositioned her glasses. "What's wrong?"

I was obviously advertising my despair on my face again. "I've found the Reverse Underground Railroad! They're kidnapping children and keeping them in a tunnel under a house on Flood Street in the Lower Ninth Ward."

Mrs. Broder's face did not exactly display disbelief, but there was ample skepticism. "How do you know that, John?" She slipped on her archivist hat. "What *evidence* do you have?"

I pulled Joseph's two crumpled handwritten notes out of my pocket and handed them to her. My hands were shaking. While she read, I explained how I had used the sounding line in the air pipes. "We've got to help them now!" I pleaded.

"My God, John. But why are you *here*? We need to go to the

police!"

"You don't understand!" I cried. "*They* are in on it! Mr. Wilson said the police didn't care about a 'bunch of runaway slaves,' but it's worse than that!" The story of Officer Craven, his lame left arm, and the wagon with the rear compartment poured out of my mouth. "We've got to get back there and get them out before they're taken away and sold as slaves!"

Mrs. Broder stood up, and it was only then that I realized how tiny she was. I wondered what in the world I had been thinking when I came here. *What can she do to help?*

"Come with me, John. We're going to the house on Flood Street," she said with a resoluteness that seemed uttered by a giant.

"But how?" I asked.

"I can get us there quicker than anyone in this city." I followed her out the back door of the offices to the stables behind that served only the paper's employees. In a stall hitched to a post was a horse attached to a contraption with two large wheels and a seat stretching between them. She untied the horse and backed him out of the stall. Mrs. Broder could see the confusion on my face. "This is called a sulky," she said pointing at the two-wheeled cart. "My hobby is harness racing, and every Thursday afternoon I take it over to the Fairgrounds to practice."

She climbed into the seat and pulled me beside her. After donning a pair of goggles, she gave the reins a shake and *we were off!* She expertly navigated the less-traveled streets of the French Quarter, and before I knew it, we were again crossing the finger of the river into the Lower Ninth Ward. As we got nearer the house on Flood Street, I explained to her about the basement of the house next door and my belief that the escape tunnel had run into the side wall of the church on the adjacent property.

When we got to the church, she dropped me off. "See what you can find," she called down from the sulky. "I'm going to get help." With another flick of the reins, she was gone.

I ran along the scraggly hedge between the church and the house until I reached the spot that I had sighted as being on the path of the tunnel. Although the foundation of the church was stacked stone like the house next door, there was a newer jut-out supporting a small addition above that was built out of wood. *If this wood extends below ground, this has to be it!*

I walked around to the back of the church looking for a way in, and I found a small window that was unlocked. I climbed up and squeezed my way into the basement. The window provided enough light for me to look along the side wall for the wood jut-out. Where it should be, I found a closet door which was also unlocked. Inside the closet were some boxes that I moved out so that I could see the back wall. *It is all wood!*

I took my fist and beat it against the base of the wall. There was a hollowness to my *thumps* that gave me hope, but I needed something stronger than my fist to use. I looked in the boxes that I had pulled out, and one contained a small toolbox that had a ball-peen hammer inside like the one that Simon used for odd jobs around my father's farm. I hoisted it in my right hand and began hammering the wood wall, oblivious to the noise I might be making. After I made some dents, I got down on my hands and knees and put my ear to the wall.

Do I hear a sound? I hushed my breathing and listened. *I do hear something!*

The light of a moving lantern spilled into the closet as I heard a voice from the dark: "You need to step out of there and tell me what you're doing." I continued to hold my breath as if I could vaporize into thin air. *I did hear something! Was it just my own heart pounding?*

"I'm going to have to get the police if you don't come out of there." I backed out of the closet on all fours and tried to look up past the glare of the lantern. The man looked back at me quizzically in recognition. "I didn't expect to see you again so soon, young man."

I could now see his silver hair and white clerical collar. "Father Andrew?" I asked.

Before he could respond, we heard loud footsteps running above. The echoing clatter moved to the stairs and descended to us. Mrs. Broder walked into the light followed by a dozen Black teenage boys carrying axes, picks, and shovels. Not at all nonplussed by the sight of the priest standing above, with me on my hands and knees, she announced, "Meet our paperboys."

Chapter 8

I expected Father Andrew to be furious about this destruction and disruption of his church, but instead, he began offering suggestions. "I would focus more on the floor of the closet at the base of the wall if the tunnel is coming up from below," he said as he pointed at the dirt floor. "Plus, that's our new organ above here," he continued as he redirected his finger to the ceiling of the closet. "We don't need this wall falling down."

We rotated in ten-minute shifts because of the strenuous work and the tight quarters. During the pauses between shift changes, we listened for any signs of life beneath us. *Had I just imagined hearing sounds from the other side of the wall?*

The paperboys were strong and determined as we made incremental progress digging through the wall and floor. We found buckets in a cleaning closet in the basement and carried the dirt we extracted out to the backyard. While dumping the dirt, one of the paperboys named Tobias found a few landscape timbers that bordered a small flower garden. "My father is a carpenter in the Garden District," Tobias said, "and he's taught me a few things. We could use these timbers to shore up the floor above." With Father Andrew's permission, we brought them in and hammered them into place.

After an hour's work, the hole in the floor was big enough for someone to fit their shoulders through, but I voiced my anxiety about the red-headed man and Officer Craven returning to the house on Flood Street. "Father Andrew," Mrs. Broder asked, "how do you get up to the bell tower? I'm not helping any down here. I can go stand lookout." He left with her to show her the way.

After another hour, we were angling down, now outside the exterior wall of the church. Tobias was in the hole swinging a pick when we heard him whisper, "I think I see light."

I climbed into the hole beside him. I took the ball-peen hammer and tapped at the tiny, sparkling hole. Dirt gave way as the circle of light grew bigger. I pushed the hammer through and began making ever-wider circles with the head of the hammer. I was going to push my head through the hole when I heard a distinct *Shhhh!* come from the other side. Father Andrew leaned into the closet with the lantern just as there was movement from the hole. A brown hand covered in dirt and blood reached out towards the light. I recognized the leather and metal bracelet on his wrist immediately.

"Joseph!" I whispered, "It's me—John!" I grabbed his hand in mine.

Tobias jammed into the hole beside me and urgently dug with his bare hands around Joseph's and my clutched hands— *Don't let go.* After several false attempts, we finally enlarged the hole enough to pull him through. Joseph was unrecognizable once he stood outside the closet in the church basement. He was covered in dirt, and his hair was matted down with sweat and blood from hitting his head on the rough ceiling of the tunnel.

"We're all lined up," he whispered.

Tobias reached into the hole and took the hand of the next prisoner and pulled him out. This boy was also covered in dirt, but what was so startling was his physique—he looked like a walking skeleton. "Tom's been in here the longest," Joseph said to me as Tom blinked hard at the daylight coming in through the basement window.

The next paperboy reached in and took a hand, pulling a young girl out of the tunnel, through the closet, and into the basement. Just as he did, Mrs. Broder walked in. "Oh, my God, you poor thing," she said as she wrapped her arms around the little girl. Mrs. Broder looked at me and Father Andrew: "We need to get them blankets and food." She added with alarm, "And a wagon just pulled up at the back of the bad house."

"We've got some scraps of leftover food from last night's Fellowship Dinner," Father Andrew said. "I'll scrounge it together and bring it down. I don't know about blankets, but we've got lots of choir robes we could use to keep them warm." As Father Andrew turned to go up the stairs, he looked back and said, "John, you've got to get them all out as quick as possible."

One by one, we took turns helping the children out of the tunnel. As each child got out, they were shepherded by the paperboy that had helped them. The basement was filling up as five, and then ten prisoners were welcomed back into freedom. Joseph took charge of counting the children and letting us know who remained in the tunnel. "There's four left," Joseph announced as Tobias climbed back into the hole. "Isaac is last. He's the oldest and the strongest." *He's the one I saw them take this morning.*

"Three left," he said as Tobias came out holding the hand of another little girl.

"Two," Joseph counted down, and then, "One." Joseph climbed in and helped Isaac, whose face was covered in sweat and dirt that still couldn't hide the huge smile on his face.

We heard another clamor coming down the stairs as Father Andrew, Mrs. Broder, Mr. Wilson, and a policeman entered the basement with their arms full of food and velvety choir robes. "John," Mr. Wilson said, "I'm sorry I doubted you. I'm just glad Mrs. Broder left me a note about what y'all were doing." As a seeming afterthought, he added, "And I did find a policeman who cares about these kids." Mr. Wilson looked with wide-eyed amazement at the room full of children as they were wrapped in robes and given food and water. "This is Captain Peter Martin, my brother-in-law."

In the silence following this introduction, we heard noise from inside the closet. As we looked in horror, another hand came out of the darkness of the tunnel. I looked questioningly at Joseph, but he gave me a shake of his head. I reached in, grabbed the empty hand, and pulled.

* * *

As he came out of the tunnel, I saw that his other hand wasn't empty. The red-headed man held a revolver down at his side as he cleared the narrowest part of the opening. When he started to raise the gun, Tobias swung a shovel and knocked the gun out of his hand and out of the closet. Four of the biggest paperboys jumped into the closet and pulled the red-headed man to his feet. "Get your dirty hands off me!" he shouted, but he was in no position to protest. Captain Martin pocketed the revolver and roughly handcuffed the red-headed man as the paperboys held him.

"Get me out of here! I'm stuck!" came a frantic squeal from the tunnel. I held the lantern up to the hole and saw Officer Craven wedged into the end of the tunnel, his fat belly heaving into the ceiling. His helpless, chubby right hand thrashed out in front of him. Tobias whispered to the smallest paperboy who climbed into the tunnel with a hand shovel and began clearing the dirt around Craven's snagged belly. Once it was almost clear, Joseph and I reached in and grabbed Craven's hands. The force of our pulling cleared the rest of the way as Craven came out of the tunnel crying like a newborn baby. He was roughly stood up and cuffed before he had a chance to voice a single coherent word of protest.

Other policemen arrived and took the red-headed man and Craven away. I told Mr. Wilson—who had his notepad out—and Captain Martin about Mr. Hawkins, but they both doubted whether he would ever be found. Captain Martin admitted, "I don't know whether other cops are involved—I pray to God not—but until I know, we're going to need to keep all of this quiet."

"I'll give you three days, Peter," said Mr. Wilson, "but then the *Times-Picayune* is going to run my story, and it ain't gonna be pretty for the New Or-lins Police Department. This 'Reverse Underground Railroad' was doing its business right under y'all's noses."

Captain Martin shook his head as he turned and left the basement. Mrs. Broder took both Mr. Wilson and Father Andrew by the arms and led them to a far corner. As they talked, each staked their position with eloquent gestures. In the end, Father Andrew nodded as he assumed the role of the gentle general and came to the center of the room to address his troops.

Looking in turn into the eyes of the fourteen children—and that's in fact what all of us were in the basement (including the paperboys)—Father Andrew began to share his and the other two adults' vision of their future.

"No one can understand the unspeakable horror that y'all have endured, but you have not *just* endured. You have persevered. It is our unalterable goal," he swept his arm across the basement to include everyone, "to make sure that your life—as a free person—is returned to you."

[The old man would have undoubtedly been delighted to know that one day—eighty-nine years in the future—in a banquet room in Stockholm, Sweden, his grandson would accept the 1949 Nobel Prize for Literature. In his speech Billy would say, "I believe that man will not merely endure; he will prevail," echoing the words coming from the kind Father that he had remembered from countless retellings of the humdinger of a story during his childhood.]

"For the next few days," Father Andrew continued, "you will be welcomed into the loving arms of the Charity Hospital and the university here. The Episcopal priest who started the medical school and fostered its relationship with the hospital was my mentor, Father Francis. Captain Martin is delivering a note to the hospital administrator who happens to be a parishioner of mine." Father Andrew smiled as he apologized. "Sorry, that's more than you care to know. The hospital and university staff, along with the *Times-Picayune* and the police, will be working tirelessly to quickly return you to your homes and your families." As he finished, Father Andrew made a grand gesture towards the stairs and led everyone up and out the front doors of the church. Parked at the curb were three police wagons like I had seen on Bourbon Street when the cops were corralling drunks. The problem was that they were eerily similar to the wagon used in the kidnappings by the red-headed man. No one seemed eager to move towards them.

I could see that Father Andrew sensed the freed children's fear and skepticism, and he approached me: "John, it's going to be okay. These are police wagons that will take the children to the hospital. The children trust you. If you and Joseph lead the way, they will follow."

Although I had not had the chance to have any real conversation with Joseph since he had emerged from the tunnel—the time since had passed in a blur—I walked over to him and took his hand in mine. Together, we made the slow walk to the rear of the first wagon. As we looked back, each of the children who had escaped, instinctively moved to take the hand of the paperboy who had been his or her escort back to freedom.

I could see the fear still in Joseph's eyes as he peered into the dark compartment of the wagon. "Is this how they took you?" I asked.

He nodded. "All I remember is looking into the wagon and then a sick, sweet smell. I woke up in the tunnel."

"You can trust them, Joseph," I said. "They're going to take care of all of you."

Joseph let go of my hand and began to climb in. He paused and closed his eyes as his now-free hand kneaded the leather bracelet on his other wrist. "I don't trust them," he whispered, "but I trust you." I sat by Joseph in the front of the compartment, and we were soon joined by four other children and a policeman. As the door closed, the five children began singing "Song of the Free," a spiritual that I used to hear Simon

and Mary sing as they worked:
My soul is vexed within me sore
To think that I'm a slave,
I'm now resolved to strike the blow
For freedom or the grave.

* * *

Before the door was shut, however, Mrs. Broder and Mr. Wilson's faces appeared in the crack of daylight. "Whew, we just caught you," Mrs. Broder said. "The police are going to need to talk to you, John. Do you want to ride with me in the sulky to police headquarters?"

"No," I answered, "I'm staying with Joseph. As long as there's room for me at the hospital, I'll be with them. Can't the police talk to me there?"

Mrs. Broder and Mr. Wilson looked at each other and nodded. "Sure," she said, "we'll make it happen."

"Besides," I continued, "after what I've done to Aleix at the coffee house, I don't think he will ever want to see me again, much less let me stay in his guest room."

"I wouldn't worry about that, John," reassured Mr. Wilson. "Sam and I have shared quite a few liquid lunches with Aleix, and I consider him a friend. I will go by and explain everything to him and leave a note telling Sam where he can find you when he gets back tomorrow."

"Thank you, Mr. Wilson," I said, and I suddenly felt guilty about my initial negative impression of the reporter.

"No, thank you, John!" Mrs. Broder interrupted. "All of these children have you to thank for their freedom… and their lives."

"No, ma'am," I rebutted as I interrupted her. "It was Joseph that saved *my* life."

The singing returned inside the wagon as we pulled away from the curb and began our journey to Charity Hospital. I could see out of the barred side window as we turned left onto St. Claude Avenue. The horse-drawn streetcar was on its westward run back into downtown, led by my friend, the driver. We passed Congo Square and ran north of the French Quarter along Rampart Street. *It was only five days ago that I arrived in this city with Joseph and his mother.*

After crossing Canal Street, we turned left on Common Street, where we soon approached a huge classical building fronted by a row of columns that looked like it belonged in the Parthenon—the subject of one of my other favorite illustrations in *Mitchell's Primary Geography* back at the Ripley schoolhouse. Letters across the portico read "University of Louisiana—Medical Department." The wagons stopped for several minutes before we were directed to Charity Hospital around the corner.

A team of young doctors and nurses met all the children as they climbed out of the wagons. Most still wore the choir robes to stay warm in the February chill. We were led up through a series of winding staircases and white-walled hallways to a long room lined with beds that the nurses called the "Infirmary." One by one, the children's names were taken by a doctor and a policeman, and each child was assigned a bed. When everyone was settled in, a nurse escorted Isaac through the double doors on the rear wall of the Infirmary. He returned a while later looking freshly scrubbed and wearing a hospital robe over what looked like pajamas. Joseph and I were the first to him when he got to his bed. "Where did they take you?" Joseph asked. "And what did they make you do?"

"They made me get in a pot of warm water like I was a potato ready to boil."

"You had to take your clothes off in front of them?" Joseph asked.

"Nah, just one of the man doctors was in there. He gave me a cake of soap to scrub myself with. You shoulda seen the water when I got out. It looked like a bucket of mud."

"Then what did you do?" I asked, not wanting to be left out of the conversation.

"They took me to a small room with a table and chairs, and a policeman asked me a bunch of questions like how long I was in the tunnel, what my name is, and where I'm from. He wanted to know about the red-headed man and the policeman. He got real agitated about that."

After all the children, including Joseph and I, had bathed and been questioned, doctors and nurses went bed-to-bed checking our temperatures with a thermometer that they stuck in our mouths and listening to our hearts with a new-fangled thing called a "stethoscope." A couple of the children were taken away for more examination, but as it began getting dark outside, we were all led down the stairs in a single-file line by a group of policemen to a dining hall.

As we sat at two long tables, a young doctor spoke to us: "What I'm about to say is not going to make any sense. I know you haven't eaten much for a long time and you're hungry, but you have to take it easy. If you eat too much, it will make you sick."

I don't know if it was the doctor's warnings or just sheer exhaustion, but no one overate, and before long, yawns began running back and forth between the two tables like a secret language. We were led back upstairs where no nurses, doctors, or policemen had to tell us to get in bed. When the lights were turned out, the yawns were soon replaced by deep breathing and the occasional snore. I could see the silhouette of a policeman pacing back and forth through the frosted glass in the doors at the front of the Infirmary, which was oddly reassuring. I heard the stirring of sheets and felt the weight of Joseph moving onto my bed.

"I can't stay here, John. I have to get to Mamma," he said with a whispered urgency. "The police don't need to help find my family. I know where it is. It's on a ship to Nantucket."

"I know, Joseph. I've been thinking about nothing else," I said. "We need to stay here tonight, though. Sam—Samuel Clemens—will be back tomorrow. He's a riverboat pilot, and he seems to know everybody. He helped me find a place to stay after y'all left, and pointed me towards Mr. Wilson. I think he's our best chance to get us on another ship."

"What do you mean *us*?" Joseph asked.

"I want to be with you on that ship to Nantucket." *I've got no place else to go.*

Chapter 9

Samuel Clemens strode through the doors into the Infirmary the next morning wearing the same riverboat pilot uniform as when I first met him five days ago. Mr. Wilson followed in his wake.

"John, are you drawn to trouble, or does it just seem to find you?" asked Sam with a crooked grin on his face and a twinkle in his eye. He turned his gaze to Joseph. "You must be the famous *Joseph* that John has told me so much about." He reached out and shook Joseph's hand.

Finally, Sam turned around to Mr. Wilson. "Wilson, tell John and Joseph here what you have been hearing."

"Captain Martin is my brother-in-law," Mr. Wilson began, "and I trust him, though I don't trust much of anybody else on the New Or-lins Police Department." I spun and looked at the silhouettes still passing back and forth through the frosted glass in the doors to the Infirmary. Mr. Wilson registered my alarm. "Those are two officers personally selected by Captain Martin, so they're okay. Captain Martin's not so sure about which other officers might have been working with Craven on their 'Reverse Underground Railroad.'"

"Is the red-headed man a policeman?" I asked.

"No, his name is Champ McCoy, and he works at the cargo

terminal. Evidently, he developed a relationship with Craven when he began bribing him to look the other way when smuggled goods, like guns and whisky, came into port."

"He and Craven are in jail, aren't they?" I interrupted.

"They are, John," Mr. Wilson said trying to sound reassuring, "but Captain Martin is worried that you are the only real witness to an actual kidnapping, and some of McCoy's and Craven's buddies on the force may have it in for you."

"We need to get you out of the city," Sam said.

"I'm not going anywhere without Joseph," I declared. "Can you help us get on a ship to Nantucket?"

Sam reached up and began stroking his mustache as he thought: "Probably not Nantucket, 'cause the next ship doesn't leave for over two weeks. I can get you to Charleston, though, and it will be easy to catch a ride from there to Nantucket. Let me do some checking this morning."

"Regardless," Mr. Wilson said, "we think it's best to move you out of here as soon as possible."

"Move *us*," I said emphatically as I looked at Joseph.

"Okay, the *both* of you," Mr. Wilson said irritably. "Captain Martin is going to move y'all to some unspecified location, though he's going to put out the word that he's just taking you to headquarters. You two need to be ready to leave this morning at eleven o'clock *sharp*."

I looked Joseph in the eyes, and he gave me a quick nod. "We'll be ready," I said.

Joseph spent the next hour going from bed to bed, telling his friends that he was leaving. There were many hugs and tears shed, but I could tell that Joseph was trying to be as positive as possible. He wrote down names and addresses in his diary in order to keep his promise to all of them that they would somehow meet again under happier circumstances.

At eleven o'clock sharp, Mr. Wilson and Captain Martin came into the Infirmary. Neither Joseph nor I had any possessions other than what would fit into our pockets, so it was not hard to leave. With quick waves to all, we backed out of the doors and were gone. When we got out to the street, Captain Martin waved to the driver of a police wagon stopped up the road, and it came to the curb for us to climb in. Captain Martin climbed up beside the driver in the box seat, while Mr. Wilson opened the rear door for Joseph and me to enter the cabin of the wagon.

When the three of us were seated, the wagon pulled away. In the front wall of the cabin, there was a small, square opening with vertical iron bars. I could see Captain Martin's profile as his head swiveled back and forth. After a few moments, Mr. Wilson leaned into the opening and whispered, "Do you see anyone following us?"

Captain Martin whispered back, "Yep. Two men on horseback a block back. You need to get them ready." Mr. Wilson leaned forward and flipped up a metal panel in the floor of the cabin. We could see the cobblestones of the street rushing by beneath us.

Mr. Wilson explained, "They have these to hose out the wagons after the drunks."

"Are we going to jump out?" Joseph asked.

"No, Joseph," Mr. Wilson chuckled, "it's not my job to get you run over by this wagon. We're going to stop in the next block directly over a manhole. The cover has been set aside. Joseph, we didn't know you were going to be along on this. You're going to have to crawl through an underground storm sewer pipe about fifty feet. Can you do that after what you have just gone through?"

I heard a sharp intake of breath from Joseph, but then he slowly exhaled. "Yes, sir, I can do that—if I have to." Before he had a chance to change his mind, the wagon began slowing.

"Y'all need to be quick so the guys following us won't get suspicious. When we stop, go straight down into the hole—it's not deep—and follow the string to its end. You will come up in the middle of that alley." Mr. Wilson pointed out the side window to the block ahead on the left.

"String?" I asked.

"Yep. There's kite string running in the pipe all the way to the next manhole. That was Sam's idea." The wagon lurched to a stop. We looked down, and the open manhole was right there. "Down you go, boys. Someday you're going to have to tell me how this story ends."

* * *

When Mr. Wilson slid the manhole cover back into place, it was pitch-black inside the pipe. I held the kite string in my fingers as I began crawling. "You back there?" I asked Joseph.

There was silence, and I could sense no movement behind me. "Joseph!" I barked.

"Yeah, I'm here," he said in a shaky voice. "Let's get moving." We had to crawl on our hands and knees, but luckily the bottom of the pipe was dry. I tested the height of the pipe and paid for it with a likely bruise. After a short way, the pipe turned slightly to the left, and I could see light ahead. I scrunched down for a second so Joseph could see the end. "I'm good now," he said. "Let's just get out of here as fast as we can."

The kite string angled up and extended out the manhole opening. I stuck my head up enough to see, and we were, indeed, in the middle of an alley. I spun three-hundred-sixty degrees and didn't see anyone else around. "Can you give me a boost?" I turned and asked Joseph. He interlaced the fingers of his two hands down by my right foot. I stepped into his "boost," and he lifted me up with surprising strength. I got my elbows above the opening and pried myself up. I then reached down into the hole and helped Joseph climb out.

"What now?" Joseph asked.

"I don't know." I looked to the other end of the dark alley just as two large horses passed by. They were pulling a carriage with four bright-red wheels beneath a driver's box and an open cabin. I heard a piercing whistle as the tiny driver of the carriage put his fingers to his mouth. "Come on, boys! We don't have much time." We sprinted to the end of the alley, but it wasn't a man driving the carriage—it was Mrs. Broder. "Jump in the back under the blanket!"

Crouched down in the back was Sam, wearing a fake beard and a cowboy hat. "Welcome aboard, boys. We're getting y'all the heck outta Dodge!"

It was a rough ride lying on the floor of the carriage under the blanket as Mrs. Broder navigated the tight streets of the French Quarter. When we slowed, Sam peeked under the blanket and whispered, "Be real quiet now. We're rolling onto the ferry to cross the river." I could feel the carriage rock back and forth as the ferry cut across the chop of the water. It felt just like the raft that Jim and I had floated down the river on from Norfolk Landing to Natchez just two weeks ago. Once we exited the ferry, we picked up speed on the much smoother dirt roads of Gretna.

"Y'all can come out now," Sam said as he lifted the blanket. The look on Mrs. Broder's face—under the goggles—was one of pure joy.

"I've always wanted to drive a tandem team like this before," she said as we rocketed past other people on the road, punctuated by Mrs. Broder's cackling laughter. "Yahoo!" she cried into the wind.

Sam sat on one side of the open carriage while Joseph and I sat opposite him. Sam leaned into Joseph so that he could be heard over the *galumph* of the horses' galloping hooves. "Joseph, I will understand if you don't ever want to think about that place ever again, but the writer in me has to ask—What was it like inside the tunnel?"

I had deliberately avoided asking Joseph this because I figured if he wanted to talk about it, he would—but still, I found myself also leaning into Joseph to listen for his response.

Joseph's face cascaded through a cycle of emotions: sadness, reticence, but then an affirmation. He nodded his head rhythmically as he began recounting his story: "There were ghosts in the tunnel that seeped into you. Their history became yours. Even though I was only in there for four days— some of the kids had been in there for weeks—I came out of that tunnel a changed man—or boy. I'm not sure which I am right now." He slowly brushed his fingers across the rough cords of his pants.

"There were hundreds of names, dates, and messages carved into the railroad ties that shored up the walls and ceiling of the tunnel. The earliest date I could find was 1809. Isaac told me that was right after America stopped bringing slaves in on ships. So, there had been children in that tunnel for over fifty years. They had come from all over—big cities like

Philadelphia and Baltimore, and other places like Cooba and islands I'd never heard of."

"What about the tunnel y'all dug to the church?" Sam asked.

Joseph thought long and hard before answering this. "Even though I felt dead when I woke up in that dark tunnel—like I had lost everything—I now see how lucky I was."

Sam cocked his head like this was totally unexpected.

Joseph explained, "The children in that tunnel had been digging that escape route for over twenty years, inches at a time. They used their bare hands, adding in rocks, borrowed timbers from the main tunnel, and bits of bone to shore up the tunnel. I was lucky because I happened to be put in there right as the escape tunnel was ready to break through."

I had to ask: "Do you know how the Reverse Underground Railroad worked?"

"Like I said," Joseph thoughtfully answered, "the history of the place seeped into you. There always seemed to be children who had been there awhile when new kids—like me—got thrown in. Word got passed down. Free children of color were kidnapped all over and smuggled down the 'Railroad' to here, where they were sold in secret slave markets. Some kids like me and Isaac got taken while in New Or-lins. The people running the Railroad tried to get twenty children at a time to take to the market. They were still wanting to get a few more before they sold us."

"Greedy sons of—" Sam muttered under his breath.

"They fed you and gave you water?" I interrupted.

"Sure," Joseph said. "Like cattle getting fattened up for the slaughterhouse."

* * *

After Joseph unburdened himself with his story, he laid his head on my shoulder and slept for a while, lulled by the steady bumping of the carriage. Sam moved over by me and told me the plan for getting us on the ship to Charleston. "We're meeting a good friend of mine, John Lory, who is the lighthouse keeper at Pass-a-Loutre which is right at the mouth of the Mississippi. He is going to meet us at Buras, a small settlement right on the edge of the swamp. He has arranged for the local packet boat to carry y'all to the lighthouse."

"What's a packet boat?" I asked.

"It's a small, steam-powered boat that carries mail up and down the river from New Or-lins to all the other little settlements in the Mississippi Delta."

Joseph stirred from my shoulder, eager to hear the rest of the plan.

"In fact, Joseph," Sam continued, "the ship your mother is on—the *Helen Mar*—is soon due to pick up mail by packet boat when it rounds the coast of Key West. I telegraphed the naval station there, and they're going to get word to your mother that you are on a ship bound for Charleston, and then Nantucket."

Joseph's sleepy face bloomed into a big smile. Mrs. Broder turned to remind Sam of the basket on the back of the carriage. "Oh, yeah," he said as he opened the basket and began removing sandwiches wrapped in cloth, "I bet y'all are starving." We ate as Sam told us stories of his most recent ride up the river with the gamblers, scoundrels, and misfits that seemed to populate the riverboat. From there, he expounded on his lifetime plan to travel the world and write about all the exotic locales while making lots of money. Mrs. Broder slowed the horses as the ragtag tents, cabins, and docks that marked the outskirts of Buras came into view.

"There's John Lory now," announced Sam as the carriage stopped in front of a saloon.

I didn't really get the chance to say goodbye to my family, as awful as they are, when I took off unexpectedly with Jim on the timber wagon. I didn't even say anything to Simon, Mary, Henry, Lucy, and George, though this kind family had taken me in when I was in trouble that Christmas afternoon. Now I did have the opportunity to say farewell to these two people who had accepted me exactly as I am without any hesitation.

"John," began Mrs. Broder as she slid those ridiculous goggles off her face, "I'm glad I listened to you. Fourteen young people have their freedom back because of you. Joseph, I haven't had the chance to get to know you. Do you have any siblings?"

"No, ma'am."

"I think you have one now. Y'all look after each other like brothers do. Promise me you will send me a telegram when you get to Charleston. Just direct it to the *Times-Picayune*."

"Yes, ma'am," I answered. "We will." She hugged both of us and climbed back up into the driver's seat of the carriage, leaving us alone with Sam.

"I'm afraid I'm going to demand more than a telegram," Sam said. "I've seen Joseph writing in his diary. I want a full accounting of your adventure in getting to Charleston and then to Nantucket. Mail me letters to Aleix Coffee House, and I promise I will read them. You two boys have saved each other's lives. Y'all are inextricably bound in ways that few people can be. Always keep that in mind. Like Mrs. Broder said, y'all are brothers. Keep looking after each other." Sam gave each of us a big hug before passing us off to John Lory.

We climbed aboard the packet boat with Mr. Lory after the pilot delivered the mail to the saloon keeper. As the small, steam-driven boat backed out of the slough with its smoky, puttering motor, Joseph and I looked back to our protectors. Mrs. Broder waved her tiny hand as she fitted her goggles back in place. Sam's wave seemed more like a salute. *We are on our own now.*

It took us a few hours to reach Pass-a-Loutre after skimming through the relatively quiet waters of the Mississippi River. The low winter sun was beginning to set as John Lory pointed out his lighthouse rising out of the river-hugging clouds on the pink-tinted horizon. "They originally built it a few miles from here at the Head of Passes. At that time, it was the tallest cast-iron lighthouse in America. It didn't stay that way for long, though, because it started sinking in the mud. Instead of building a new one, they just moved it here six years ago. I stayed the keeper, and they even built me a house."

As he said this, the house emerged from the fog. It was a two-story white house with black shutters and a wraparound porch. I immediately thought of the porch at the house on Flood Street and looked at Joseph, but then I realized he never saw the house that way. He just knew the tunnel.

"I've got a room up in the attic with a couple of beds for y'all to sleep in," Mr. Lory said. "The steamship to Charleston will be passing by around midnight tomorrow night." He must have noticed the alarmed looks that both Joseph and I gave him. "It's fine. The captain knows you're boarding. He's a friend of Sam and mine. There's no way he could have allowed you to board in N'Awlins without being accompanied by an adult, but on the river, *anything goes.*"

After a simple dinner and a good night's sleep, Joseph and I spent the next day exploring the swamp around the lighthouse. I had never seen cypress trees growing out of the water, with their gnarled "knees" resembling ancient stalagmites. Even though it was February, the marsh was full of color: the green of the sawgrass dotted with duckweed with its tiny white flowers, and spider lilies with their red funnel-shaped blossoms. After a late dinner of soup and bread, we waited intolerable hours until it was time to climb into Mr. Lory's small rowboat. He paddled us out through the recurring fog to board the idling steamship that would take us to Charleston.

"Are we doing the right thing?" Joseph asked me in a hushed voice.

"We're doing the *only* thing," I answered, sounding much braver than I felt.

PART THREE: New Orleans to Charleston (February-April 1861)

Chapter 10

"Boys, I'm glad to have you aboard, but I've got two problems," the squat, bandy-legged captain said to us as he paced back and forth across the narrow, moonlit deck of the steamship. Joseph and I were still breathing hard from scaling up the rope ladder from John Lory's rowboat to the deck of the ship. "First, we have our maximum number of passengers—I think people are worried that the U.S. Navy will soon blockade New Orleans—so y'all are going to have to be crew members."

When Joseph and I returned blank looks to the captain, he changed his tack: "You're both going to have to work. Second, I've only got one free hammock in the crew's quarters, so y'all are going to have to share it."

I had spent a few lazy hours in a hammock as a child, and even though both Joseph and I were thin, I didn't see how *sharing* would work, and evidently, my skepticism showed through—even in the darkness of the midnight deck.

The even-more flustered captain blundered on: "Now, I would do anything for Sam Clemens and John Lory, so we're going to make *this* work."

This? Is this making any more sense to Joseph than it is to me? My sideward glance at him confirmed that he was as confused as I was.

Finally, the captain got down to basics: "I need to know what each of you can do. Where can I put you to work?"

After an awkward silence when we could hear—and feel—the *whirring* of the propellers come to life beneath us, Joseph spoke up first: "My mother is the best cook in the State of Mississippi, and I've been helping her and learning from her since we've been on the road to New Or-lins from the plantation."

"Well," the captain replied, "I'm not sure what's left of the *State* of Mississippi, but that's all well and good. What's your name, young man?" he asked.

"I'm Joseph."

"And your surname?" Joseph gave him another confused look. "Your last name?"

Joseph seemed to answer reluctantly: "My freedom papers say *Rossiter*, but that's not *my* name. That was my master's name. That ain't me."

"I have to put something in the ship's manifest," said the captain. "What should it be?"

After a long, thoughtful pause, Joseph looked the captain square in the eye and answered, "Call me *Freeman*, 'cause that's what I am—a *free man*."

"Okay, Joseph Freeman, you're going to be working in the ship's galley for the breakfast and lunch shifts—six o'clock a.m. to two o'clock p.m."

"Yes, sir," Joseph nodded humbly. "Thank you, sir."

The captain turned his gaze to me. "What's your name?"

"John Wesley Thompson Falkner." All I could think to say regarding my work skills was to dovetail on what Joseph had said about what he had learned on the road to New Orleans.

"I know how to build fires."

Before I could elaborate any more, the captain interrupted, "Good, John. I was hoping it would be something like that. We need a man for the graveyard shift in the boiler room—ten o'clock p.m. to six o'clock a.m."

It was my turn to be confused. "Excuse me, sir, but what will I be doing?"

"You'll be shoveling coal into the furnace to keep the steam going for our engines. Like you said, you'll be keeping the fires burning." He paused to size me up from head to toe. "I hope you're stronger than you look."

The captain led us below decks to the crew's quarters where a dozen hammocks hung from overhead pipes. Snores filled the cabin as the captain silently guided us through the dark maze of sleeping men and pointed at the sole unused hammock in the far corner. Joseph and I tried to sleep together with my feet up by his head, but when the whistle sounded at six o'clock the next morning, neither of us had slept more than a wink.

While Joseph joined the other kitchen staff in the galley to work on breakfast, I explored the ship. I learned that the steamship was called the *S.S. Tribune*, and it sailed regularly between Charleston and New Orleans. One long-time passenger confided that he could remember when the steamship carried newly sold slaves between the two cities, though they were always kept below decks, out of sight of the paying, white passengers. The ship had two levels above the main deck that were framed by two black, smoke-spewing iron stacks. Where the stacks extended below the decks would become my workplace for the foreseeable future.

Our staggered work schedules allowed Joseph and me to

each separately have the hammock for sleep. He slept during the night while I worked in the boiler room, and I slept in the morning and early afternoon while he worked in the galley. Ironically, I had kept the bandana that the bad man had used to gag my mouth when he tied me up by the creek, and it served as a sleep mask to filter the sliver of daylight that eased into the crew's quarters during the day. Joseph and I had between two o'clock in the afternoon and ten at night to explore the ship, eat dinner, and plan our futures in Nantucket. At the end of my shift, my face was always covered in black coal dust, while Joseph's face was usually covered in white flour from the biscuits he would make for breakfast in the galley. Some of the Cuban crew members that I worked with in the boiler room joked that Joseph and I must be "twins," calling me *el negro* (the "Black One") while Joseph was *el blanco* (the "White One").

* * *

I'm sure it was because of his friendship with Sam, but the captain was quite kind to me as we began our voyage to Charleston. He allowed me to look at the navigational charts in the pilothouse when I was not in the boiler room or the hammock. Once the *Tribune* exited the mouth of the Mississippi at Pass-a-Loutre, it sailed eastward in the Gulf of Mexico, passing south of Mobile and Pensacola. Joseph joined us in the pilothouse the second afternoon and excitedly explained the Gulf Stream to us: "My father said that the Gulf Stream is like a warm river running in the middle of the ocean. He compared it to riding a racehorse in a gale wind—when you're with it, you're flying, but when you're against it, it's like you're standing still."

"Your father is right," said the captain, "and right now we're sailing with the stream, and we're flying." We went out on deck, and we were close enough that we could see the white beaches of the Florida Panhandle pass by. "Look to the port side!" yelled the captain. When Joseph and I both gave him our oft-repeated looks of confusion, he repeated, "Look to the left. *Port* is left, and *starboard* is right." As we looked down through the roped railing running along the port side of the ship, we could see two porpoises riding high in the waves beside us—like they were our personal escorts. "That means good weather ahead," exclaimed the captain. He pointed overhead to a squadron of pelicans flying eastward. "They know that springtime is not far away."

At night I would get breaks from the boiler room, and I liked to go out on deck and see the fires burning on the beaches as we headed south along the western coast of Florida. In broken English, the Cuban sailors would explain how the few remaining nomadic Seminole Indians moved from beach to beach trying to stay ahead of the U.S. Army soldiers who were trying to eradicate them. "*Luchadores feroces…* fierce fighters," the sailors said. "Never give up."

Another Spanish phrase that I soon learned from the Cubans was *cuarto de fuego,* which translates to "fire room." The boiler room—or fire room—where I spent eight hours each night, was located below decks at the rear of the *Tribune.* It was adjacent to the engine room where the turbine transformed the steam produced by the boiler into a massive turning propeller that projected out the back of the ship. At night, the fire room had a hellish glow from the raging, carnivorous furnace whose insatiable appetite us "stokers" kept fed with a never-ending supply of coal. Overhead, in the high ceiling of the fire room hung the black, sucking oculus—the base of one of the tall stacks that sucked out the smoke.

Although I had grown up on a farm, it wasn't until that first night of shoveling coal that I realized what a pampered life I had lived. Juan and Fidel, the two Cubans who also worked the graveyard shift in the fire room laughed at my weakness and ineptitude, but they also showed me the right way to bend my knees—instead of my back—as I lifted and threw the coal from the storage bin into the furnace. They shared the ginger root that they chewed on at the end of the shift, which miraculously took some of the pain away.

Joseph laughed at my bent-over posture when we met up the first afternoon after each of us had worked our initial shifts: "What did they do to you last night?" he snickered. "Take you up on deck and beat on you?"

I began to plead with self-pity about how hard I had worked, but mid-sentence it struck me: *This is how hard Joseph—as a slave—has had to work his whole life. This is the life that Simon, Mary, Henry, Lucy, and George have known from the cradle to a probable too-early grave.* I was just about to tell Joseph how that fire room was my own personal hell where I was sent to atone for all my sins, but luckily, I kept my mouth shut. I was having to work for a living. *Big deal.*

The next night of work was hard… and painful… but I was better at it, and the next night even a little better. I felt muscles growing—albeit sore ones—where none had existed before. Likewise, Joseph talked about all the cooking tricks he was learning from the Greek woman who was the lead cook in the galley: "Miss Lydia keeps some butter frozen that she uses in making the biscuits, and they come out as flaky as the pages in a book. Mamma is going to love to try that out." *Joseph is already looking ahead. He has put the tunnel behind him.* "And Miss Lydia salts and peppers the eggs while she is cooking them, and they taste *so much better* that way." Joseph bundled up some leftovers from the galley for me each day because I slept through the breakfast and lunchtimes, and he was right—even cold, they were the best-tasting eggs and biscuits I had ever had.

On the evening of the fourth day of our journey across the Gulf of Mexico, Joseph and I stood in the pilothouse as the captain pointed to our progress on the nautical chart stretched across a table: "We've just about reached the southernmost part of our voyage, and we'll be turning eastward shortly. We'll be threading the needle through the triangle created by Cuba, Key West, and the Bahamas. As we pass by the Keys, we'll be rendezvousing with a packet boat which will be delivering any mail to us."

"That's how Sam was getting word to your mother that you were safe," I said to Joseph.

"I wonder if the man on the packet boat will be able to tell me that she got Sam's telegram?" mused Joseph. "Maybe my mother left a message for me."

"We'll find out tomorrow morning," the captain said.

As our conversation paused, we began to hear music from the deck behind the pilothouse. We left the captain to explore the music's source. We found three of the Cuban crew members sitting on barrels playing a guitar, a fiddle, and a strange-looking drum.

* * *

"We're serenading our home," said Juan who spoke the best English. He pointed out to the starboard side of the ship with the bow of his fiddle. "Those lights you see over there are Havana, our home."

"Why did you leave?" asked Joseph as he looked out across the dark water.

"No work," Juan answered. "Years ago, when America stopped taking in new slaves, they got sent to Cuba. Why pay Cubans to work when slaves do it for nothing?"

Joseph frowned as he began to reply, but I touched his elbow. "When I heard your music," I said as I tried to detour the conversation, "it made me think of Congo Square."

Juan nodded his head and smiled: "I love Congo Square. We go there when we are in the city. We get to eat *ropa vieja* and listen to *salsa* and the beat of the *tumbadora*." He pointed to the drum that his compatriot was playing. "Congo Square lets us find a piece of home."

Joseph and I found barrels to sit on, and we listened in the dark as the Cubans played their homesick tunes. Despite the quiet mournfulness of the music, I could tell that Joseph was restless. "It's not like slaves work *for free*," he whispered as he let Juan's statement rustle around in his head like a trapped mouse. "We never had a choice. It was work or die."

"I know," I said. "I made the mistake of whining about my lack of choices to Jim, the old man I shared a raft with down the river. He set me straight real quick about what it truly means to never have a choice."

"I would like Jim," said Joseph as the bitterness in his voice subsided. "I understand the frustration that he felt. Now I *do* have choices," he said as he yawned, "and I'm choosing to go get some shuteye." We heard a whistle sound from the pilothouse. "And it's time for you to get to work," Joseph said as he playfully returned a tap to my elbow.

When I finished my shift at six o'clock the next morning, there was a commotion up on deck. As I exited the ladder leading from the bowels of the fire room, I could see several crew members crowded at the portside railing. The captain walked up as the crew parted to allow him to the front. Joseph, with his face covered in white flour, followed in his wake. As I turned to look at what was drawing everyone's attention, I was suddenly overwhelmed by the traffic in the harbor we were entering. There were steamships similar to ours as well as massive sailing ships with masts supporting billowing white sails. Servicing these ships were squat tugs, barges, and tenders scurrying around between ships like waiters in a fancy Bourbon Street restaurant.

Cruising straight towards us was a packet boat almost identical to the one that we had boarded in Buras with John Lory. Instead of John standing at the prow of the ship, however, there stood an elderly, bearded Black man who reminded me of General Washington crossing the Delaware in the painting that hung in our Ripley schoolhouse. "I don't know who in the world that is," said the captain, "but, evidently, he wants to see *you*, Joseph." The captain placed a gentle hand on Joseph's shoulder, attempting to reassure my puzzled friend. "I'm pretty sure he's bringing good news to you." The captain looked over Joseph to me, and I thought I detected a panicked look of uncertainty pass across his face like a foreboding cloud.

"Why does everyone seem so excited about him?" I asked.

"Oh, it's not him that all the rest of the crew is excited about," the captain laughed with relief. "The packet boat has mail, and some of these men have been at sea for months."

The mysterious Black man struggled as he climbed the rope ladder up from the packet boat to the deck of the *Tribune*. He hobbled with a cane, walking with a noticeable limp, so the captain moved quickly towards him to reduce his walk. After thanking the captain for allowing him to board, the man announced in a loud, gravelly voice, "I have come to talk to Joseph."

Joseph shyly stepped forward, not knowing what to expect from this stranger.

"Joseph," the man began, "my name is Sandy Cornish, and it is a privilege to meet you. Now, I must confess that I learned about you from a spy I have in the Western Union office here in Key West. He alerted me to a telegram sent by a Mister Samuel Clemens to the captain of the *Helen Mar*, where he described the plight of a young, Black boy—*you*, Joseph—who had won his freedom only to be kidnapped by white devils attempting to put him back into slavery. This telegram was asking the captain to tell the boy's mother, a passenger on the *Helen Mar*, that the boy had escaped these devils and was now on his way to the North on another ship. Is this the truth, Joseph?" I saw my friend nod his head almost imperceptibly.

"When I was a young man, Joseph," Sandy Cornish continued, "I was a slave, but I worked for nine years up in the Florida Panhandle on a railroad job that allowed me to make some money, and I bought my own freedom. But I lost my emancipation papers in a fire, and I had no way of proving it. I got kidnapped by slave traders, but I, too, escaped, and before they could catch me again, I stood in front of a mob of people in Port Leon and stabbed myself in the leg and cut off one of my fingers." There was a collective gasp among the people listening to Cornish as he held up his four-fingered left hand. "I'd be damned—sorry for my language, Joseph—if I was ever going to be a slave again. My friends hauled me off in a wheelbarrow, and I never saw those traders again. No one wanted to buy a pitiful, lame, one-handed slave."

The crowd that had now gathered to listen was struck silent by his story.

"About ten years ago," he concluded, "my wife and I moved to Key West and started farming, and I dare say—without bragging, mind you—that I'm one of the richest men on this island. I wanted to meet this brave boy whose story sounded so familiar. I'm having a talk with the captain about the remainder of your journey because your new life begins now."

I don't know what Sandy Cornish said or did, but I do know I did not work another night in the fire room. Instead, I found myself again washing dishes in the galley—as I had done at Aleix Coffee House—while Joseph worked his breakfast and lunch shifts nearby, and we both started getting paid a nickel an hour for our work. And miraculously, another hammock suddenly appeared so that Joseph and I both slept during normal nighttime hours. The only inkling I had of the source of Cornish's influence was when a large load of fresh fruits and vegetables were ferried out to the *Tribune* before we cast anchor that night.

Joseph and I were sitting out on deck before we set sail from Key West, watching all the activity around us. After Cornish's bounty was unloaded, U.S. Customs officials came out in an official-looking boat to inspect the *Tribune*. "What was Mr. Cornish able to tell you about your mother?" I asked.

Joseph's eyes lit up: "She definitely got the telegram. The messenger recalled her response as being 'Sweet Jesus, the Lord is good.' Now all we have to do is *actually make it to Nantucket*. She should be getting there any time now." Joseph squinted into the glowing orange sun that was setting behind the brick arcades of Fort Taylor on the southern tip of Key

West. As another tender sped to the side of the *Tribune,* we saw a bearded and distinguished-looking white man wearing a derby and a long coat that blew in the wind. "I wonder if they found room for another passenger," pondered Joseph.

We watched from a distance, while the captain approached the new passenger when he climbed aboard and took the folded papers that the man handed him. After a cursory perusal of the documents, the captain returned them to the man who nodded. A steward gathered his belongings and ushered the man into the hallway leading to the main deck suites.

After the sun set, a deep, moonless darkness descended on us in the harbor. A light spread across the deck as the pilothouse door opened and the captain exited. There was a wobbliness to his gait that reminded me of my father after he had been drinking his Macallan whisky. "G'd evenin'," the captain slurred as he walked up and looked over the railing at the darkness below. "We'll be gettin' und'r way in a few minutes."

"We got a new passenger onboard," I half stated and half asked.

"Yeah," the captain replied. "S'spicious, f'reign fellow."

"Suspicious in what way?" Joseph asked.

"Talks with a funny accent. And very secretive about what he's doing here. I'm wonderin' with Florida having seceded from the Union if he might be a Yankee spy." As he said this, I felt a slight jolt to my feet like something had bumped into the ship.

"Did you feel that?" I asked Joseph and the captain.

"Feel what?" said the captain. *In his current state, I don't think he's feeling much of anything.* He bid us goodnight as he wobbled back to the pilothouse. Luckily, I knew that the *Tribune* had a very capable pilot who would guide the ship safely out of the harbor.

"I felt something too," whispered Joseph after the captain had left. "Like something hit the ship." We walked over to the opposite—and darker—side of the ship and peered down. Just as we did, the newest passenger appeared at the railing.

"I thought I zaw a shape in the water," he said in accented English that reminded me of Antoine at the pension in the French Quarter. "Eet iz zo dark tonight."

Indeed, it was so dark that I couldn't see any details of the man's face. He was just a disembodied voice. "We thought something bumped into the ship," I said cautiously, "but I guess it could just have been a log or something. I saw a dead palm tree float by this afternoon."

"Maybe zo," he admitted, "but on the ship I waz on to Key West, the crew waz talking about a zea monster in the Triangle."

"Where did you sail from?" asked Joseph.

"Up north," the stranger answered vaguely, only increasing the mystery surrounding him. He reached into his overcoat pocket and withdrew something that he tucked under his arm. His hand flashed across the top of the metal rail and a spark grew in his hand. The lighted match brought detail to his face as he placed the stem of a bulbous pipe between his thin lips and began to draw in air as the tobacco lit. This illumination seemed to unbutton his personality, and he continued his story. "I zailed over from Cherbourg at zee end of last year, and I'm afraid I've gotten the 'zailing bug.' I've been going up and down zee East Coast collecting information."

Even though I wanted to ask the question, I refrained, but

Joseph blurted it right out, as he was wont to do. "Are you a spy?"

The mysterious air surrounding this foreigner evaporated as a broad smile appeared across his bearded face. "*Mon dieu,* no," he laughed. "Eez that what they are zaying of me?"

"Maybe," Joseph said as his reciprocal grin showed in the glow of the man's pipe.

"Worze than a spy," he said with a fake, threatening voice. "I'm a writer. I've been gathering zcientific information for a novel I am planning to write about zee dangers at zea." He pulled a small sketchbook out of another pocket and flipped through the drawings and notes that covered the pages.

"I met another writer who keeps a journal just like that," I said.

"What eez hiz name?" the man asked.

"Mark Twain… or Sam Clemens," I said, but the stranger shook his head at both names.

"Never heard of him. My name is Verne," he announced to us. "Jules Verne."

* * *

We made good time cruising the Gulf Stream up the eastern coast of Florida. After we finished our shifts the next day, we ran into the captain on deck. "I am a bit ashamed of my behavior last night," he said. "I'm afraid I might have sampled a little of the contraband that Customs had seized from another ship—some fine Cuban rum—and I wasn't at my best."

Joseph and I acted like we didn't know what he was talking about, and I do have to admit that I had also forgotten about the bump we felt that the captain had been oblivious to.

Nothing seems to have come of that anyway. The Tribune is sailing smoothly.

This peaceful interlude, however, was not destined to last. "Hark! Eyes to the portside," yelled a crewman as passengers and stewards rushed to the railing. The water was churning as several "beings" surfaced out of the waves only to splash back down into the depths, creating a whirlpool of turbulence. Jets of water shot up, spraying the deck of the *Tribune*, as scared passengers rushed for cover under the overhanging floor of the second deck. The solitary witness to this maelstrom of marine madness was Jules Verne. He steadfastly remained at the rail pulling out a telescope from his seemingly endless supply of tools in the pockets of his overcoat.

"Is it the sea monsters?" Joseph gasped as we made our way to Verne's side.

"I don't theenk zo," replied the unflappable writer as he squinted into his telescope.

He opened his sketchbook and looked at a hand-drawn map.

"By my calculations, we should be about two hundred nautical miles up zee coast."

"Then what is it out there?" I yelled over the roar.

"A pod of excited humpback whales." His eyebrows arched comically. "Mating zeazon." We later saw Mr. Verne seated comfortably in a deck chair scribbling furiously in his sketchbook about the excitement that we had witnessed that afternoon.

We sailed steadily northward that night along the Florida coast. The next day was uneventful, though the clear, blue skies gave way to clouds and a rising wind. The captain ordered the deck crew to raise some supplemental sails that increased our speed and took some of the load off the steam-driven turbines. With this easing of the need for coal, I saw some of the Cuban crew that I had worked with in the fire room up on deck at odd hours. A couple of them whispered and gave me sideways glances that raised the hair on the back of my neck. "They look like they'd like to slit my throat," I said to Joseph.

"I wouldn't worry about it, John," replied Joseph. "That's the way they've looked at me since the first day we boarded."

We woke the next day to a steady rain, and the drabness of the weather seemed reflected in the collective personality of the crew as they sat silently in the galley sipping their coffee after breakfast. The mood did not improve during lunchtime as both passengers and crew picked at their food while the ship rolled in the tempestuous seas. After Joseph and I finished our shifts, we visited the captain in the pilothouse as he directed the pilot to bring the *Tribune* closer to shore for another rendezvous with a packet boat. This delivery was coming from Fort Clinch at the northernmost point of Fernandina Beach on the border between Florida and Georgia. "If the weather doesn't deteriorate any further," the captain said as he pointed to the charts, "we should pass by Savannah late tonight and reach Charleston by day after tomorrow."

Mary, George's daughter on my father's farm and wife to Simon, used to say, "If wishes were fishes, we'd had some fried." So, the captain's "*If* the weather doesn't deteriorate" was just a wishful prelude to a fierce, inevitable storm. By the late afternoon, sheets of rain pelted the deck of the *Tribune* as all crew and passengers hunkered down in a dry space. As nightfall enveloped the ship, flashes of lighting strobed the decks followed by deep rumbles of thunder.

The captain ordered all crew members to don the cork

lifejackets that had just recently become mandatory on ocean voyages. We all scurried about on deck securing sails, and mooring lines and chairs against the wind that whipped across the ship. During one lightning strike, the shocking image of Mr. Verne peering through his telescope seared itself onto my retina. Ignoring the rain, he stood soaking in his ever-present overcoat. "You shouldn't be up here, sir," I yelled amidst the crash of thunder. "It's not safe."

"There's zomething out there," he yelled back, pointing to the starboard side of the ship.

When the next lightning flashed, others joined in spotting the intruder. "Hark, to the starboard side, there's a beast in the water!" cried the lookout who was poised halfway up a mast that secured his tether.

"It's the sea monster we were warned about!" another crewman exclaimed in a heavy Scottish brogue.

I grabbed Joseph's hand as we braced ourselves against the railing to get a view of *whatever it was* in the water. "Is it another whale?" I asked Mr. Verne.

"I don't zeenk zo," he replied in an unsure voice.

"I can see the beast's head and its fiery eyes," yelled the lookout. "And it's swimming straight at us!"

In a near-continuous string of lightning flashes, I finally saw what everyone was yelling about. It was swimming low in the water. It appeared to be covered in black, shiny scales like the huge rat snakes we used to chase out of the vegetable garden in Ripley. Its squat head stuck out of the water with two flanking, fire-glowing eyes. Growing out of the top center of the sea monster's head was a thin, telescoping horn. "It *is* a sea monster, isn't it, Mr. Verne?"

"No, John," he answered. "But it might be zomething worze."

* * *

"But it's got scales and a horn!" I protested loudly through the noise of the storm. It did not take a navigator to realize that we were on a collision course with this monster.

"Eetz not a horn," Mr. Verne answered with an eerie calm. "Eetz a cannon, and it can blow this ship right out of the water. Thoze aren't scales either. They are a metal skin. That 'monster' eez a French broadzide ironclad ship. Zee first one left the port of Toulon two years ago. I have talked to the naval architect who dezigned it."

"But what is it doing here?" Joseph asked.

"There'z been rumorz that zome rogue Frenchmen have been aiding the zecessionist states by zmuggling gunz into Florida through Cuba in exchange for cotton. Major Beauregard evidently haz reached out to zome of heez French kinzmen for help. Thiz ironclad must be part of that operation. I need to talk to zee captain right now."

When he turned and began walking to the pilothouse, I felt an arm lock around my throat and the cold metal of a gun barrel pressed against my cheek. In the little bit that my head could pivot, I saw that Joseph was also being held by one of the Cuban crewmen who had looked at us with such hate. Just as a violent collision of the two ships seemed inevitable, I felt the vibration of the engine stop. *Mr. Verne must have made it to the captain in time.*

They dragged Joseph and me down the stairs to a lower deck of the ship. We were pushed through a hatch that led to a forward cargo hold. While one of the Cubans held his pistol on Joseph and me, the other cranked open a cargo door that was just above the level of the churning water outside. Like magic, a small rowboat appeared at the opening, and a man tossed a mooring line from the rowboat to the Cuban at the door. All of this was happening on the port side of the ship while everyone's attention was attracted to the attacking ship on the starboard side.

The Cuban with the gun yelled to Joseph and me in broken English: "Load crates onto boat." He pointed to two large unmarked wooden crates wedged against the hull of the ship.

Joseph whispered to me as we bent down to pick up the first crate, "That's the bump that we felt in the harbor at Key West. When they were sneaking these crates on board."

I whispered back, "If what Mr. Verne says is right, they're full of guns."

"Shut up talking and get to work!" hissed the man as he waved the pistol wildly at us. We picked up the heavy crate and carried it to the cargo door. While the man in the boat locked arms with his compatriot on our ship to steady the connection, we stepped across and dropped the crate onto the floor of the rowboat. I lost my balance and was headed overboard, but Joseph grabbed my upper arm. We repeated this with the second crate and retreated back into the cargo hold, thinking we had satisfied the demands of the Cuban crewmen; instead, the man with the pistol again pointed it at us. "Now, you get on boat and row it to other ship."

Again, faced with the hopeless dilemma of no choices, Joseph and I rowed the boat around the bow of the *Tribune* while the man in the boat sat and pointed yet another gun at us. "They're going to think we were in on this," said Joseph. The storm had quieted, and we were able to make slow progress to the backside of the ironclad, away from any view from the *Tribune*. When we were tied up to the shiny, metallic side of the foreign ship, another cargo door opened, and we unloaded the two crates in the same manner that we had loaded them.

"They're going to kill us," I said to Joseph as we laid the second crate down. "We know too much now."

"Despite what you may think, we are not monsters," uttered a new voice that resembled Mr. Verne's. Judging from his uniform, the captain of the ironclad was now addressing us. "We do not kill children. I will at least give you a fighting chance." *Like the bad man by the creek.*

We were ordered to get back into the rowboat, but this time without the man who had accompanied us from the *Tribune*. "The prevailing winds are blowing to the west, so with any luck, you should reach the Georgia coastline by daybreak. If the winds change, the cloudy skies tonight are going to be of no use to you, but by morning you'll want to row against the rising sun." He gave us a menacing smile and a subtle bow as the cargo door closed over him.

We quickly drifted away from the French ironclad, but any hopes we had of rowing back to the *Tribune* were dashed as it moved even more swiftly away from us. As a brief break in the clouds allowed a sliver of moon to shine through, we watched as the deck lights of the *Tribune* flickered and then disappeared into the distance, leaving us alone at sea.

"We've got to keep the boat pointed north in the direction the *Tribune* is headed," I said to Joseph in the silence of the suddenly calm sea. I looked over my shoulder and added, "The moon is at four o'clock."

"That only helps if the moon stays out," Joseph answered. *He is right, and our chances aren't good.*

As it turned out, we had luck on our side that night. The clouds cleared, the moon shone, and the rowboat stayed on a northward course, no doubt aided by the Gulf Stream. As the sun began to peek above the horizon, the sky turned from darkness to pink and then to a deep blue as a crystal-clear morning presented itself. The steady current of the Stream meant that we did not have to row much. This allowed us to save our strength, which was especially important because we had nothing to eat or drink. The ironclad's captain may not have considered himself a monster, but his failure to provide any essentials left Joseph and me a very narrow window in which to survive. That window widened a bit when we began hearing and then seeing seagulls swooping down to us. Within an hour of that, we spotted a distant tree line on our port side.

Chapter 12

Our boat seemed to be pulled to the distant beach by some inexorable force. We could hear breaking waves ahead of us, and we rode their crests as we got closer to shore. We grounded on a sandy beach that converged into a low rock outcropping emerging out of the sand. Nestled into the pockets created by the intersection of sand and rock were hundreds of clamshells garnished with wispy garlands of rust-colored seaweed. Fortunately, Joseph and I were both wearing shoes when we were forced below decks of the *Tribune* at gunpoint. If we had had to navigate our way barefoot across the jagged rock, our feet would have been ripped to shreds.

After a short walk, we encountered a brackish saltwater channel that separated us from a sawgrass marsh that reminded me of Pass-a-Loutre. With the sun at our backs, we waded across the channel and through the marsh until we came to solid ground. We passed into the shade of a forest of twisted live oaks and scraggly pines where we found a clear pool of fresh water to satisfy our thirsts. The ironic first signs of human life we literally stumbled across were some mossy-covered graves crowned with rugged, carved headstones. These were hunkered into the shady corner of a small cemetery that was partially bordered by a split-rail fence. On the crooked gate that was the entrance hung a rough-hewn, hand-carved sign reading "Tombee Cemetery—St. Helena Island, South Carolina."

"Somehow, we sailed right past Georgia," I said to Joseph as I pictured a map of the Southeast from our school textbook in my head. "Charleston is in South Carolina, so maybe we're not too far away."

"How do we know how to even get started in the right direction?" Joseph asked me.

"The ocean—and the sun—is at our back, so I say we just head inland." To one side of the gate was a grave that looked freshly dug. The newly turned soil was compacted by multiple bare footprints skewed in all directions as if the mourners had danced in a frenzy. Littered on the grave were bits of broken dishes and bottles. "Looks like somebody had a pretty wild party here," I said to Joseph as he bent down to examine the colorful shards.

"Looking at all these busted dinner plates reminds me that I'm starving," Joseph said. "I wish we had picked up some of those clams on the beach."

As we exited the cemetery through the gate, I said, "Maybe we can find some food if we start walking again." There was a rough dirt road the width of a single wagon leading from the cemetery, so we began there. After about an hour with the warming sun at our backs, we came upon an abandoned shack set back into the woods. As if a genie had come out of a bottle to grant us our wishes, we found several bowls of freshly cooked food laid out on the front porch.

We did not want to just help ourselves to what was someone else's food, so we gently rapped on the unlatched front door which pushed open. "Hello!" I called out. "Anybody home?"

We tiptoed cautiously into a rear bedroom where a bare mattress lay askew on a simple wood bed frame. Joseph whispered, "Someone has turned the mirrors into the wall. My mother once told me that this was a voodoo custom so that dead people wouldn't be reflected."

"This might be the home of the person we just saw buried in the cemetery," I offered.

"I'm sorry for whoever that is," replied Joseph, "but if that's true, they ain't gonna be eating that food on the porch anytime soon."

Sitting together on the front steps so we could see if anyone approached, we shared this feast that evidently had been lovingly prepared for the spirit of the recently departed. We devoured a delicious stew of shrimp, sausage, potatoes, corn, and onions. Joseph smiled as he murmured, "This tastes just like Mamma's cooking. I can feel her here."

"I've eaten all of these foods before," I said as I scraped the bottom of my bowl, "but I've never tasted them together. It is *so* good!" I filled my bowl with another helping.

"Mamma calls this 'Lowcountry' cooking," Joseph explained as he also refilled his bowl. "Her mother was from South Carolina, so she learned from her." After stuffing our bellies (and after a rough night in the rowboat), Joseph and I both needed naps. There was a tiny barn behind the shack that was practically hidden in the woods, so we felt we would be safe for a little while. We climbed a primitive ladder up to the loft and fell asleep immediately.

I awoke with low, sharp rays of sun burning across my face. Joseph was still breathing heavily beside me, though he had an intermittent raspy catch that I thought would wake him.

I waited a half hour before I roused him. *We can't wait any longer.* We needed to put some more miles behind us while we still had daylight. Surrounded by tabletop-flat fields bordered by cedars and oaks festooned with Spanish moss, I remarked as we resumed walking, "It's easy to see why it's called the Lowcountry. I feel like we can see all the way back to the ocean, and that's got to be ten miles."

"It feels like we've walked a hundred miles," croaked Joseph as he struggled beside me.

"I've been thinking," I said trying to take his mind off the walking, "that we literally escaped with just the clothes on our backs. I didn't really have anything to lose, but what about you, Joseph? Did you leave anything on the ship that you need?"

Joseph reached in his back pocket and pulled out the journal that Father Matthew had given him. He opened the book to a thin, red gingham packet tucked between the pages. "My freedom papers. Mamma gave me this piece of an oilcloth tablecloth to keep them dry. That's all that I need," he said as we passed a printed bill hanging on a tree. I thought of the "Missing" headline and the Black boy's face on the poster that Officer Craven had snatched off the pole on Flood Street. This notice was offering a hundred-dollar bounty "for the successful capture of any runaway slaves from the Frogmore Plantation."

* * *

It was a starless night. As we continued along a straight, flat, dirt road through fields of rice, Joseph began having a dry cough. When we stopped for a drink of water, I could

128

see Joseph's face glistening in sweat. "I'm okay," he insisted. "We've got to keep moving."

After another hour of walking, during which the frequency and severity of Joseph's cough increased, we saw a fire in the distance and heard the faint echo of singing or chanting. As we got closer, we could discern dozens of Black people dancing around the fire to a song with words in a strange language. That morning's feast on the porch of the shack now seemed an eternity ago, so we hoped they might have some food.

"Welcome, strangers!" said a large woman who put down a basket she was weaving when she saw us approaching. "Come join us by the fire."

"Are you slaves?" Joseph asked the woman as he smartly took the lead.

"Yes, we are, but we are much more than that. We are Gullah."

"We are from Mississippi," Joseph replied, "and I have heard of the Gullah from stories that my grandmother told my mamma, but I've never met one. My friend John and I are traveling to Charleston. We're really hungry and willing to work for some food."

The woman smiled. "We have food for you—and you don't have to work for it. Look at you, though," said the woman as she took Joseph by the arm. "It is a cold night, and you are soaking wet." She waved to an old man who was dancing beside the fire. "Bala, come here. My new friend needs some of your Hoodoo."

"Hoodoo?" I asked as the strangely dressed man looked at Joseph.

"Bala is a root doctor. He knows the ancient art of herbal, or

Hoodoo, medicines. He has saved many of us from the fevers of the Lowcountry. My name is Mariama. I am his niece."

"Very nice to meet you both," Mariama continued, but she focused her attention on Joseph as she patted him on the head. "You have such beautiful hair. In our culture, hair is a sign of strength and courage. I see many great adventures in your future. We are so glad that you and your friend have found us. Now, how about some of that food you were asking about?"

As I sat beside the fire, Mariama went to prepare a plate from a table on the other side. As I looked around, I heard the Gullah people talking in a language that sounded at times like English, but featured many words which I did not recognize. Mariama handed the plate to a girl about my age who brought it to me. "Here's your food," the girl said as she sat down beside me. "My name is Jilo."

"Thank you," I said. "Are you Gullah?"

"Yes, we all are here. We try to stay together as much as we can."

"What is Gullah?" I asked.

Jilo was small and thin with lustrous dark skin and large brown eyes. Her head was wrapped in a bright-green scarf which seemed to make her eyes look even larger. "Our ancestors were from the Gola tribe in West Africa. They were brought to America on slave ships to work the rice fields here. Our elders tell us many stories of our ancestors—our family—so we will not lose who we are and where we came from."

I could see Bala, the root doctor, preparing a steaming pot for Joseph. Mariama sat with him as he also ate from a plate of fish and rice. There were several women with braided hair weaving intricate baskets as they talked by the fire. "The baskets are beautiful," I said to Jilo.

"They are another African tradition. They are called *fannah* baskets, and we use them out in the rice fields to separate the chaff from the hull. The Gullah have been weaving them for hundreds of years."

When I rejoined Joseph by the fire, he already seemed better and was anxious to talk: "Though these people are slaves like Mamma and I were—and Daddy still is—they seem to possess a freedom that comes from having a past—they call it a *heritage*. Although I have a family, as a slave, I never felt connected to anything larger."

Joseph and I sat by the fire for many hours listening to stories and songs such as "Cum Out De Weederness," that seemed at once very foreign and very familiar. Though we were on our way to what we felt was true freedom in the North, I could have happily stayed with Jilo and the Gullahs for a long time. When we woke up in the morning, Joseph's fever had disappeared.

We found Mariama by the fire making coffee, but almost everyone else was gone. "We saw a notice on a tree yesterday," Joseph said. "Do all of you work at the Frogmore Plantation?"

"Most of us do," she answered. "As plantations go, I guess it could be worse, but our brothers and sisters are always trying to escape."

"Where do they try and go?" I asked as I thought about the path ahead of us.

"Most are so desperate to get away," she said in a voice full of resignation, "that they don't have a plan. I'm afraid most never make it out of the marshes. Whether it's the snakes or the alligators, or malaria or the fever like Joseph had, it's a hard place to survive for more than a few days. Where are y'all planning to go?"

"We need to make it to Charleston," said Joseph. "My mamma is on a ship to Nantucket. My daddy bought our freedom," he said as I saw him reach back and unconsciously pat the bulge in his back pocket, "and we are going to catch the next ship north."

"We can help you with that," Mariama said. "My cousin fishes all the rivers between here and Charleston, and he should be able to take you there on his boat. His master has fled the island because he's afraid that the U.S. Navy will be freeing us as soon as the war starts."

* * *

As Joseph and I boarded the long, flat-bottomed dugout boat with Jah, Mariama's cousin, I thought, *And just like that, I'm back on the river.* I was reminded of Jim and me drifting down the Mississippi River on our homemade raft as well as the "pee-row" boats that Joseph and I hid under when the militiamen attacked Mr. Boudreaux's Cajun outpost. *Was that a month ago or a year ago? I have lost all concept of time.*

Jah told us that he was twenty years old, though he could have passed for our age. He was first reluctant to talk, as befits a fisherman who spends most days in the quiet solitude that the profession requires. Joseph and Jah soon hit it off, however, and they would talk back and forth a mile a minute. Unfortunately, the boat did not move nearly that fast. In the shallow sections of the narrow river that we started out in, Jah would use the opposite end of his long oar as a pole to push us along, like the Venetian gondoliers that I had seen pictures of in my school geography book. In deeper channels, either Joseph or I would join Jah in tandem with a second oar that was strapped along the side of the long boat. After dark, we would alternate rowing and holding the gas lantern that lit our way through the eerie, shadowy marshes.

"I'm not just a fisherman," Jah told us as we approached a camping spot for our first night. "I'm a hunter too." As we unloaded our gear and pulled the boat up on the shore, Jah pointed out his bow and woven quiver of arrows. "Even though the Indian tribes that lived in the Lowcountry—the Edisto, the Kiawah, and the Santee—are long gone from here, their culture and traditions remain in the Gullah. I learned how to hunt with a bow and arrow from my grandfather, who did live alongside the Edisto." As darkness crept into the woods beside the river, Joseph stuck like glue to Jah as he hunted—and killed—a beaver and a wild turkey that we cooked on the campfire that I had built while they hunted.

Joseph soaked in all that Jah had to say on how to cook the game. After dinner, I saw him chronicling all that he had learned in his journal. "Mamma knows more than anybody about cooking," Joseph said as he looked up, "but she would love to learn what Jah knows."

Seeing Joseph's journal reminded me of my confusion that morning as we had started out on the river. "Do you know what day it is?" I asked Joseph. "I have lost all track of time."

"Yes, as Sam told me I should do, I write a little bit each day. It's the First of March. It was a month ago that my mother got on the ship, and I ended up in the tunnel."

We traveled in the boat with Jah for almost two weeks as we stayed on the smaller creeks and tributaries that we hoped would inevitably lead us to Charleston. Jah seemed to be known by all the other fishermen on the river, so we did not seem to arouse anyone's suspicions. He introduced Joseph as his cousin from Georgia, while I hid under a blanket on the flat bottom of the boat when we encountered other people on the river. *I understand better now what it means to stand out because of the color of your skin.* Each evening we would stop and hunt or trap our dinner before sleeping the night away beside the fire.

Joseph woke one morning with a curious smile on his face. "I know that there are dangers out there—like the bad men who tied you up beside the creek in Mississippi—but this is the most fun I've ever had in my life. I like playing *Cowboys and Indians* with a bow and arrow." Joseph had gotten nearly as good as Jah with the bow, although we both still had a lot to learn from Jah about tracking animals. "I miss Mamma—and I can't wait to see her again in Nantucket—but I almost wish we could just take our time in getting to Charleston."

As I listened to Joseph, a weight of guilt lifted from my shoulders. *I've been thinking exactly the same thing.* I had felt like we needed to keep pushing forward out of an obligation to reunite Joseph with his mother, but I could now admit to myself what *I* was feeling:

This has been the best two weeks of my life.

The next morning, however, Jah announced to us that we were nearing the end of our journey with him. He took an arrow out of his quiver and scratched a rough map into the dirt with its sharp point. "We'll be turning into Wappoo Creek today, and it's only about half a day's paddle to the McLeod Plantation landing. We'll avoid the plantation, but all you will need to do is climb the ridge just east of it, and you will be able to see all of Charleston right below you."

"How do you know all these names?" I asked Jah as we began

loading up the boat for one last time. "All these creeks and rivers look the same to me."

Jah laughed, "There are some Gullah slaves at the McLeod Plantation who make their way south to us every now and then. Lots of the masters around Charleston head west in the summertime to avoid the heat and the fevers, so their slaves have a freedom they don't normally have. They are the ones that have taught me the names of the rivers and landmarks around here."

When we reached the landing, Joseph and I hugged Jah and thanked him for all that he had done for us. Before climbing back into his boat, he again pointed out the path we should take up the ridge. As he disappeared up the creek, Joseph and I were faced with the frightening prospect of being on our own again. We each hoisted up the white fannah baskets with orange straps that Mariama had given us when we left the Gullahs. They now held a day's worth of food.

As we approached the top of the ridge, we heard a constant hum from the other side. We crept up on our hands and knees through the dense brush to see where this noise was coming from. When we peeked over the edge, we saw a sea of tents spread across a valley like the red fire ant piles I used to see scattered across my father's bean fields. Beyond, we could see what had to be Charleston. Too late, I heard the sharp *crack* of a twig snapping behind us.

"You boys need to come with us," we heard a voice say as I again felt the touch of a cold steel barrel on the back of my neck.

PART FOUR: Charleston
(March–April 1861)

Chapter 13

When Joseph and I were allowed to turn our heads, we saw two boys not much older than us dressed in drab gray uniforms and peculiar flat-billed caps. "I think we've found us a couple of spies," announced the boy who had first confronted us from behind.

"We're not spies," I returned in a dry voice. "We're just trying to make it to Charleston."

"Well, welcome to Charleston. You're our prisoners now," said the other "soldier" as he too raised his rifle. "Y'all need to drop those baskets. We're taking you to the general."

We were led down off the ridge through the tents that were laid out in sinuous curves following the topography of the valley. The tents were staked into the lush grass of the slope that was punctuated with odd potholes filled with dark sand. We looked ahead and saw a central area of larger tents radiating from a flagpole topped by a red flag, which was crisscrossed with diagonal blue stripes containing white stars. Oddly enough, there were small holes scattered throughout the tented area which were marked with tiny white flags.

There was activity all around the tents as men of all ages dressed in the uniforms of our captors scurried to don their packs and prepare their rifles. "Clear ahead!" yelled one of the boys "escorting" us. "We need to see the general!"

We stopped in front of the biggest tent, and—judging from the more elaborate uniform—an officer stepped out of the gap at the front of the closed tent. "What's all this noise out here?" asked the officer. "You're disturbing the general."

"We caught these spies creeping along the top of the ridge," announced one of the boys self-importantly. "We knew that the general would want to be notified of this immediately."

"The general is busy right now," declared the officer. I could see the two boys who had captured us deflate a bit as their importance was challenged.

The officer looked at us dismissively and told the two soldiers, "Hold your so-called 'spies' over by the latrine until the general is ready to see you."

As we waited, holding our noses in the foul air by the communal latrine, I looked further down the valley where we could see the city of Charleston rising up beside the harbor that was guarded by a red brick fort. I watched the faint outlines of ships entering and leaving the harbor in the glare of the morning sun. To distract him from the serious fix we were in, I tried to direct Joseph's eyes to the harbor and our ultimate destination. Joseph nodded in recognition.

From our malodorous detention area, we had a view of the rear of the large tent. After a few minutes, we saw the bottom flap at the rear of the tent rise, and a young, dark-haired woman emerged surreptitiously. She wore a light-pink, lacy robe that she gathered around herself as she got herself clear of the tent flap. Seeing us being held at gunpoint, she scrunched her eyes in confusion and hurried away towards another tent further down the hill.

"Bring the prisoners around!" ordered the officer. The two

boys raised their rifles at a threatening level and marched us back to the front of the large tent. "I'll take them from here," said the officer as he dismissed the two boys with a flick of the wrist. He opened one of the tent flaps and told us to step in.

The interior was dark, but we saw the silhouette of someone step forward and turn up the light of a gas lantern that sat atop a table in the middle. In the back corner of the tent, we could see a curtain hanging from the ceiling that was meant to hide a disheveled bed. We could now clearly see the man who stood before us dressed in a red satin robe, boots, and nothing else. He was thin and only slightly taller than Joseph and me. He had dark, oiled hair and a black goatee that framed his olive-toned face. His heavy-lidded eyes gazed at us with seeming amusement. "So, you are the big, bad spies?" he asked us as he measured us with his eyes from head to toe.

The officer spoke up: "Two of the new recruits found them at the top of the ridge looking down at our camp. They brought them straight to you, General."

The general's eyes pivoted from the officer to me as if to educe an explanation from me. Instead, it was Joseph that spoke up: "We're not spies. My name is Joseph, and I am a freed slave, and this is my friend John, and we are just trying to make it to Charleston so we can get on a ship to Nantucket to meet my mother." He blurted this so swiftly and breathlessly that the general just smiled in response.

"Please, sir," I picked up, "you've got to believe us."

"I don't *have* to believe *anything*," replied the general with a lilting accent that reminded me of Mr. Verne. "You have interrupted our war games, and I have anticipated all along that Major Anderson would grow curious about what we were doing up here in the hills. I just didn't think he would send boys to do a man's job."

"We don't know any Major Anderson," I objected. "Joseph is telling you the truth. We're just trying to get on a ship so he can get back to his mother." When I looked at Joseph, he had a weird, mischievous spark in his eye.

"What are *war games*?" Joseph asked.

The general seemed to temporarily table his suspicions as he looked at Joseph anew. He paused and poured himself a drink of amber-colored liquid from a sparkling crystal decanter on the table. "It's where we practice having a war," he explained, almost patiently.

I had learned to appreciate Joseph's openness and absolute courage in asking direct questions, but I held my breath as I looked at him and tried to see into his mind. *What is he going to ask next?*

"Wouldn't it make more sense to practice *not* having a war?" Joseph asked.

* * *

The general exploded with rheumy laughter that his officer parasitically joined in on. "Ah, Joseph!" the general guffawed, "If only I could have you as an envoy between Lincoln and Jefferson Davis. Maybe, years of misery could be avoided."

I began breathing again as the tension in the tent seemed to have dissipated like smoke out through the open front flap. The general turned his attention to me. "What's *your* story? I think I might even believe Joseph's."

"My name is John Wesley Thompson Falkner, and I ran away from my home in Ripley, Mississippi. I met up with Joseph and his mother along the way, and we traveled together to New Orleans. He got separated from his mother, who ended up on a ship to Nantucket, so Joseph and I have been trying ever since to get him back to his mother."

"You said 'Falkner'... from Mississippi?" inquired the general.

"Yes, sir. I was hoping to meet someone that my father knew in New Orleans that might help us, but he wasn't there."

"John, did your father fight in the Mexican War? A lieutenant?"

"Yes, sir."

"Just so I can be sure you are who you say you are," the general probed with increasing intensity, "what was your father's favorite liquor?"

"He only drinks Macallan Scotch. Still does. *Way too much* of it."

"I must apologize to you two boys," the general said gently as he stood up straight. "I've been rude and failed to introduce myself." He placed his drink on the table and approached Joseph and me. He held out his hand to shake. "John, I am Brigadier General G.T. Beauregard, and I owe your father my life. How may I be of service?"

Joseph and I stood speechless. *Someone is offering to be of service to me?*

"Captain Lee," Beauregard ordered in the wake of our shocked silence, "take John and Joseph over to the mess tent and get them something to eat. I will get dressed and meet you there shortly."

As we walked by the flagpole, I asked the captain about the unusual design of the flag flying at the top: "Is that the South Carolina flag, now that the state has seceded?"

Captain Lee squinted as he looked into the sun towards the flag. With the subtlest of smiles, he explained, "No, that's a flag designed by General Beauregard. He's hoping that the Confederacy will adopt it as its battle flag. He sent a copy to President Davis by armed special courier, but he has not heard back if it has been accepted."

While we drank coffee and ate hardtack in the mess tent, the captain gave us a brief history of General Beauregard's tenure in Charleston. "He arrived on March 3rd—eleven days ago— the day before Lincoln was inaugurated—and immediately began overhauling Charleston's defenses. His specialty is artillery, so he has been fortifying the batteries scattered around the city, especially as they relate to Fort Sumter."

"Is that Fort Sumter I saw at the mouth of the harbor?" I asked the garrulous captain.

"Yes, it is."

"Why is it so important?" Joseph inquired as he joined in the conversation.

"Even though South Carolina seceded from the Union almost three months ago and formed its own army that General Beauregard now commands, Fort Sumter is still under federal control. In January, a few shots were fired at a ship, the *Star of the West*, that came into the harbor to resupply Fort Sumter, and some were afraid that would be the start of the war, but cooler heads prevailed. I don't know how much longer that can hold, however."

The captain abruptly jumped to attention as General Beauregard entered the mess tent. He wore a tunic-length gray coat that tapered at his thin waist, which was circled by a gold belt matching the gold buttons of the coat. Gold-fringed epaulets adorned the shoulder of each sleeve that terminated in matched gold cuffs. He wore gray pants with gold stripes running down each leg that disappeared into high, black riding boots. *There is no doubt who is in charge here.*

"Let me show you around the camp," the general said as he beckoned us out of the mess tent. "Like I said, we are holding 'war games' right now to prepare our new recruits for battle." When we were away from Captain Lee and any other soldiers, the general continued speaking in a low, conspiratorial tone: "These South Carolina boys are tough, and they know how to shoot, but they're also raw and undisciplined."

As we walked around one of the potholes filled with sand with its accompanying small hole and tiny white flag, I asked the general, "What are all the holes around here?"

Beauregard smiled ruefully as he withdrew the flag from the hole. "Evidently, many years ago, some of the rich Scottish merchants in Charleston decided for some reason that they needed a 'golf club'—copying the one in St. Andrews, Scotland. They walk around this beautiful valley whacking at a little ball with a stick. *Mon dieu!*"

"I did like the Scottish flag that they flew over the club, however," the general declared, "so I used its diagonal-crossed stripes in the design of our new Confederate battle flag."

"Captain Lee told us about that," I said.

"He did, huh? I might need to talk to him about that. *Loose lips—*"

"You said that you owed my father your life," I interrupted. "My father tends to exaggerate, especially when he has been drinking, so I wasn't sure there was anything to it—"

"Oh, I do," he interrupted back, "and I would love to settle this debt."

* * *

"I was a major during the Mexican War, serving as an engineer under General Winfield Scott," Beauregard began recounting as we sat on a bench beside one of the potholes. "I had survived several of the bloodiest battles without a scratch, but my horse got shot out from under me at Chapultepec, and it was your father, who was a lieutenant in the Mississippi Army, who pulled me to safety. I was bleeding from my shoulder and thigh pretty bad, and your father poured that damn Macallan Scotch over my wounds." The general reached up and touched the epaulet on his left shoulder. "It burned like hell, but it probably saved me from dying of gangrene."

"That Scotch has caused nothing but misery to my family," I said quietly. "I'm glad to know that it was good for *something*."

"Your father and I stayed in touch for a short time after the war," the general replied, "and he never missed the opportunity to remind me that I owed him." He suddenly smiled to himself as he obviously was thinking back. "I never thought I would get the chance to return the favor." Just as quickly, he left the past behind and refocused on Joseph and me. "As I said when I belatedly introduced myself, how can I be of service?"

"We just want to get to Nantucket as soon as possible," Joseph answered frankly.

"We were on a ship from New Orleans to Charleston—the *S.S. Tribune*—when we were attacked by an ironclad ship," I further explained, "and we were forced off the ship by gunrunners."

Joseph again stepped in with his characteristic bluntness: "A passenger on the ship thought that you might be behind this ironclad. He said it was built in France."

The general's eyes narrowed. "Who was this passenger accusing me of this?"

"He is a French writer," I replied. "Jules Verne."

"Never heard of him," the general said in a dismissive tone. He deftly danced around this discussion of the ironclad. "Two weeks ago, it would have been no problem getting you on a ship to Nantucket. But with Lincoln's inauguration, tensions along the East Coast have ratcheted up significantly. We are limiting the ships that come into Charleston Harbor to keep Fort Sumter from being resupplied—"

"Yes, Captain Lee told us about the *Star of the West*," I interjected.

"He did, huh? I think I really need to have a talk with the good captain." A scowl appeared on the constantly shifting canvas of the general's face. "Anyway, it may take a couple of weeks to find suitable passage for you to Nantucket."

Joseph's face immediately reflected his disappointment. "Is there another way for us to travel there?" he asked desperately. "Railroad?"

Beauregard shook his head emphatically: "Putting you on a train headed north right now would be a death sentence." In an eerie echo of the captain's words when we had our midnight boarding of the *Tribune* at Pass-a-Loutre, the general said, "I need to know what each of you can do. How can we keep you busy and out of trouble for two weeks?"

"Joseph is a great cook!" I offered. "His mother is amazing, and he has learned everything from her. He worked in the galley of the *Tribune* until we were forced off."

"Interesting. I know of a place that is always in need of a good cook," the general said as Joseph got quiet all of a sudden. *He's thinking of his mother.* "And what about you, John? What job did you have on the *Tribune*?"

"I worked in the fire room, and then I got moved to washing dishes in the galley. I also washed dishes at Aleix Coffee House in New Orleans."

"Aleix's? One of my favorite spots."

"Do you know Samuel Clemens? Or, he has another name… Mark Twain?"

"Riverboat captain with a bushy mustache?" the general asked.

"Yes! He's the man that helped us get out of New Orleans," I answered. We had arrived at the bottom of the valley where a gravel drive circled a small hut. A soldier ran from it and immediately presented himself at attention before General Beauregard with a crisp salute.

"At ease, Private," the general said with a reciprocal, nonchalant salute. "I need my carriage to take me and my two guests into town." A carriage materialized out of thin air, drawn by white horses under the reins of a uniformed driver. Another soldier with a long rifle sat on the driver's box. The private opened the door, and the general directed us to climb in.

After we had settled into the plush leather bench on one side of the carriage, the general, sitting across from us, restarted the conversation: "I want to hear how you two boys came to be traveling together. It sounds like a grand adventure."

Joseph rediscovered his voice as he told the general about his father using his winnings as a jockey to buy Joseph's and his mother's freedom. He described Mr. Hallahan and his tinker's wagon, and how he found me tied to a tree by a creek in southern Mississippi.

"I understand what it means to owe someone my life," I interrupted.

"This is even grander than I imagined!" the general said in glee.

The carriage stopped as we came to what looked like a tall wall across the road. "This is the new drawbridge across the Ashley River that allows ships through," the general said.

I looked down into the river and saw the sun reflected off the black scales of a too-familiar ship riding low in the river. "Joseph, look!" I whispered urgently as I pointed down.

The general said with a quiet, calm voice, "Whatever you think you see… you don't."

Chapter 14

"I need to know that I can trust you… both of you… even with secrets that might mean the difference in whether we go to war or not," the general said after the drawbridge had lowered allowing us to cross. He looked at Joseph and me with a disarming intensity. Then, his eyes shifted to looking through us and beyond us, focusing on the city ahead. "I'm a stranger here in Charleston, and it's a snake pit full of spies, radicals, and sycophants." His focus returned to us: "Can I count on you,"—his thin, almost delicate hands swept in front of us indicating that he meant both Joseph and me with his collective *you*—"to help me for the next two weeks until we can safely put you on a ship to Nantucket?"

Joseph and I looked at each other. *What choice do we really have?* Joseph nodded with a single dip of his chin, and just like that, we were committed.

"We are headed to McCrady's Tavern, the oldest in Charleston, and I feel sure that the owner can use Joseph in the kitchen. John," the general said cryptically, "I have some jobs for you. But now that that's settled, I want to hear about how Joseph got separated from his mother."

As the carriage entered the busy part of the city, Joseph and I alternated telling the story of the red-headed man and the wagon… and the tunnel. Beauregard's heavy-lidded eyes closed, seemingly in pain, when I explained my theory of the Reverse Underground Railroad.

"I cannot believe," the general grumbled, "that such a thing could have been going on in *my* city under our very noses." He was intrigued, however, with Joseph's experience inside the tunnel. "I am very sorry you had to go through that, Joseph, but how did you feel when you woke up inside the tunnel? Where did you think you were?"

Joseph replied quickly as if the answer lay near the surface: "I thought I had died and gone to hell." He paused as he dug deeper. "I would have died—or worse—if not for John."

I shrugged my shoulders: "I would have been a rotten corpse tied to the bottom of a tree if not for you, Joseph. Like General Beauregard said, it felt good to settle my debt with you."

The general also seemed fascinated by how I found Joseph and the tunnel. "So, you were able to follow the wagon all across the French Quarter and into the Lower Ninth Ward without being seen?" he asked.

"I guess I just blended in," I answered. "I don't think there's anything that makes me stand out."

"That's exactly what I need!" exclaimed the general. "Somebody that can blend in and be my 'eyes and ears' for these next two critical weeks."

"What's going to happen in two weeks?" Joseph asked.

General Beauregard smiled in that rueful way that I was already getting familiar with: "That's a secret I'm not quite ready to share yet." He leaned forward towards the small, barred opening in the front wall of the carriage and asked the driver, "How much longer to McCrady's?"

"Ten minutes, General. Unless you want me to push it."

"No, Private, we're fine back here. Getting to know each other." The general asked me to tell the story of how I used the sounding line to lower messages into the tunnel through the air pipes. After I finished, he again said excitedly, "That's exactly what I need! Someone who is clever and can think on his feet without having to be told everything to do. John, that's a talent you can't learn. They try to teach that at West Point, but I'm convinced you just have it, or you don't. How did you end up getting help from the priest at the church?"

"That was pure luck," I replied.

"Well, we all need some of that too," said the general as the carriage came to a halt.

McCrady's Tavern was—at first glance—a nondescript, three-story brick building with a masonry arch framing the entrance door. We were met by a short, red-bearded man with the blood-vesseled nose of a heavy drinker—an attribute I had first noticed in my father. He greeted General Beauregard with great enthusiasm and ushered him (and us, his peripheral guests) into his self-described "humble establishment." As the general introduced Joseph and me to the owner, Mr. Tisdale, I felt a sudden *I have done this before.* I thought back to Sam taking me to Aleix Coffee House after Joseph disappeared and securing me both a short-term job and a place to live.

Mr. Tisdale seemed genuinely excited to have Joseph come work in the kitchen—after he had carefully examined Joseph's emancipation papers—but was significantly less enthusiastic about finding a spot for me "maybe washing dishes." After the general produced a handful of crisp, newly minted Confederate bills, Mr. Tisdale also agreed to let Joseph and me stay in a furnished room on the third floor for—as the general assured—"only a couple of weeks."

Once this business was taken care of, I looked around the dark interior of McCrady's Tavern that was endowed with a "split personality." Half reminded me of Aleix's and other drinking establishments I had seen in Oxford and Ripley, but the other half evoked the ethereal aura of a church—an odd juxtaposition for the typical, sinful ambiance of a tavern. Blue, red, and green light filtered through several semi-circular panels of stained glass that were set into wide, brick arches that ran along one long wall. In the part of the tavern in which we stood, the ceiling had an alternating pattern of white plaster crisscrossed with dark-stained half-timbering, but when we crossed into the adjacent part, the ceiling sparkled with pressed tin tiles that resembled those that I had glimpsed in the foyer at the house on Flood Street.

"I feel like I have lived through all of this before," I said to Joseph.

"There is a French phrase—*déjà vu*," said the general, "that translates to *already seen*."

* * *

For the next two weeks, Joseph stayed busy in the kitchen, and though he was exhausted at the end of each day, he was enlivened about the cooking experience he was gaining and what he was learning. I helped out washing dishes during rush hours, but General Beauregard kept me otherwise occupied being his errand boy, messenger, spy, and general 'eyes and ears' around Charleston. My most frequent errand was delivering notes to stately houses located along the Battery, a seawall and promenade overlooking the harbor and its sturdy protector, Fort Sumter. The general's handwritten notes were always addressed exclusively to "The Lady of the House," and they oftentimes resulted in a reciprocal perfumed note that I would take back to the general. This was usually followed by the general's discrete departure from his headquarters in his carriage for an afternoon *rendezvous*—another French word I learned from General Beauregard.

The seriousness of my errands escalated tenfold, however, during the first week in April when the general confided in me about a letter he had received from Francis Pickens, the governor of South Carolina. It relayed a message that the governor had received from President Abraham Lincoln concerning the resupply of Fort Sumter. "An attempt will be made to supply Fort Sumter with provisions only," wrote Lincoln, "and that if such attempt be not resisted, no effort to throw in men, arms, or ammunition will be made without further notice, [except] in case of an attack on the fort."

"I'm afraid this is our last chance to avoid war," General Beauregard said privately from behind his large desk. "I have one last thing to try before another confrontation occurs like with the *Star of the West* in January. If shots are fired on a resupply ship this time, I don't think there will be any holding back. I need to convince the commander at Fort Sumter to evacuate before that ship gets to Charleston, and I'm going to need your services to make that happen."

Again? I can be of service? "I'm not sure I see how I can help here," I said.

"Don't sell yourself short, John," the general replied. "You're able to disappear among the populace, you possess cleverness and initiative, and maybe—just maybe—you'll turn out to be my good luck charm. I need you to deliver something to the U.S. Army commander at Fort Sumter."

I don't understand half of what he just said.

"The commander's name is Major Robert Anderson," the general plowed on, ignoring my confusion. "When he was an artillery instructor at West Point, he took a young man— much like you—under his wing and served as his mentor. That young man was me. Major Anderson is a good man, a kind man, but I know him, and I think he can be persuaded that it is futile to continue to occupy the fort when he is surrounded by Confederate forces. I want to take a non-threatening approach with him, however, and that is where you come in. Please meet me in the alley behind McCrady's at seven o'clock sharp tomorrow morning."

That night after Joseph and I had finished our shifts in the kitchen at McCrady's, we each lay in our beds in the attic room, and I explained what the general was asking of me. "It sounds dangerous, John," said Joseph cautiously.

"General Beauregard said that if it were not for South Carolina's secession, he and Major Anderson would be friends," I answered with more confidence than I was really feeling.

"That's a big *if*," Joseph replied. "I don't mean to complain— I'm learning so much from the chef here at McCrady's—but are we getting any closer to getting on a ship for Nantucket?"

"I feel like things are coming to a head with the letter from President Lincoln," I said. "When I meet the general tomorrow morning, I will press him about us leaving."

"You might remind him—as he said your father always did— that the slate has not been wiped clean yet. You're the one who has been doing all the favors for *him*. And with the war sounding so close, we're *both* putting our lives in his hands by staying in Charleston."

It was still dark when I met General Beauregard the next

morning in the alley behind McCrady's. He was standing beside a wagon and talking with the owner, Mr. Tisdale, when I walked up. "Good morning, John," the general said cheerfully. "Mr. Tisdale has agreed to loan us his buckboard for you to make your delivery this morning. I think he just about has the package ready in the kitchen."

We walked through the back door into the kitchen where the chef—Joseph's boss—was placing some bottles in the top of a wooden crate that sat atop a table. "That should be all," the chef said as he placed the wooden top on the crate and nailed it shut with efficient strokes of a hammer. "Three bottles of our best whisky, three bottles of brandy, and four boxes of Cuban cigars. I don't know *how* you managed to get those." I remembered back to the Cuban crew members on the *Tribune* and thought, *I bet that wasn't just guns in those crates that Joseph and I moved to the ironclad... the same boat that I'm pretty sure I saw crossing under the drawbridge.*

The chef and I carried the crate to the back of the buckboard. I climbed into the driver's box as Mr. Tisdale handed me the reins to the calm mare that stood just in front of us. "She's as gentle as she can be, John, and she knows this city as well as most humans do. Just follow this map I've drawn for you to Fort Johnson, and there will be a ferry to Fort Sumter waiting."

I sat up straight—girding my spine—to confront the general as I promised Joseph I would, but before I could say anything, Beauregard reached his hand out for me to shake. In his other hand he held two envelopes. "Thank you for doing this, John. I know how much Major Anderson loves his liquor and his cigars—almost as much as your father does," he said as he smiled, "and this should get you in to see him. Here is the letter I need for you to give to him." I looked expectantly at the other envelope that remained in his hand. "Oh, yes… here are two tickets for a ship leaving for Nantucket tomorrow night. I'm going to miss you and Joseph."

* * *

I nodded dumbly as Mr. Tisdale gave a soft swat to the mare's flank, and the wagon began rolling to the end of the alley. Before I turned onto the busy street, however, the general was striding quickly beside me. "One other thing, John," he whispered. "While you're in the fort, count how many guns they have pointed at us." He winked at me, and then he was gone.

I stowed the two envelopes into the pockets of my trousers. One envelope held the future for Joseph and me, while the other possibly held the future of our nation. I tried not to think of them as I instead focused on the map that Mr. Tisdale had drawn for me. As he said, the horse seemed to know exactly where she was going. I only needed to subtly prompt her a couple of times. We crossed back over the drawbridge leading to Beauregard's war game troop encampment that now resembled a huge checkerboard spread out on the side of the hill above the marsh that was labeled "James Island" on Mr. Tisdale's map. I steered the mare onto Fort Johnson Road which wound its way through sawgrass and scrub oaks until it straightened out into a long run terminating into the hulking presence of Fort Johnson.

"Who goes there?" asked a young rebel soldier who was squatting behind a black metal tube pointed into the air.

"I have a message from General Beauregard to take to the commander at Fort Sumter," I declared, trying to sound official.

"I heard someone would be coming. I didn't know it would be a *kid*," said the soldier who was really just a kid himself. He called out to an older soldier positioned on another part of the earthen wall overlooking the harbor and Fort Sumter, who trudged down to a boat resting at the water's edge. "That's Joe," the young soldier said. "He'll ferry you across. His cousin Tom is a Yankee guard over on Sumter, and he'll meet you on the other side."

Joe helped me load the wooden crate onto the boat with no questions asked. At the base of the brick fortress wall surrounding Fort Sumter, we were met by a Union soldier who gave a subdued wave to his cousin. He demanded to see the note from the general before helping me unload the crate onto a makeshift wheelbarrow. I followed him as he disappeared through a dark hole at the base of the wall with the general's crated peace offering. When we reemerged into the harsh sunlight of the inner court of Sumter, I found myself looking up at the tops of the walls that were ringed with cannons pointed back at the city of Charleston.

One... two... three... I mentally counted as I was led to a uniformed officer who stood in the center beside a flagpole where the red, white, and blue American flag hung limply in the windless sky. The soldier pushing the wheelbarrow stopped and saluted the officer and announced my presence: "Major Anderson, sir. This boy comes with a note from General Beauregard. And this..." he said as he pointed to the crate.

"Who do we have here?" asked Major Anderson as he peered down at me with his hawk face and intense blue eyes.

"My name is John Wesley Thompson Falkner," I said with

an embarrassing squeak to my voice as I handed him the note from the general.

Anderson looked at me sardonically as he took the note. "Why has he sent you, of all people, to deliver this?"

"I think he trusts me, sir," I answered. "My father served with him in the war."

"The Mexican War, I assume you mean; a skirmish in which I, too, had the *pleasure* in serving," the major said with odd formality. "You said your last name is *Falkner*?" he asked. "I met a Falkner from Mississippi at Vera Cruz. Good soldier, but a drunk," he said.

"That would be my father, sir."

Major Anderson addressed the soldier who still stood at attention beside us: "Private, carry this crate into my office and bring me a pry bar." As we walked to his office, the major read the note from the general. I believe I heard a brief chuckle escape from the major as he stuffed the note into the front pocket of his army jacket.

The soldier returned to the office and pried the top off the crate. After removing some of the straw that the chef had placed in the crate to cushion the contents, the major extracted a bottle. "Bardinet Napoleon V.S.O.P. Brandy," he read as he examined the label. "Pierre—your good general—was always a sucker for anything to do with Napoleon." He reached further into the crate and pulled out a box of the Cuban cigars. He broke the seal on the box with his thumbnail and lifted the lid to his nose. "Ummm…" he moaned as he breathed in deeply. "Pierre isn't making this easy," the major said, "but, Private, find a hammer and put the top back on this box of bribery." He tucked the cigars and the brandy back into the crate.

"General Beauregard is a brilliant artillery strategist," Major

Anderson continued, "maybe the best student I ever had, but he is *not* a good judge of character. He thinks everyone else will just do what *he* would do. I'm not about to abandon my duty as an officer in the United States Army and betray my country for *thirty pieces of silver*." He waved the back of his hand in the air in front of the crate as if to swat it away. "Take this back to the general and tell him 'Thanks, but no thanks.' We will just have to let history judge us for the decisions we make here today." He abruptly turned on his heels and strode out of his office.

With the help of a Union soldier on one side of the harbor and his Confederate cousin on the other, I returned the crate in the buckboard to McCrady's Tavern. When the general showed up in the dining room that night to hear my report of the day's events, he seemed disappointed but unsurprised by the outcome. Shrugging his shoulders, he merely said, "*C'est la vie.*"

Chapter 15

When I awoke the next morning—our last day in Charleston—Joseph's face was scrunched in deep thought as he wrote in his journal on a page that had the amended heading of *Wednesday, April 11, 1861*. When he finished his writing, he carefully began tearing out the pages, separating them from the binding of the journal. "I promised Mr. Clemens that I would send him my account of our 'adventure' in getting to Charleston, so I need to mail these pages today to Aleix Coffee House. Do you know its address?" Joseph asked me.

"Yeah, 240 Bourbon Street. I've thought about sending a telegram to Mrs. Broder at the *Times-Picayune* like I promised, but I've been embarrassed to because I'm afraid word has gotten back to New Orleans that we were working with the smugglers on the ironclad."

"I think with everything that Mrs. Broder and Mr. Clemens did for us, we owe it to them to let them know we are alive and on our way to Nantucket," Joseph said.

"You're right," I conceded. "The Western Union office is over by the post office, so I will send it when we walk over to mail your letter."

When we got out on the street that morning, the atmosphere

seemed charged like the humid air before a thunderstorm. People hurried about talking animatedly to each other while pointing to headlines in the *Charleston Courier* that they had just purchased at the corner newsstand. *War Is in the Air,* was the thought I kept seeing as a headline in my mind.

Joseph and I turned onto Broad Street, a main thoroughfare, just as a platoon of South Carolina soldiers—probably fresh from practicing their war games—marched down the middle of the street, led by the Confederate battle flag of General Beauregard's design. A lone bugler walked at the rear playing "God Save the South."

Joseph turned to me and whispered, "I think we're getting out just in time."

On the corner of Broad Street and Meeting Street stood the massive white granite edifice that housed both the courthouse and post office for Charleston. Joseph approached the counter with a thick envelope. The postal clerk was a kindly, elderly woman who read the carefully lettered address on the envelope that Joseph handed to her. "New Orleans is it, young man?" she asked. "Let me look at my chart here. New Orleans is about seven hundred miles from here—as the crow flies—so that's going to be at a rate of five cents per half ounce." She placed the envelope on a scale on the counter and calculated the total in her head. "That will be forty cents."

Joseph emptied the coins from one of his pants pockets onto the counter. "It's U.S. money, ma'am. Is that okay?" Joseph asked.

"Yes, we're a Confederate post office now, but we still take the Union money."

As Joseph began counting out the money from the pile of coins, he said, "This is the first time I've ever paid for something with money that I earned. Even though I like saving up money, it feels good to spend it."

Two doors down from the post office stood the main Western Union office for Charleston. The clerk at this counter was a thin, nervous young man who displayed none of the patience that the kind woman had shown to Joseph at the post office, but the clerk perked up when he saw that I actually had money to pay for a telegram.

"What is your name?" the clerk asked.

"John Wesley Thompson Falkner." I handed him the text that I had written out earlier. He started reading it, but a frown came to the clerk's face. "Wait. Your name is *Falkner?*" he asked.

"Yes, sir." My thoughts immediately went to the concerns that I had voiced to Joseph earlier that morning about people suspecting that we were involved with the smugglers. *Are the police looking for me?*

"I have a telegram that was sent to you via *general delivery,*" the clerk said as he searched through a pile, "because the sender evidently did not have an address for you."

"Joseph, I got a telegram!" I called out. The clerk handed me a piece of crinkled yellow paper that I began to read aloud to Joseph as I stepped back from the counter:

JOHN AND JOSEPH *STOP* HEARD FROM TRIBUNE CAPTAIN THAT YOU DISAPPEARED FROM SHIP *STOP* DID YOU MAKE IT TO CHARLESTON? *STOP* SEND WORD TO MRS. BRODER *STOP* WE ARE WORRIED *STOP* IN NANTUCKET CHECK WITH HARBOR MASTER FOR JOSEPH'S MOTHER'S LOCATION *STOP* YOUR FRIEND SAM CLEMENS *STOP*

"My mother made it!" Joseph yelled with pure happiness when I read the last sentence.

"I'm ready to send *my* telegram," I declared to the back of the clerk who was tapping out a message to someone new on his telegraph key. He shifted to the message I had given him:

MRS. BRODER *STOP* JUST READ TELEGRAM FROM SAM *STOP* JOSEPH AND I MADE IT TO CHARLESTON *STOP* WE WERE FORCED OFF SHIP BY SMUGGLERS *STOP* WE HAVE BEEN HELPED BY GENERAL BEAUREGARD HERE *STOP* BOARDING SHIP FOR NANTUCKET TONIGHT *STOP* YOUR FRIENDS JOHN AND JOSEPH *STOP*

After leaving Western Union, we went to a general store where we each bought some clothes and cheap toiletries—soap, toothbrushes, and toothpaste—for the voyage to Nantucket. Joseph wasn't the only one to feel good about having some money to spend that had been honestly—more or less—earned with my own labors.

When we got back to McCrady's, Captain Lee was pacing the sidewalk. He handed us the fannah baskets that had been seized when we were captured. "I thought you might need these on your voyage. The general wanted to come in person to say goodbye to you," he explained, "but unfortunately, he is tied up in meetings all day." I wondered if these were related to Major Anderson's blunt refusal to accept the general's gifts. *Are we on the brink of war?*

* * *

"He also wanted me to make sure you understand," the captain continued, "that the ship you will be sailing on is not a 'luxury' ship like the *S.S. Tribune* was." *It wasn't a luxury to me in the fire room,* I thought, *and not for Joseph in the dark, cave-like galley.* "This is a whaling ship. One of the last few sailing out of Nantucket, but you should only be on it for four or five days. General Beauregard had to pull a lot of strings to get you two boys on board."

"Please tell the general that we appreciate everything that he has done for us," I said. "One way or another, I will get word to my father that the general's debt has been settled."

The captain lowered his head and chuckled. "You don't have to worry about that," he said. "The general ordered me to send a telegram to your father in Ripley both telling him where you are and how the slate was now clean. I arrived at Western Union just as you were leaving. The general will be relieved to know that other people know of your whereabouts as well."

I don't really care if my father knows where I am.

Mr. Tisdale had told Joseph and me that dinner for our last evening in Charleston was "on the house," and we could have anything we wanted. "You're the expert on food now," I said to Joseph, "so you choose."

"We're in Charleston," Joseph replied grinning, "so I gotta go with a Lowcountry boil."

I don't think it was lost on either of us as we enjoyed our "Last Supper" in McCrady's dining room that Joseph's choice had been the same meal that we had eaten on the porch of the shack after we had washed ashore on St. Helena's Island. "I wish we could somehow get word to Mariama and Jah and Jilo that we're okay," I said as I added a few more shrimp to my plate.

"Yeah," Joseph said with a mouthful of food. "We never would have made it without them. Maybe someday we will get the chance to settle our debt with the Gullah."

After dinner, we loaded up our purchases into our fannah baskets and walked a short distance to Union Pier. Our ship, the *Charles W. Morgan*, was a hub of activity as we walked to where it was docked. The huge wooden vessel might not be a "luxury ship" as defined by General Beauregard, but it was impressive, nonetheless. As we climbed the gangway to board the ship, I could see gleaming bits of live oak, hemlock, and copper bolts holding everything together. Furled sails hung loosely from the two tall masts that dominated the skyline of the pier.

We presented our "tickets" to a crewman who beyond everything else seemed exhausted. His jacket was stained a dark red that glowed as he stood in the last rays of the setting sun. I could see Joseph's nose crinkle when we both caught a whiff of odor from the man's clothes.

"I don't know who you boys *know*, but they must be *real* important. We were on our way back home to Nantucket after two years hunting whales in the Pacific when we got a telegram in Key West saying that we needed to make a stop in Charleston. Lucky for y'all, we also needed to make a minor repair to our keel, and Charleston was as good a place as any to get that done."

"What are we supposed to do while we are on board?" Joseph asked, as I think he was experiencing a moment of *déjà vu* himself. "I mean, what are our jobs? On the last ship we were on—the *Tribune* from New Orleans to Charleston— we worked in the galley." *Please don't say anything about me working in the fire room!*

"The *Tribune*, huh? We heard in Key West that it ran into some trouble off the coast of Georgia—a sea monster, or something. Anyway, what jobs are y'all supposed to have? I don't know," the crewman said shaking his head. "The captain didn't say anything. He just said to take y'all aboard." He scratched his head as if to shake something loose. "We did just load a few special South Carolina cattle. Do y'all know anything about taking care of livestock?"

I gave a sideward glance to Joseph who spoke up enthusiastically: "Yes, sir! I've been taking care of animals my whole life."

"All right," the crewman decided, "that's y'all's job, but otherwise, stay out of everybody's way. The whole crew is tired and dirty, and we just want to get home."

So do we, I thought, *but we just don't know where "home" is yet.*

The crewman showed us a dark corner below decks where we could stow our baskets and sleep. Joseph and I easily found the cattle by using our noses and made sure that they had hay and water in the buckets mounted on the side of the pen. Despite the familiar aroma of the cattle, the entire ship seemed to possess a different, pervasive odor emanating from its very bones. The same dark red stain on the crewman's jacket appeared countless other places on the deck of the ship, even as crewmen swabbed the stains with soapy water and grumbled elbow grease.

Grumbling started among the crew as our appointed departure time came and went with no movement away from the pier. As darkness fell upon Charleston, Joseph and I could see lights scurrying around the horseshoe-shaped harbor. Finally, the captain came out on deck and announced to the crew that they were waiting on permission to leave from the harbor master. "Something is going on, but I don't know what it is," admitted the captain.

I gazed out to Fort Sumter, but there didn't seem to be unusual activity there. I remembered Lincoln's letter to the governor. "I wonder," I posited to Joseph, "if this delay has anything to do with that ship that was supposed to be coming to resupply Sumter?"

We both looked past Sumter to the mouth of the harbor, but we could not see the lights of any approaching large ships. The stalemate in the harbor lasted for hours and—resigned to the delay—crewmen went below and retrieved musical instruments. Accompanied by an accordion, a sailor sang mournfully in a deep Scottish brogue as my eyelids grew heavy.

* * *

"John!" Joseph said to me as he shook me awake. "We're moving."

As the ship sailed out of Charleston Harbor into the ocean's darkness in the early morning hours of April 12, 1861, Joseph and I—at his urging—dropped down on our knees on the rolling deck and prayed for a safe voyage to Nantucket. When we stood, we were nearly knocked to our knees again by a huge blast behind the ship. I was reminded of the fireworks I had watched during the 4th of July celebrations in Ripley.

Still feeling the heat of the blast on my face, I looked up as I saw a huge, bearded sailor slide down the masthead. I turned to Joseph and asked, "Fireworks?" but instead of my friend's voice, I heard the sailor yell from across the ship as the sky filled with fire and smoke and light.

"That ain't fireworks, kid. The Rebs are shelling Fort Sumter. *It's war!*"

[*"To this day, Miss Betty,"* the old man paused, *"I still hang on to the belief that General Beauregard delayed the barrage of Confederate artillery fire until Joseph and I were safely out of the harbor. When I first mentioned this to Joseph, he told me that his mamma always said that 'prayers can work in mysterious ways.'"*]

In the five days it took us to sail to Nantucket, the brown-bearded sailor who was built like a bear began calling me "John Boy," while he said, "Call me Mr. Herman." Even though I was supposed to stay below decks with the animals, Mr. Herman loaned me books from the large trunk he kept in the crew's cabin, and I would sit in a hammock on deck and read about faraway lands in a way that I had never enjoyed reading before. During most of the day, Joseph and I were kept busy caring for the cattle in the deep holds of the ship, far below the water level. We fed and slopped them, taking note of any cows that might be sick. It wasn't fun by any means, but we tried to care for the animals as Joseph's father had taught him.

Mr. Herman would sometimes meet us out on the deck at night, and he showed us the basics of navigating by the stars. Sitting on the rough planked deck, he taught us how to use a sextant, and together we plotted the course of the *Charles W. Morgan* on the map. As we followed the warm Gulf Stream waters up the coasts of North Carolina, Virginia, and Maryland, some nights we could see dolphins, with their silvery skin reflecting the moonlight, riding the crest of the waves alongside the ship.

"That is what freedom looks like," Joseph said as we watched.

"Makes you want to dive in right after them, doesn't it?"

asked Mr. Herman.

Joseph hesitated before answering, "I can't swim." *He has never confessed this to me.*

Mr. Herman laughed and said, "Joseph, you *do* realize you'll be living on an island at Nantucket?"

"Yes, sir. But it doesn't mean I have to get in the water."

One night as Mr. Herman and I were sitting on the deck looking at the map by the light of a gas lantern, the sailor in the crow's nest yelled down from the darkness, "Herman, kill the light. Pass the word for total darkness and silence. There's a runner off our starboard bow."

"What's a runner?" I whispered to Mr. Herman.

"It's a Confederate warship that runs Union blockades. There's been rumors that Raphael Semmes has been running a ship out of the James River. They attack merchant ships like ours and take the sailors hostage." As word passed around the ship, other sailors came onto the darkened deck, whispering as they tried to see the lights of the ship in the distance. At one point the runner seemed to turn towards us and pick up speed. Silently, the men went below decks, some returning with rifles or pistols. "There's no way we can match their firepower," Mr. Herman whispered back. "We'd be better off trying to outrun them."

As if on cue, a loud bell began to ring, and a sailor cried out, "Full speed ahead!"

"You and the captain must think alike," I said to Mr. Herman.

He smiled slyly as he began to untie one of the riggings: "We should—he's my brother." Our ship shot forward in the night, its tall sails catching the stiff wind blowing from the south. A low, far-off rumble could be heard in the distance—maybe thunder, maybe something else—but before long, the lights of the other ship were just a distant memory. We ran hard throughout the night. Joseph joined me on deck as we watched the black water race by beneath us like the track of a fast racecourse. I knew what he was thinking: *Daddy would love this.*

When daylight came, we could see the beaches of Long Island as seagulls flew overhead searching for their morning food. We docked in Nantucket late that afternoon. I saw Mr. Herman walk down the gangway where he was met by a woman and three little kids. He waved us over and introduced Joseph and me to his family.

"I come through Nantucket pretty often," Mr. Herman said, "and I'm going to look you up." He handed me a leather satchel full of books: *David Copperfield, The Voyage of the Beagle, The Scarlet Letter,* and others.

I didn't know what to say, but I did stretch out my hand: "Thanks, Mr. Herman."

He laughed, taking my hand into his huge paw. "You're welcome, John Boy. Just make sure you read that thick book. Even though I didn't sell many copies, it's a *whale* of a good story."

After he had left with his family, I opened the satchel and took out the thick book. It was a beautiful, brand-new, leather-bound edition. I turned to the title page which read *Moby Dick* by Herman Melville. My eyes moved to the opposite page where there was an engraved portrait of Mr. Herman. Beneath his picture was a handwritten note:

To my good friend John. You may not understand all these books now, but someday they will change your life. Best wishes from your sailing companion, Mr. Herman

PART FIVE: Nantucket (April 1861-December 1862)

Chapter 16

Excerpt from Joseph's journal dated April 17, 1861:

Even though the ship's crew—the ones that would talk to me—warned me about the whales before we docked, nothing could have prepared me for the sensual onslaught that hit me when I stepped off the Morgan. Looking up the gradual slope rising from the harbor, Nantucket at night looked like a million fireflies ready to take flight. Although the gas lights lining the cobblestone streets were no longer fueled by whale oil—another fact shared to me by a particularly loquacious (and inebriated) crew member—there were still scores of barrels of pale-yellow whale oil waiting to be capped along the docks branching off the ironically named Easy Street in the center of the harbor. Nothing seemed "easy" about this town.

On our voyage, I had learned that whaling ships were not just vessels. They were floating factories where captured whales were tied to the side of the ship while out at sea and butchered for all the products they had to offer the consumer: meat, skin, blubber, and organs were vitamin and mineral-rich foods; baleen, the bristly filtering system inside the mouths of baleen whales, was used in weaving baskets and fishing line; and the bones of the whales were made into tools and ceremonial masks.

As I crossed from the port to the starboard side of a docked whaling ship—surprisingly small considering its prey—a blast of reeky wind hit that nearly dropped me to my knees. This gagging gale emanating from the carcass of a whale bypassed my nose and went straight into my mouth. I tasted the thick muskiness of the whale detritus down into the back of my throat. I walked cautiously along the dock with John, careful not to step into the amalgamated stew of fish guts, blood, vomit, and who knows what else that covered the gray, splintered planks leading to the harbor master's office. I was about to find out where my mamma was.

"I've been waiting for you two boys," the elfish harbor master said after we had given him our names. "As well as frequent visits from Miss Estelle, I've gotten telegrams from a Mr. Clemens, a Mrs. Broder, and a Mr. Cornish, all telling me to be on the lookout for you." *Nothing from a Mr. Falkner.* "Welcome to Nantucket!" he greeted. "The *Little Grey Lady of the Sea!*"

I could see Joseph trying to keep his patience, but he cleared his throat—maybe just trying to get rid of the whale musk— and it drew the harbor master's attention. "Of course, you want to know where Miss Estelle is—your mother, I mean," he said as he focused on Joseph. "She is the cook at the Carter House Inn on North Water Street, and word is already spreading across the island about how good the food is there now. Just the other day—"

"Excuse me, sir," Joseph interrupted, his patience at an end. "How would we get to the inn from here?"

"Oh, yes… sorry, son. I *do* prattle on," the harbor master stammered. "Just start walking up Broad Street a couple of blocks and then turn right on North Water. The Carter House Inn will be about five blocks on the left. Their sign has a big, winged whale on it."

Although the walk through nighttime Nantucket with its gas streetlights sparkling above the cobblestone streets was breathtaking, Joseph might as well have been wearing blinders, like the racehorses that his father rode, because he had a focused singularity of purpose as he strode—almost running—up the hill from the harbor. He was *this close* to making it back to his mother.

We were met in the foyer of the inn by a plump, white-haired, elderly woman who introduced herself as the owner, Mrs. Carter. "I've heard so much about you, Joseph," she gushed, "and you are exactly as your mother described you." She paused for a second as she led us to the back of the house. "And you must be John. I can't believe y'all are both finally here. Estelle is in the kitchen finishing up the prep for tomorrow's breakfast."

As we neared the closed door into the kitchen, Joseph slowed and held a finger to his lips. "If you don't mind," he whispered, "I would like to be the first into the kitchen."

"Of course, Joseph," Mrs. Carter purred. "Be my guest," she said as she stood to the side while Joseph quietly pivoted the swinging door open.

As I watched through the opening, his mother was standing with her back to the door at the counter on the opposite wall of the kitchen. She was wearing a light-blue smock, partially hidden by the straps of the white apron that crisscrossed her back. Her hands were mixing flour in a large wooden bowl, and I could hear her humming a hymn.

Despite Joseph's request, Mrs. Carter couldn't help herself in being the first one to speak: "Estelle, I think I've found the right person to help you in the kitchen."

Miss Estelle began a slow turn towards Mrs. Carter, a look

of skepticism already forming on her face. Before it could set, however, she saw Joseph out of the corner of her eye. Almost afraid to confirm—or discredit—what she thought she was seeing, her neck continued to turn at its deliberate pace. "Sweet Jesus," she finally sobbed as Joseph stepped into her hug.

Her white, powdery hands wrapped around her son's face, leaving two defined handprints on his cheeks that were soon turning into a gummy paste as Joseph and his mother's tears mixed. "I never gave up hope," she said, "but I also wasn't sure I would ever see this day."

"I wouldn't have made it without John," Joseph said as he found his voice. "It turns out we make a good team."

Miss Estelle's warm arms enveloped me in a hug that felt like an absence—something that had been missing from my life since... *Since the phantom pain of my own mother's missing touch.* "Thank you for taking care of my son, John," Miss Estelle whispered in my ear.

We took care of each other... like brothers are supposed to.

* * *

It wasn't until the next morning when I woke early needing a walk that I got a feel for our new "home." The Carter House Inn was located atop a bluff overlooking the picturesque town and its harbor. Occupying the former home of a whaling captain, the inn was wrapped in Nantucket's trademark gray shingle siding with crisp white trim and black shutters.

When I returned, I found Mrs. Carter sweeping the front walk and ready to share the history of the inn. It had been purchased by her late husband after his return from the

Mexican War in the late 1840s. Unfortunately—according to Mrs. Carter after she sipped from a cup of coffee that smelled suspiciously fortified—he was a much better soldier than he was an innkeeper, and he had tragically fallen to his death from the roof while fixing a loose shingle ten years ago. She loved the inn, however, and managed it very capably—"If I say so myself," she said with a wink—with a staff including herself, Joseph's mother, and a local married couple who performed maid and handyman duties. "Unfortunately, the husband informed me this morning," Mrs. Carter confided, "that he got the dang fool idea of enlisting in the army."

She led me on a brief tour of her cherished inn, during which she constantly wiped her hand across various surfaces to check for dust. The house had seven guest rooms located on the second and third floors with a parlor, library, sitting room, dining room, and kitchen on the main level. There was a large front porch spanning the entire width of the house with many rocking chairs which she said had become "the desired place to be on a hot summer afternoon." There was a smaller back porch off the kitchen which looked onto the graveled rear yard with the stables and the servants' quarters where Joseph and I had slept the night before in a room beside his mother's. A large elm behind the house shaded the rear porch and the stone path to the well that supplied the water for the inn.

The handyman's "dang fool" idea of enlisting seemed to be contagious, as the ranks of the Massachusetts army swelled over the next few weeks, creating a shortage of available labor on the small island of Nantucket. Even though Joseph and I had only recently turned thirteen, we were put to work by Mrs. Carter—with the blessing of Miss Estelle—performing a variety of duties around the inn.

Each of us settled into a work routine that was both comforting and challenging. Joseph naturally helped his mother in the kitchen preparing meals for the guests at the inn as well as caring for the dray horse and the three riding horses in the stables using the talents and knowledge he had gained from his father. I assumed the handyman duties of the now-enlisted husband who at last word was training with the 18th Massachusetts Infantry Regiment at Camp Brigham in Dedham, just outside of Boston. When I heard where he was stationed from Mrs. Carter, I immediately thought of General Beauregard's tent encampment at the golf club in Charleston. For me, being a handyman was largely a "learn by the seat of your pants" kind of job, but I just tried to make my mistakes little ones that might not be too hard to repair. I also did most of the shopping in town for the inn as well as making deliveries, a job that I had plenty of experience with through the general's handwritten notes to the ladies of Charleston.

When the wife of the ex-handyman left Nantucket at the start of the summer to work at a field hospital in Virginia, I began helping clean the inn along with transient housemaids that Mrs. Carter was forced to rely on. Mrs. Carter showed me the right way to use a feather duster, so I cleaned all of the photographs and drawings which hung in frames on the wall of the small sitting room outside the library. Likewise, I dusted the shelves in the library that held all the books which I one day hoped to have the chance to read. After I finished cleaning downstairs, I moved up to the guest rooms where the housemaids were changing linens, putting out fresh water, and polishing the furniture. Most of the new housemaids were German girls fresh off the boat from Europe and worked part-time at all the inns on the island. I loved listening to their constant cheerful chatter laced with only a smattering of English which I could understand.

Joseph's and my routines were abruptly interrupted in late August when Miss Estelle and Mrs. Carter informed us that we would be starting back to school on the island in September. "We've had a busy summer," said Mrs. Carter to Joseph and me, "and I couldn't have survived without your help, but things around here will be slowing down some with the escalation of the war. As much as I forget it sometimes, y'all are both just thirteen, and you need to be in school."

As usual, Joseph beat me to the punch in asking the difficult questions: "Will we be at different schools like it was in Jackson? White kids at one, and the Black kids at the other?"

Miss Estelle answered, "No, Joseph, it's one of the wonderful things about Nantucket. Even though we're not Quakers, you'll both be going to a school set up by the Quaker community at the Friends Meeting House—an easy walk away."

Mrs. Carter picked up the narrative: "Y'all will be in school from nine o'clock in the morning until two o'clock in the afternoon. When you finish at school, you will walk home and get started on your duties at the inn."

The number of guests did decrease in the fall, so Joseph and I usually managed to stay caught up with both our studies and our jobs. We were among the older students at the school, and we sometimes found ourselves being asked to help tutor the younger students. When Joseph told his mother that "we made a good team," that seemed to apply to our reciprocal academic strengths as well. Joseph was usually asked to help students with mathematics and science, while I helped them with reading, writing, and history.

* * *

Although I had always liked reading, the gift of the books from Mr. Herman seemed to activate a much deeper love. I also liked reading and replying to the letters that I received from Sam Clemens and Mrs. Broder, while Joseph had developed a pen-pal relationship with Sandy Cornish, who loved hearing of Joseph's progress in the North. The one person I did not hear a word from was my father who had to now know of my "relocation" to the North. In this regard, Joseph and I were also inextricably tied together, as he and his mother had not heard anything about his father since their tearful goodbye nine months ago at the Raw Cedar Plantation.

"I know how much it hurts to not hear from your father," I spoke into the darkness late one night as Joseph and I lay in our beds in the servants' quarters, "but you know that if there was any way that he could, your father would get in touch with you. But he doesn't have a choice." I paused for a second to see if Joseph would respond. *Silence.* "My father *does* have a choice, and he is choosing to pretend that I no longer exist."

"I guess," Joseph said quietly, "but that really doesn't make it hurt any less. You at least can assume that your father is safe—he's not a slave."

"You're right, of course," I replied, "although I'm sure my father is fighting for the Confederacy now. Fighting is all he knows how to do. I don't know if I would feel anything if I found out that he had been killed. It's funny… I only knew General Beauregard for three weeks, but he acted more like a father to me than my real father ever did. I *know* I would feel sad if I heard that the general had died."

"Even though he is fighting to keep slavery? To keep my

daddy a slave?"

"I know… it makes no sense." *How can I tell him that I am jealous that his father loves him and my father has never loved me? I haven't met Joseph's father, but I just know it's true.*

Joseph and I both became friends with a girl named Deborah who was in our "grade" at school. She had grown up a Quaker in Nantucket, and she seemed fascinated with our previous lives in the South. "My mother and father are very strict Quakers," she explained to us at lunch one day, "and they will not allow anything in our house that was produced with slave labor."

I had noticed that she seemed to wear heavy, wool clothing even on warm days. "So, you're not even allowed to wear cotton imported from England or France?" I asked.

"No," she answered, "because my parents say that the raw cotton would have been picked by slave labor here in America and then sent to Europe to be made into clothes."

"I was raised in a small church in Mississippi," Joseph said. "How is the Quaker religion different from what I learned from my minister?"

Deborah bit her lip as she considered her reply. "Quakers believe in each person having a *personal* relationship with God. We don't necessarily need ministers or even churches to express our love for God, but lots of Quakers believe in Christian values."

It was mid-November, and Joseph and I had just finished helping Mrs. Carter decorate the inn for the holidays. "Do Quakers celebrate Thanksgiving and Christmas?" I asked.

Deborah smiled. "Not really. We believe that *every* day is a good day to celebrate God, so we like to think that we treat every day like it was Christmas."

She could see that both our faces were filled with bewilderment. "It would be great if you all could come to one of our Friends meetings here on Wednesday nights. My mother and father would love to hear about your journey from Mississippi to Nantucket."

It was not easy, but Joseph finally convinced his mother to accompany Joseph and me to the Friends Meeting House—our school during the daytime—for the next weekly Wednesday meeting. "I don't know what to wear," Miss Estelle complained as we got ready after dinner.

I could tell from the look on Joseph's face that he was thinking—just like me—about what Deborah had said about not using anything produced by slave labor. He gave me a brief glance with raised eyebrows that I immediately understood: *Keep my mouth shut.*

"You look fine, Mamma," Joseph reassured. "These are just normal folk."

The Meeting House was a simple building wrapped in traditional Nantucket siding with a single entrance door centered on the front topped by two flanking second-story windows. As we arrived, the attendees were beginning to filter in. It was a very diverse crowd: men and women, young and old, and—most surprisingly—an equal number of Black and white people. The interior of the Meeting House was a bright, white-painted, double-height space that resembled any traditional church. Although Joseph and I spent some of our school day in this main meeting hall, most of our time was spent in the school's basement rooms.

"Welcome, friends. I am Christopher Hussey," spoke Deborah's father as he opened the meeting. "We would like to begin with our usual 'silent prayer': In the silence I am trying to center myself, which means to lay aside distractions of the world, and to listen carefully to the inward teacher, the inward guide, the inner Christ, that within me which is… also beyond me."

At the end of the short meeting, which was marked with frequent opportunities for silent reflection, Joseph, Miss Estelle, and I were approached by Deborah's father: "I am so happy to finally meet you all. Deborah has told me so much about you." As he steered us to a corner of the hall where we could "speak more privately," he said that he was anxious to hear about our journey to Nantucket. As we began sharing our stories, he was joined by Deborah's mother and two other Quaker "elders" who also listened intently. The hall was almost empty as we finished. Deborah's father swapped glances with the other elders who gave him silent approval to proceed. He asked us—almost in a whisper, "What do you know about the Underground Railroad?"

Chapter 17

Warm temperatures came early to Nantucket in March of 1862, so the inn was bustling with guests from the mainland after what had been a very slow winter. During busy times, I often helped with the breakfast service in the dining room while Joseph and his mother did the cooking. After the rush of diners, I was cleaning the tables on a Saturday morning when I found a discarded copy of the *Inquirer*, Nantucket's daily newspaper. Although I didn't often get the chance to read it, I tried to keep up with what was happening in the war. I knew that General Beauregard had been transferred from Charleston to Virginia and had commanded Confederate forces at Bull Run. He had recently been reassigned to Tennessee as second-in-command of the Army of Mississippi. *Is he going to be fighting with my father again?* I wondered.

Before I could read any of this newspaper, however, Miss Estelle came into the dining room with Joseph and gave us an assignment. "We haven't had any good seafood to eat in ages," she said. "I want you and Joseph to take the fishing gear over to that pond that Mrs. Carter is always bragging about and see if you can catch me some fish to cook. Y'all have been working really hard both here and at school, so maybe it will be a chance to have a little fun too."

We got directions from Mrs. Carter to Sesachacha Pond which was on the eastern end of the island. "It is a great fishing spot," she said, "because you've got the freshwater pond that's chock full of bass and bluefish, while the ocean is just a narrow strip of beach away. Joseph, it will be a great chance for you to add to your seashell collection, and you'll be able to see all kinds of birds flying north over the beach. Y'all take the wagon in case you get a big catch."

By late morning, Joseph and I were standing on big rocks that preternaturally projected out into the pond, preparing our fishing gear. Miss Estelle had given us some leftover sardines to use as bait, and Joseph was carefully threading our hooks through the gills of the tiny fish.

All I had ever fished with before were the cane poles that Simon and Henry, my father's slaves, let me use when I had gone with them to the small pond near my father's farm. Our potential seemed infinite as Joseph and I cast our baited hooks out into Sesachacha Pond then set the lines with minute rotations of the heavy brass reels at the base of our bamboo rods.

The sky was a bright blue and the sun felt warm on our backs as we pulled off our shirts.

"Look at that heron over there," Joseph said as he pointed at a long-legged white bird perched in a patch of cattails on the eastern shore. "They're supposed to know where the fish are."

We stepped across the tops of the large rocks to get closer to the heron. I heaved my cast as far as I could. It *plopped* into the water about six feet to the right of the bird who barely moved at the sound. After only a few seconds of zig-zagging my line across the water, I felt a hard strike. "I've got something!" I yelled. After a flurry of reeling alternated with letting the fish take more line, I lifted a rainbow-striped fish out of the water that was the length of my forearm.

Ough! Ough! I heard coughs coming from behind as I held the fish up for Joseph to see. "That's a mighty fine-looking bass," I heard an unknown voice say coming from the direction of the coughing. I turned to see a thin, bearded man gliding between the rocks in a canoe. Even though his face with its defining long, angular nose still appeared youthful, his movements were those of an old man. The canoeist touched one of his paddles to a rock and stopped his glide. "These rocks must make fishing really convenient," he remarked to Joseph and me.

Joseph looked down at the rock he was standing on as if he was noticing it for the first time. "They do, now that I think of it," said Joseph. "It's almost as if God spaced them this way to allow you to walk across the pond."

The man chuckled and stifled another cough. "This is not God's work," he followed. "As I hear it, the local tribe put these into the pond long ago so they could spear fish from them."

I looked down into the deep-blue pond between my feet as I straddled two rocks, and—sure enough—I could see fish darting between the rocks. I looked over at Joseph, and he was doing the same thing. "I could see how spears might be the way to go," Joseph said dreamily.

"Looks like you're doing just fine with those rods," the man said. Joseph now stood beside me on the adjacent rock. The man waved to us: "My name is Henry, by the way. I've been at Cape Cod for a few weeks, and I was invited to come to Nantucket for a couple of days."

"I'm John, and this is Joseph," I replied. "We both work at the

Carter House Inn if you need a place to stay." I knew from that morning's breakfast service that there were vacant rooms.

"Thanks," Henry said, "but I'm staying with friends."

"How did you know about the rocks?" Joseph asked.

"Oh, as I've gotten old, I've gotten more interested in the history of places. I like studying the plants and trees and even the way lakes and rivers got formed. I lived beside a pond for a few years when I was younger, and it's amazing what you can learn just by keeping your eyes and ears open."

"But you're not old," Joseph rebutted.

"Maybe not in years—I'm forty-four—but I am in miles," Henry said as his head seemed to drop into his shoulders. A fit of coughing racked his thin frame as he lay the paddle down. "I've had tuberculosis for a long time…" He paused and took a handkerchief out of his pocket to pat his mouth. "It was in remission, but last year foolish me stayed out late on a rainy night counting rings in the tree stumps in a forest near Concord, and I've been in a downward spiral ever since." He smiled thinly but made forceful eye contact with both Joseph and me with his piercing blue eyes. "The woman I'm staying with looked at my current appearance and asked me if I had 'made my peace with God.' I told her, 'I did not know we had ever quarreled.'"

* * *

After Henry said goodbye and continued his canoe trek across the pond, we resumed fishing. Inspired by the notion of spearfishing, Joseph retrieved his fannah basket from the wagon that held a bow and arrows that he had gotten in a trade with a local Wampanoag Indian for one of his mother's apple pies at a "Support Our Troops" swap meet. He tied a fishing line to an arrow just above the fletching. "I hope I still remember everything that Jah taught me," Joseph said as he targeted a fish swimming between the rocks. He did, and as the sun began falling behind the trees on the west side of the pond, we packed up our gear and our "big catch."

Joseph noticed the newspaper that I had stuffed into my knapsack and forgotten about. "My father used to wrap his fish in paper before he took them back to my mother," Joseph said. "Sometimes, my mother would cook the fish in the paper. She said it kept all the juices in."

We began taking the folded newspaper apart and wrapped each sheet around a fish. When I got to the front page, however, the headline caught my eye: "Ironclads Monitor and Merrimack Battle Off Virginia Shore."

"Look, Joseph," I said, straightening out the front page of the *Inquirer* so that he could see the drawing under the headline. "The Union ship, the *Monitor*, looks just like the ironclad that attacked the *Tribune*."

"Would the Union have had time to copy Mr. Verne's French ironclad?" Joseph asked.

I had to count my fingers to answer his question: "That was eleven months ago." *Could they have built a ship that quickly?* "I think war speeds everything up," I concluded.

When we got back to the inn and began unloading the fish for a delighted Miss Estelle, we were surprised to see our classmate Deborah walk around to the back of the inn where we stood by the wagon. "Hey, John and Joseph. I don't mean to interrupt your work, but I've been sent by my mother and father to invite you to a special meeting tonight."

Joseph's *suspicious* look surfaced on his face: "What kind of meeting?" he asked. He added skeptically, "And I'm not sure I can get my mother to come to another one."

"That's okay," Deborah said. "The elders just want to talk to you and John." When I tried to get more clarity about what they wanted to speak to us about, Deborah just held up her hand dismissively and breezily said, "Don't ask me. I'm just the messenger." She tossed her long, blonde hair back as she spun on her heels and headed back out the gravel drive.

"What was *that* about?" Joseph asked as he shook his head.

"Don't ask me," I laughed.

We dutifully arrived at the Friends Meeting House that night for the meeting, but there were only a few people inside when we entered. I recognized Deborah's parents, Christopher and Elizabeth Hussey, and two of the elders that we had met at the previous meeting. Mr. Hussey beckoned us forward: "John, Joseph! Thank you for coming." *Did we really have a choice?*

We sat at a table across from the adults and briefly made small talk: "Today was such a lovely day," Elizabeth Hussey said. "I hope you boys were able to be outside."

Before we could answer, we saw the adults' eyes raise over our shoulders as we heard footsteps approaching from behind us. "Sorry, I'm late," we heard a vaguely familiar voice say. "I found a meadow full of Arrowwoods that just lured me in. I sat with my back against this beautiful, twisted, black oak to read for a while, and before I knew it, I was sound asleep."

"No problem, Henry," Mr. Hussey said. "Let me introduce you to—"

The newcomer interrupted as Joseph and I turned in our chairs to see him: "We've already met, Christopher. I had the pleasure of running into John and Joseph at the pond today."

Surprised, Mr. Hussey turned to the elders at the table:

"Well, for those of you who have not had the pleasure, let me introduce our esteemed guest, Mr. Henry David Thoreau."

He coughed as he slowly settled into a chair at the head of the table. I was reminded again of how his aged movements contrasted with his youthful face. "Thank you for inviting me to your lovely island," Mr. Thoreau said. He turned his blue-eyed gaze to Mr. Hussey and got down to business. "Now, Christopher, tell me why you wanted me here."

"The war has caused a major disruption in our… venture, shall we say," Mr. Hussey said.

"Are we going to be able to speak openly, or not?" quizzed Mr. Thoreau as he shifted his glance to Joseph and me.

"Yes, absolutely, Henry," Mr. Hussey said almost in apology. "John and Joseph are why we're here tonight."

"Then let's not beat about the proverbial bush," spoke Mr. Thoreau tersely. "I don't have the time or the inclination to tap dance around the truth." A spasm of coughing followed.

"Sorry, Henry… the truth, then. We have been running the Nantucket station of the Underground Railroad for a few years now, and we know that you were the conductor in Concord before the war. The need for the Railroad is greater than ever now—so many of our brothers are at risk because of the war—and our lines have been disrupted. We have been trying for a long time to get a network established in the Lowcountry to help slaves trying to escape from the rice plantations around Beaufort and Charleston, and we think John and Joseph have information that can help us. We need your expertise and experience to come up with a plan."

Joseph looked at me out of the corner of his eye, as I am sure he was thinking the same thing that I was. *So, we can be of service.* As I looked back at him, I gazed past him and for the first time noticed a small, Black woman dressed in military clothes sitting in a chair off in the shadows. I returned my attention to Mr. Hussey with questioning eyes, and he immediately understood.

"Don't worry about her," Mr. Hussey explained. "She's with us. That's Mrs. Tubman."

*　*　*

"John and Joseph," Mr. Hussey said, "please tell everyone here the story that you told us at our previous Friends meeting."

"Where do you want us to start?" asked Joseph.

"Why don't you begin when you were forced from the ship off the coast of South Carolina," Mr. Hussey said. "And please remember, you're among friends."

"We figured out that some of the Cuban crew members were helping smuggle guns to the Confederacy," Joseph began, "by sneaking them onto the ship we were on, the *Tribune*, while we were docked at Key West." Joseph looked to me to continue.

"We were attacked by an ironclad ship one night," I said, "that looked a lot like the *Monitor* I saw in a picture in the *Inquirer* this morning. Mr. Verne said it was a French ship."

"Mr. Verne?" Mr. Thoreau asked as he sat up in his chair.

"Jules Verne," I replied. "He's a French writer who was traveling on the *Tribune*."

"Y'all know *Jules Verne*?" Mr. Thoreau seemed incredulous.

"Yes, sir," Joseph said as he resumed our narrative. "The captain of the ironclad put John and me in a rowboat and told us how to reach shore, which we did the next morning. We landed on St. Helena's Island in South Carolina. We knew that from a sign we saw at a cemetery."

It was now Mrs. Tubman's turn to sit up as we just seemed to gain her attention. "After we walked all day," I said, "we came upon a gathering of the Gullah people by a campfire. They fed us and took care of Joseph, who had a fever."

"You met the Gullah?" Mrs. Tubman asked. Her eyes blazed with intensity. "Where?"

"We were near the Frogmore Plantation where many of them were slaves."

"What else did you do with the Gullah?" Mrs. Tubman next asked us.

"The woman who first welcomed us there—Mariama—had a cousin named Jah who was a fisherman. He took us in his flat-bottomed boat..."

"A canoe?" Mr. Thoreau suggested eagerly.

"No," I answered, "it was more like the 'pee-row' boats the Cajuns use in Louisiana."

Joseph continued, "Jah took us from St. Helena's to a landing just outside of Charleston."

"How long did it take you?" quizzed Mrs. Tubman.

"About two weeks," Joseph patiently answered.

"Who did you run into on the river as you traveled?" Mrs. Tubman interrogated.

"Just other fishermen who all seemed to know Jah." *I am happy for Joseph to handle our end of the interrogation.*

"Most importantly," said Mrs. Tubman as she came out of the shadows and sat next to Joseph at the table. Her withered hands unrolled a sheaf of maps that she pulled from a bag hanging from her shoulder. "What was your path?"

Joseph looked over to me and beckoned me with his eyes. I moved from my chair to the one on the other side of Mrs. Tubman. Joseph and I—two thirteen-year-old boys—towered over her as we each pointed to the map. I started, "It's been almost a year since we did this, but I know we put in here at the Combahee River and rowed across to Edisto Island."

Joseph remembered, "Jah told us we would be on the South Edisto River for a good while, and he told us the stories of the Edisto Indians that he remembered from his grandfather. I wish that I still had all my journal entries that I wrote from that part of the trip."

"What happened to them?" Mr. Hussey asked with a suspicious tilt to his head.

"Mr. Clemens wanted me to mail them to him in New Orleans," Joseph answered.

"And who is this *Mr. Clemens*?"

I intervened. "His name is Samuel Clemens. He is a riverboat pilot in New Orleans, but he's also a writer. He goes by the pen name of *Mark Twain*."

"Never heard of him," interjected Mr. Thoreau.

"Mr. Clemens," I continued, "along with Mrs. Broder at the *Times-Picayune*, helped Joseph and me escape New Orleans after we discovered the Reverse Underground Railroad…"

"The *what?!*" Mrs. Tubman hissed as she jumped out of her chair.

Joseph looked at me with wild eyes. *He needs me to handle this part of the interrogation.*

"Joseph was kidnapped by two men after he had boarded the ship in New Orleans with his mother to go to Nantucket. They took him in a wagon to a tunnel that lay beneath a house in the Lower Ninth Ward—on Flood Street. I followed the kidnappers when they took another boy, and along with Mrs. Broder and a priest, we helped everyone escape from the tunnel."

"*Everyone?*" queried Mrs. Tubman.

"There were fourteen of us," Joseph said quietly. "We were from nearby. From cities like Philadelphia. Some from the Caribbean. All *free* people who were going to be sold *into* slavery."

"I am aware of the existence of the Reverse Railroad," Mrs. Tubman said. "But I've never met anyone that escaped it… and I didn't know that this evil extended to New Orleans."

"General Beauregard was shocked to hear about it too…" I said.

"Wait!" Mr. Thoreau interrupted. "You know *Beauregard* too?" The group at the table devoured our story—punctuated with myriad questions—over the next two hours. We told them about the red-headed man and the cop with the lame arm, the paper boys with their shovels, General Beauregard's debt to my father, and the war games being staged on the side of the hill.

"War *games?*" Mrs. Tubman said as her bowed head shook in exasperation. She paused. "Boys," she said as the smallest of smiles crossed her face, "what you have told us changes all the rules of *this* game."

Chapter 18

The next morning, I went to the Nantucket Atheneum, the white-columned temple of learning that was home to the local public library. While sitting at a solid, burnished oak table in the corner of the Reading Room, I learned from a newspaper that Mrs. Harriet Tubman was one of the earliest "conductors" of the mysterious group called the Underground Railroad. It was rumored that she was now serving as a scout and a spy in the Union Army. I pictured this tiny woman with blazing eyes in her military fatigues, and I wondered if I would ever cross paths with her again. Two months later, while I was sitting at that same table, I read in the *Inquirer* that Henry David Thoreau had died in his hometown of Concord. Already, Joseph and my late-night interrogations at the Friends Meeting House seemed like a distant, fading memory.

It was only when school started back in the fall that the subject of that meeting resurfaced. Joseph and I left the Meeting House at the end of a school day, and Deborah caught up with us as we walked up Fair Street towards the inn. "John, Joseph! Slow down, guys," she said as she struggled to catch her breath. "Y'all walk *really* fast!" she gasped.

Joseph smiled and said, "We've still got our jobs to do at the inn. We don't get to just go home and have tea and crumpets."

"Oh, shut up!" Deborah said as she gave Joseph a playful punch in the shoulder. "I have chores to do too. In fact, my father gave me this letter to give to y'all. He said it was *real* important that no one sees me giving this to you." We all involuntarily looked around for anyone that might be watching.

I took the letter from her as she said goodbye. Joseph and I continued to walk until we came to a shaded bench in a secluded "pocket park" off Centre Street. I slipped my fingernail under the red embossed wax seal across the flap on the envelope and opened the letter.

Dear John and Joseph,

Even though it is against Massachusetts law for the police or government to aid in the capture of a fugitive slave, there are still private "bounty hunters" who show up on our island to perform this despicable act. As employees at the Carter House Inn, you are in a perfect position to be our "eyes and ears" as far as identifying strangers who are up to no good who might be staying or dining at the inn.

All of us on the Railroad Committee trust you and Joseph after what you have lived through, and we appreciate your help in this matter. If you notice anything out of the ordinary, take a piece of chalk from the school and mark an "X" at the far-right side of the bottom step at the front of the Meeting House. We will contact you after we see your signal.

Destroy this letter <u>immediately</u> after reading it.

C. H.

"Eyes and ears, huh?" Joseph said as he finished reading the letter. "I've heard that before." I thought back to our carriage ride with General Beauregard when he told us that he needed me to be his "eyes and ears" in the snake pit that he called Charleston. *Why do these people all seem to trust us and expect us to be of service to them?*

"Notice how there is no question in this letter, like 'Would you be willing to help us?'" I said to Joseph as I reread the letter and began tearing it into tiny strips.

"You mean like we don't have a choice?" Joseph followed.

"Exactly," I said. "I guess—like it or not—we'll be their spies, though I don't know when we will ever see anything *out of the ordinary.*" Actually, we didn't have to wait long at all.

On the morning of December 23, 1862, I was working in the side yard of the inn when two men in black suits and black bowler hats rode up on horses. As they climbed the stairs to the front porch, they were met by Mrs. Carter, and I overheard the name "Pinkerton." The two men spent the rest of the morning touring the house and the grounds of the inn with her.

After the two men in bowler hats had completed their inspection and left, Mrs. Carter gathered the staff together in the kitchen for instructions: "We're going to have some special guests at the inn over the next few days, and none of you can talk to anyone about this. Those men you saw this morning were from the Pinkerton Detective Agency, and they will be coming back tonight. Under no circumstances is anyone to be in the stables after dark tonight. If you are caught outside of your quarters, you will be arrested!"

After the meeting, Mrs. Carter told me to help the house-maids clean and prepare all the rooms. We started to work on the main floor as I polished the oak paneling in the parlor and brought in firewood, which I stacked on the large stone hearth. I filled the brass lanterns with fuel and trimmed the wicks. As I left the room, it smelled of oak, linseed oil, and kerosene.

As nighttime came, I was reading *David Copperfield* by an eyebrow window in the roof of the attic room of the servant's quarters. I heard footsteps in the gravel as I looked out to see a polished black carriage pull into the yard, escorted by horses carrying the same two men who visited this morning. The driver on top of the carriage wore a red scarf around his face to keep dust and sand from his mouth and nose. Though the windows of the carriage were foggy from the cold, damp evening, I could just barely make out the profile of the only passenger. *It couldn't be!* Arrest or not, I ran down the stairs and out the back. I climbed up a chain to the hayloft on the back side of the stables just as the carriage pulled inside. Peeking through the cracks of the loft floor, I watched as a tall, thin man removed his top hat before stepping out of the carriage.

* * *

"What are you doing here?"

Though the words were challenging, Joseph's familiar voice wasn't. I turned to see the shadowy outline of his dandelion hair sticking above a hay bale. I crawled on all fours over to where he stood in the darkness of the loft.

"I heard footsteps, and now that I'm a spy, I figured I ought to check them out. How did you get up here?" I asked.

"I saw the lights. I was in Mamma's room, but she was asleep, so I climbed out the window and jumped out to the big tree behind the house. I climbed up the chain right before you did. Is that who I think it is?"

"I believe so." I looked at my friend as he shivered beside me. He was wearing only a thin wool coat over a flannel nightshirt. His long, skinny legs showed between the bottom of his nightshirt and his rough leather shoes. As I leaned closer to whisper to him, I could see the dried residue of tears beneath his bright, alert eyes. "What were you doing in your mother's room?"

"We were talking about my daddy. It's been a year since we left Raw Cedar and a year since we last saw him."

"Couldn't you try writing a letter or sending a telegram?" I asked gently.

"Daddy can't read," Joseph answered, "and even if he could, Mamma says a letter or telegram would never get to him. Old Man Rossiter would intercept it and destroy it. Besides, the war has changed everything."

"How is your mother?"

"She tries to put on her usual brave, cheerful face, but she misses him too. We shared a lot of tears tonight. So many, it just wore us out. We were both asleep when the lights woke me."

"Come on, Joseph. Let's get out of here." We climbed back down the chain and crept in the shadows back to the main house, hiding behind a woodpile by the kitchen just as the stable door opened. The two men in the bowler hats came out—one carrying a lantern and the other what looked to be a rifle. The tall man walked closely behind, with the fourth man with the red scarf bringing up the rear. They walked right by us crouched behind the woodpile, up onto the back porch, and into the rear door of the kitchen. After they were inside, Joseph and I tiptoed onto the back porch and peeked into the window.

The four men stood at the fireplace with their backs to us stomping their feet and holding their hands to the fire. Mrs. Carter began pouring steaming coffee into china cups on the kitchen table as the men took their seats. I could see her chattering nervously as she started opening cabinet doors and drawers looking for things. I guessed that the men must be hungry, but I had never seen Mrs. Carter do so much as boil an egg. Miss Estelle and Joseph did all the cooking at the inn, and I think that Mrs. Carter realized in that moment what a treasure she had in Miss Estelle. She gave up trying to find what she was searching for and walked out the back door onto the porch, standing less than six feet from where Joseph and I were crouched in the shadows. She took a small silver bell out of her housecoat and began ringing it. Before long, I saw a light come on in Miss Estelle's room. After a few moments, Joseph's mother descended the stairs of the servants' quarters and began walking across the rear yard. As she approached the rear porch, Mrs. Carter said, "I'm so sorry to get you out of bed, Estelle, but we need you."

"That's fine, Mrs. Carter. I wasn't sleeping." As Joseph's mother stepped up into the light of the porch, I could tell from the slackness in her face that she *had* been asleep. She smiled at Mrs. Carter as she walked into the rear door of the kitchen. As Miss Estelle entered, the tall man at the head of the table stood—and she fainted dead away into the arms of Abraham Lincoln.

Joseph jumped up from where we were hiding on the porch and started for the door. "Joseph!" I whispered to him. "You can't just rush in. We're not supposed to be here! Your mother just fainted. She will be fine." I remembered Mrs. Carter's warning: *If you are caught outside of your quarters, you will be arrested!*

"But it's my mamma!" We again peeked in the window, and his mother was now sitting in the armchair by the fireplace with a washcloth on her forehead. Miss Estelle was smiling as she shook her head back and forth. President Lincoln came around beside the chair and took her hand. I was afraid she would faint again, but whatever the president said to her made her laugh.

I could feel Joseph shivering beside me. Suddenly he jerked as he sneezed into the arm of his coat. I saw the man with the red scarf look towards the window as I dropped down to the porch floor. Joseph and I rolled off the side of the porch into the bushes at the base of the big elm tree. We heard the door open and footsteps on the porch. "Who's out here?" he asked.

I looked through a bush to see the man with the red scarf standing right where we had been on the porch. His eyes scanned the rear yard, but we got down as close to the cold ground as we could. He stood dead still searching for any movement, but soon the man stuck his hands in his pockets and stomped his feet. He was getting cold. He gave up after a few more minutes, muttering to himself as he walked back into the kitchen.

After we were sure he was not coming back out, we climbed from the bushes. "Joseph," I told him as I helped him up, "that was way too close. We need to get back to our room before you catch your death of cold." Joseph nodded in stubborn agreement, and I watched in amazement as he scampered up the elm tree like a squirrel and was back through the window into our room in a flash. I quietly walked across the rear yard and climbed the stairs to our room. When I awoke in the middle of the night, I wondered if it had all been a dream.

* * *

Miss Estelle always woke earlier than us so she could get breakfast started for the staff and the guests. As I walked across the rear yard towards the kitchen trying to shake the weight of sleepiness from my shoulders, I could smell biscuits, bacon, and coffee. A hot plate of food was waiting for me at the table where Joseph was already seated. Mrs. Carter was talking to his mother, so I didn't get a chance to ask her about the night before. Besides, I was not supposed to be there, and I was certainly not supposed to know who our guest was.

When Mrs. Carter was finished giving instructions for the morning to Miss Estelle, she next turned to me: "John, there's an axe out in the storage room in the stables. I need you to walk down the hill to Mr. Brayer's lot at the end of North Street and cut us a Christmas tree." *She obviously doesn't know my doomed history with Christmas trees.* "Mr. Brayer is expecting you, and he has a six-foot tree selected. You can just throw it over your shoulder and carry it back. Put it in the back corner of the stables for now." She added vaguely as a slight blush came to her face, "I'm hoping we won't need this tree, but I want to be sure…" She next told me that after I returned with the tree, I should bring the inn's passenger wagon around front because she needed Joseph and me to accompany her to collect our other three guests. We rode in the back of the wagon to the harbor—bouncing along on the cobblestones of Lower State Street—where a tall clipper ship named the *Flying Cloud* stood docked at the wharf.

Mrs. Carter talked to us in her steady, cheerful manner as we approached the ship: "I know both of you have probably already heard all these stories, but these docks used to be home to the largest whaling fleet in the world. There were eighty-eight ships based out of Nantucket that sailed as far away as South America to hunt whales for their oil."

Joseph asked, "What happened to them?"

"There was a huge fire in 1846, and all the wharves and part of the town burned to the ground. My husband was away fighting in the Mexican War, so I went to live with my family in Boston until he returned. Most of the whalers never came back. The town built the docks back, but now it's mostly tourists and merchant ships that come." I thought back to the whaling stories that Mr. Herman told us on our voyage from Charleston to Nantucket. As I listened to him, I had sensed the bittersweet nostalgia that he felt for a time in history that had passed.

Heading to the docks also made me think of the journal entry that Joseph had shared with me in which he wrote of his first impressions of Nantucket after we had gotten off the ship. He wrote powerfully of the sights, sounds, and smells that we encountered in this new place that was now our home in a way that I could never express or even observe. "How do you know all these words like *sensual*, *loquacious*, and *detritus*?" I asked Joseph after reading his journal.

"Father Matthew encouraged me to keep a list of words I didn't know and their definitions," Joseph answered, "so I started writing words in the back pages of my journal. When I heard or read a new word, I would just add it to the list." He flipped through the back of his journal, displaying a dozen pages filled with his tiny, precise handwriting.

As we rode, jostled in the back of the wagon, an irony jarred me like a bump in the road. *At school, I typically help the younger students with reading and writing, while Joseph helps them with math and science. We have this exactly backwards! It is obvious to me now that Joseph is the writer on our team, while I am the "numbers" man.* Since I had begun doing the shopping for the inn, I had become adept at handling money. Mrs. Carter now trusted me to collect payment from our guests and even enter these payments into the thick ledger that she kept on the top shelf of the "check-in" counter at the inn. *Is this pointing me to a future career in handling people's money? I like doing it. Is Joseph destined to be a writer like Sam, Mr. Verne, Mr. Herman, and Mr. Thoreau? I always thought the future writer would be me.*

Mrs. Carter ended her story that had become just background noise to me as she pulled up to the docks. "Oh, one last thing," she said. "Do you boys know who our guest is who arrived last night?"

Joseph and I glanced at each other furtively with, nonetheless, completely guilty looks, giving us away immediately. "Yes, ma'am," I answered softly.

Much to our surprise, Mrs. Carter smiled and said, "I thought so. Well, you're in for another surprise in a few minutes." With that, she led us over to where the dockworkers were unloading the baggage from the *Flying Cloud*. Our guests' luggage had been pulled off to the side, and Mrs. Carter pointed them out to Joseph and me so that we could begin loading them. Mrs. Carter walked towards the ship to locate her arriving guests.

Joseph lifted a brown leather valise sitting on the ground. "This has to belong to a very successful man, right? This stitching reminds me of the saddles that my father mounted on racehorses." *He's still thinking about his father.* He pointed to the top of the case between the brass locks where the initials *C.D.* were engraved. *Again, he observes things I never would.*

"And this man has traveled the world," I said trying to match him as I picked up a worn black suitcase that was covered with colorful labels that were applied with paraffin wax. *Sydney, Cape Town,* and *Rio de Janeiro* were all visible on the sides of the tattered case.

"The initials also say *C.D.* on that luggage, but it *must* belong to another man," Joseph said as our competition gained steam. "The same man would never own such different suitcases."

"And this trunk reminds me of one my father bought secondhand in Oxford," I countered. "The owner of this is a working man—not a gentleman. My father dreams of being a gentleman who travels to exotic places, but all he'll ever be is a drunk and a fighter."

"My daddy's a dreamer too," Joseph said, "but all he's ever dreamed of is us being free."

"Well, your father has succeeded. You and your mother *are* free, and I am sure your father will be free himself soon. My father dreams, but he has never succeeded at anything."

We just finished loading the last piece of luggage when Mrs. Carter walked up with three bearded men. "Boys," she said, "I would like to introduce you to our guests from London. This is Mr. Darwin, Mr. Marx, and Mr. Dickens. They are here at the request of President Lincoln."

Chapter 19

All I could think about as we rode back to the inn was the satchel that Mr. Herman had given me that now lay under my bed. Those books had come to life and were riding with me in this wagon. I had read Charles Darwin's *The Voyage of the Beagle* that summer, often while sitting in a rocker on the front porch where I could see the tall ships coming into the harbor. As I read about Mr. Darwin's voyage to South America, Africa, and Australia, I thought about Sam, and I wondered if the war was preventing him from fulfilling his dream of traveling the world. I had finished Charles Dickens's *David Copperfield* just last night when I woke up in the middle of the night and couldn't get back to sleep. It had taken me a month to read, but while I was reading it, I felt like the main character David was my best friend in the world—except for Joseph, of course. I had tried to read Karl Marx's *The Communist Manifesto*, but I think it was one of those books that—as Mr. Herman wrote—I was not meant to understand now.

The three men's appearances were humorously analogous to their luggage. The expensive-looking valise belonged to Mr. Dickens who was similarly dressed in a fine-tailored suit. He was the shortest of the three, though his dark curly hair bunched up on top of his head. His cheeks were cleanly shaven above his dark, neatly trimmed beard. Like his well-traveled suitcase, Mr. Darwin looked somewhat the worse for wear. Although he was the tallest of the wagon's riders, the stoop in his shoulders made him look shorter. He was mostly bald and appeared to have recently begun growing a beard. Echoing his working man's suitcase, Mr. Marx was dressed in a worn suit with his shirt sleeves showing through the holes in his jacket's elbows. His long, bushy white hair and beard looked untamed, but his eyebrows were dark and loomed above his intense, shining eyes. His conversation with the other two travelers was punctuated by a sporadic, racking cough that reminded me of the late Mr. Thoreau.

The three famous men seemed to genuinely enjoy each other's company. Mrs. Carter asked them about their voyage across the Atlantic, and they eagerly traded stories about their adventures on the ship. Mr. Dickens laughed as he needled Mr. Marx about getting seasick: "No wonder they call the ship the *Flying Cloud*. Karl was sending every meal he ate off the side of the boat in a *flying cloud*."

"Yes, that is true," Mr. Marx came back, "but no one told me that a fifth of Scotch each night was the antidote for seasickness, like *you* obviously knew."

Mr. Darwin joined in the fun as he added, "Yes, but the result was the same. Dickens was always hungry on board because he was losing *his* lunch in the saloon every night."

They slapped each other on the back in raucous laughter as Mrs. Carter graciously asked, "Is there anything special you men would like when we get to the inn?"

"Yes!" the three men said in unison.

"A warm bath!" said Mr. Marx.

"A warm meal!" said Mr. Dickens.

"A warm bed!" said Mr. Darwin as he yawned heavily. They all laughed yet again as the wagon pulled into the drive of the inn. When we stopped in front of the house, there was yet another bearded man sitting in a rocking chair on the front porch with one of the men in the black bowler hats. They appeared to be looking at a piece of paper together. The white-bearded man came down from the porch and met our wagon as we tied up the horse.

"Charles, it's so good to see you, old friend," he called up to Mr. Dickens in the wagon.

"Henry, it's a pleasure as always," said Mr. Dickens as he helped the other men climb down. "Let me introduce you to my illustrious travel partners. Karl Marx and Charles Darwin—I would like you to meet my good American friend, Mr. Henry Wadsworth Longfellow."

"How is your son, Henry?" Mr. Dickens asked Mr. Longfellow.

"I am worried sick, Charles. He is serving in the Army of the Potomac, and they were on the front at the Battle of Fredericksburg which went badly for the Union. It's been two weeks, and I haven't heard a word from him. But enough of my family problems. It's the future of our fragile nation that brings you here. I am grateful that Nathaniel was able to persuade you to come. Fredericksburg has really shaken President Lincoln, and I fear for his resolve."

Mr. Longfellow introduced the man in the bowler hat to the just-arrived travelers: "Gentlemen, this is Mr. Allan Pinkerton, the head of President Lincoln's security detail. He has the unenviable task of protecting our president from all the lunatics that have surfaced since he was elected two years ago."

Mr. Pinkerton doffed his hat to the three men as he shook hands all around. "It is an honor to meet such an august group of men," he said humbly with a bowed head. "My team and I will do everything we can to minimize any disruptions to your meetings with the president. Please do not hesitate to report anything you might see that appears suspicious."

I noticed that the piece of paper that he and Mr. Longfellow had been looking at slid out of Mr. Pinkerton's pocket and blew off the porch into the shrubbery below. After they had all gone inside, leaving Joseph and me to deliver the luggage to their rooms, I retrieved the paper, which turned out to be a short, one-line letter. It was written in scarlet ink with a delicate longhand script bearing the letterhead of the American Consul to Liverpool:

Dearest Henry,

I have made a terrible mistake. One of the men is not who he pretends to be.

As ever your friend,
Nathaniel Hawthorne

* * *

Joseph read over my shoulder as I knelt on the ground by the porch. I felt a chill pass over me as a cold wind blew in from the harbor. "This is not good," said Joseph.

"Yeah, we need our eyes and ears open," I whispered back. "Let's keep this between us." Joseph nodded—*We are a team, and we are in this together.*

We walked back up to the porch just as Mrs. Carter came

out the front door. She gave us the room numbers for each of the guests and told us to deliver the suitcases to their rooms. "Be quiet when you're on the third floor," she warned us. "President Lincoln is resting."

I grabbed the handsome brown leather valise and climbed the stairs to the second floor. I knocked on the door at the end of the hall and was told to enter by a deep, friendly voice. Mr. Dickens had taken his coat off and was standing in front of the mirror. As he brushed his thick beard he asked me, "What are your stories? How did you and Joseph come to work at this inn?"

I gave him a condensed version of the fiery Christmas story and my decision to run away from home—but mostly from my father. I then shared Joseph's story of how his father bought Miss Estelle and Joseph's freedom from his jockeying earnings.

"Do you ever hear from your father?" Mr. Dickens asked.

"No, sir. He knows where I am, but I have not heard a word in two years. I could give him the benefit of the doubt that he is fighting in the war, but he doesn't deserve even that."

"I'm so sorry, John. I'm sure your father misses you and is worried about you, but sometimes fathers don't tell their children what they need to hear. My father was a good man, and I know that he loved me, but he just wasn't very good at saying it. He tried his best to take care of my mother and my seven siblings, but he eventually got overwhelmed by circumstances."

"What happened?" I asked.

"My father could never seem to keep his head above water when it came to money matters, and when I was twelve—just about your age—he got put in debtors' prison at Southwark in London. My mother and my younger brothers and sisters went to live with him in the prison, while I got passed around among ever more peculiar 'family friends.'"

Mr. Dickens laid down his brush and looked at himself in the dressing table mirror. *Is he seeing the twelve-year-old he used to be?*

He shook his head and looked at me in the reflection of the mirror as he continued *his* story: "My mother died after a year in the prison, and I soon found myself working in a blacking warehouse where I made pots and pans to help pay down my father's debts. I was thirteen and on my own, so, John, I'm afraid I do understand what you're going through."

"Did you ever get back with your family?" I asked.

"Not really," Mr. Dickens replied vaguely. "I got sent off to school—a horrible, depressing place. In fact, it was my inspiration for Mr. Creakle's establishment in a book I wrote called *David Copperfield*. After two years under the headmaster's brutal hand, I left to go work at a law office where I began to find the person I wanted to be. I met a young German student last year named Friedrich Nietzsche when I was traveling in Switzerland, and he told me, 'Out of life's school of war—what doesn't kill me, makes me stronger.' I like that quite a lot. I told Friedrich he needed to use that in a book before I beat him to it."

"So, you feel like all that pain made you stronger?" I asked hopefully.

"I do… But enough about me. Has Joseph heard from his father?"

"No, sir. Joseph says that even if a letter or telegram got through to the plantation in Mississippi where his father is a slave, his master would never let him see it. Aside from that, his father never learned to read and write."

"Slavery is a curse on this land, John. I gave a series of lectures when I was here twenty years ago, and everything I warned about has come true. Slavery has torn this country apart." Mr. Dickens suddenly looked very old as he sat at his dressing table. "Do you enjoy reading, John?"

"Oh, yes, sir! My class read *A Christmas Carol* last year and—believe it or not—I just finished *David Copperfield*. While I was reading it, I imagined that David was my best friend."

He smiled as I said this. "That's why I write books. I feel like all my characters are my children, but if I had to choose a favorite child, it would be David Copperfield."

I told him about the satchel of books that Mr. Herman had given me, and how it had opened up a whole new world to me. "But, John, that is uncanny," Mr. Dickens said. "That is exactly how it happened with me. When I was a child, we had a small room in the attic where I discovered some boxes. In one, I discovered the worlds of *Don Quixote*, *Robinson Crusoe*, and *Tom Jones*. I would take scenes from these books and place myself as a character in them. I could talk to Robinson Crusoe, and he would talk to me. That box of books changed my life."

"That's exactly what Mr. Herman wrote in a note to me."

"I have never had the pleasure of meeting Mr. Melville, but he wrote a note to me as well. It seems he admires my book *Bleak House*. He obviously has excellent taste in literature," Mr. Dickens said as he winked at me. "Now, Mrs. Carter has promised me a good, warm meal. Do you think Joseph's mother can make a proper plate of fish and chips for me?"

"Yes, sir! Joseph swears she's the best cook in Mississ… uh—Massachusetts."

I walked down with Mr. Dickens and out to the front porch. He spoke plaintively as he looked across the front yard to the town and the harbor beyond. "This is such a beautiful place, but I cannot forget the reasons we are here. I hate to be pretentious and quote myself, but it seems in your America right now, it truly is the best of times and the worst of times."

* * *

I next took up Mr. Marx's old black case, but when I knocked at his door, there was no answer. I cautiously cracked open the door to his room and slid his case inside. I could hear water splashing. I glanced across the room, and the door to his bathroom was partially open. Evidently, Mrs. Carter had already prepared his requested warm bath. As the splashing continued, Mr. Marx began singing what sounded like one of the German drinking songs which I had heard coming from the tavern in town where the housemaids liked to go to after cleaning rooms at the inn. In mid-verse, his voice shifted into English in a clear, smooth baritone just like the singing sailors I had heard on the decks of our Gulf and Atlantic voyages:

"Here's to our mare, and to her right eye,
God send our mistress a good Christmas pie;
A good Christmas pie as e'er I did see,
With my wassailing bowl I drink to thee."

With all the excitement of last night and this morning, I had forgotten that today was Christmas Eve! While the fiery fiasco two years ago had soured me on Christmas, last year's celebrations at the inn with Mrs. Carter, Miss Estelle, and Joseph had somewhat revived my joy of the holiday.

I eased backwards out of the room and went downstairs.

Joseph was taking care of Mr. Darwin's luggage, so I went to my room in the servant's quarters to confirm my thoughts. *One of the men is not who he pretends to be,* the letter had said. I pulled *David Copperfield* out of the leather satchel and turned to the engraving of the author opposite the title page. There was no doubt that the man I had just talked to was indeed Charles Dickens. *One down, but how many to go?* I sat on my bed and pondered this for several minutes. *Who all could the letter be referring to?* I walked down the stairs, across the gravel yard, and into the back door of the kitchen.

Joseph and his mother were sitting at the long table talking to Mr. Marx. He had dressed after his bath, but his wet hair and long beard were a tangled mess. Miss Estelle looked up as I walked in, and she waved me over with a spatula in her hand. "John, Mr. Marx was just asking us about our life here in Nantucket. You are the one who has read all the books. I always thought Joseph and I were just slaves, and then we were ex-slaves. But Mr. Marx says we are now the oppressed working class—the *pro-le-tar-i-at.* Do you think we are being—what was the word?—Oh, yes... *ex-ploited?*"

I had never been asked such a question in my life, so I stood there awkwardly, trying to think up an appropriate answer. Joseph rescued me when he voiced with his youthful wisdom, "I would rather be free and exploited than be what we used to be. I think Daddy would agree."

I was afraid Joseph's response would upset his mother, but Mr. Marx spoke up enthusiastically: "Good answer, Joseph. Your mother speaks of how smart you are, and I can see why. She is so proud of you." He paused a moment before continuing. "I lost my only son seven years ago, and it still leaves a hole in my heart."

"I'm so sorry, Mr. Marx," said Miss Estelle.

"Thank you, Estelle, but please call me *Karl*. Edgar was seven years old when he died. My family and I were living in London in such poverty that I sometimes felt like we were characters in a novel by my new friend, Mr. Dickens. I was working for the Communist League as I had previously in Paris and Brussels, but it paid very little. I was struggling to feed my family by writing articles for several newspapers. When Edgar got sick, we had no money to get him a doctor's treatment."

I spoke up, hoping to divert Mr. Marx from the agony that he was reliving: "I saw one of your articles in the *New York Daily Tribune* in the parlor here at the inn."

"Yes, John, but I am afraid there will be no more paychecks coming from the *Tribune*," sighed Mr. Marx. "It is the new policy of the newspaper's editors that the Union should find a way to make peace with the Confederacy, even if it means keeping slavery intact. I told them *To hell with that notion*, and they informed me that my writings were no longer welcome."

"I have written about slavery in such theoretical terms," Mr. Marx continued very deliberately, "that I often lose sight of what it really means in flesh and blood. I have spent half of my life it seems sitting at the British Museum studying economic theory. I have even written the foolish notion that the slave needs the slaveholder as much as the slaveholder needs the slave. Now that I am here in America, all I can say is 'Balderdash!' I have cast slaves as mere machines in a capitalist society, but machines do not have mothers and fathers or sons and daughters. I am here to help your President Lincoln understand this."

Joseph's mother said, "I got the chance to speak with

President Lincoln last night about our family—about how my husband bought our freedom and now seeks his own. The president is a good man. I think he understands."

"I believe he does, Estelle," Mr. Marx agreed. "He *is* a good man—a great man—in a most difficult time. I have written him several letters about the war and about the evils of slavery, and he has always responded kindly and intelligently. I think he has lost confidence, however, in knowing what is right."

I looked at this burly, wild-haired man in his old, ill-fitting clothes and realized something—this highly-educated intellectual was talking to Miss Estelle person-to-person—as a fellow human being—and not just talking down to her as some sort of servant. *I think he is maybe more comfortable sitting with her in the kitchen than being in the parlor with the other guests.* Joseph's mother continued to sit and chat with him while Joseph and I brought in firewood to the kitchen. I liked and trusted Mr. Marx immediately. *Two down.*

Chapter 20

When I had finished my other chores, I walked into the parlor and found Joseph and Mr. Darwin looking through a magnifying glass at a moth which had lighted on one of the brass lanterns. Mr. Darwin was pointing out to Joseph the difference in the markings of this moth as compared to the moths in England. "It's all a survival mechanism. Let me explain to you about natural selection," Mr. Darwin said as he took a notebook out of his pocket to show Joseph a sketch that he had drawn. *Just like Mr. Verne*, I thought.

Charles Darwin was bald with the beginnings of a scraggly, white beard—he looked the part of a scientist and spoke to Joseph in a patient, scholarly voice: "I saw your seashells out on the front porch. When I was your age in England, I had a wonderful natural history collection. I gathered shells, insects, fossils, and I especially loved bird eggs and the skeletons from birds. We need to go to the beach tomorrow morning to look at the birds. They are the easiest place to see evolution's undeniable face."

Joseph said, "I would like that very much. I love watching birds and wondering where they have been and where they are going. Sometimes I dream that I am flying myself."

Mr. Darwin patted Joseph on the back and replied, "I will try to convince you that birds evolved from creatures living in the sea. Scales became feathers and fins became wings. So would you believe that what we know now as birds were once fish?"

Joseph smiled sheepishly and answered, "That might take some convincing."

Just as Mr. Darwin was making his argument to Joseph, Mr. Dickens walked in the front door from a walk and caught the tail end of the conversation. "I say, Charles," said Mr. Dickens, "were you discussing lunch? Did I hear you mention fish?"

Oh, no, I thought frantically, *I forgot to mention the fish and chips to Miss Estelle!*

But just as I realized this, Mr. Marx came into the parlor with Miss Estelle, each carrying a tray with glasses and a large bowl. The man in the bowler hat from the front porch entered from the front hall, nervously patting his pockets. I snuck a glance at Joseph, and he winked back at me. The man was soon joined by his two colleagues—the man who had carried the rifle and the driver in the red scarf.

Mrs. Carter next emerged from the kitchen wearing a festive green and red apron covered in stars and holly berries. Her white hair featured a large red velvet bow which made her round, smooth face appear even pinker than usual. There was a curious twinkle in her eye as she began dipping the glasses into the bowl of hot yellowish liquid which smelled of apples, cinnamon, and something else very strong. "My dear guests, it is time for us to share our Christmas wassail. This is an old family recipe that has been used in holiday toasts for five generations. Drink up!" Mrs. Carter handed glasses to Messrs. Darwin, Marx, and Dickens. Mr. Pinkerton—

the original man in the bowler hat—took one whiff of the hot drink and politely declined with a smile and a shake of the head. His colleagues, "Rifleman" and "Red Scarf," also reluctantly declined in turn.

The glasses were frequently replenished as the volume in the room grew steadily louder and louder. Mr. Darwin and Mr. Dickens walked over to where Mr. Marx stood with Miss Estelle. Mr. Darwin noticed Mr. Marx's wet hair and said, "Speaking of things which evolved from the sea. Karl, has anyone ever told you that you resemble a walrus?"

Far from being offended, Mr. Marx roared with laughter. "Believe me, Charles," he said, "I have been accused of much worse than that."

"As have I," Mr. Dickens added. "I think that all of England sees us three as godless heathens. So, for now," he laughed as he raised his glass in a toast with the other men, "God bless America!"

I tried to get over to Miss Estelle so I could whisper to her about Mr. Dickens's lunch request, but Mrs. Carter spoke up before I had the chance: "My dear guests, while we are all here together, I would like to invite each of you to the traditional Carter House Inn Christmas Eve dinner tonight. I can assure you that Estelle will make it a memorable evening. We will have an informal social time beginning at seven o'clock, and dinner will be served immediately after."

As she was talking, I kept trying to catch Miss Estelle's eye, but I could tell she was already thinking about tonight, as her eyes looked wildly all around the dining room. *She is planning a menu for a room full of men from other countries that have their own food cultures that she has never experienced.* Mrs. Carter continued talking, "And in honor of our English guests, Estelle has prepared a delightful lunch of fish and chips." *I now know that I should never underestimate the cooking skills of Miss Estelle.*

I let out a loud sigh of relief as Mr. Dickens came over to me and whispered, "Good show, John. I knew you would take care of me." After Mrs. Carter had finished addressing the guests, she beckoned Joseph, his mother, and me to her side.

"John and Joseph, because of the holidays and the war, you're all the staff that I have for today and tomorrow. Estelle, would you mind if Joseph helped serve tonight?" As she said this, I remembered Joseph telling me the story of his serving Christmas dinner two years ago at Mr. Rossiter's plantation, right before they left in the tinker's wagon. *It seems a lifetime ago.*

"Of course, I don't mind, Mrs. Carter," his mother answered. "Joseph will be happy to do whatever you need him to do. Isn't that right, Joseph?"

"Yes, ma'am," he replied quickly. I knew that his mother wasn't really asking a question. As I looked around the room at all the guests, I could not help but wonder where the president was, what he was doing, and which person *is not who he pretends to be.*

✳ ✳ ✳

It was the tradition at the Carter House Inn to save all the decorating for Christmas Eve, so after lunch, Mrs. Carter and Miss Estelle put Joseph and me to work cleaning and decorating the dining room while all the guests retired to their rooms for a much-needed nap. Mrs. Carter told me that there was a small Christmas tree already on a wooden stand out on the front porch. "We're not going to need that tree you put in the stables," she added.

Joseph's mother asked Mrs. Carter, "Did that Mr. Early bring this tree to you?" During my regular duties of purchasing supplies for the inn, I often found myself in the small shop on Candle Street where "Early's Floral and Landscaping Supplies" was located. Its owner, Mr. Travis Early, a short, plump, white-haired old gentleman, never failed to ask how Mrs. Carter was doing, and he never missed the opportunity to drop by the inn to personally deliver a vase of flowers or a potted plant to the widowed owner.

Mrs. Carter blushed a little and answered, "Yes, he did. Mr. Early served with my husband in the Mexican War, and ever since my husband passed, he has delivered a fresh-cut fir tree to my front porch every Christmas Eve. I didn't know if he would this year with the war going on."

"I do believe Mr. Early might be sweet on you," Miss Estelle teased. "Did you leave him one of the fruitcakes I made?"

Now Mrs. Carter really blushed, as her pink face turned closer to the red in the ribbon in her hair. "I did, because it's the neighborly thing to do."

"You ought to invite Mr. Early over for dinner one night," Miss Estelle said as she winked at us. "John and Joseph probably get tired of being the only men of the house."

I'm sure Joseph wasn't conscious of it, but his mother and I both witnessed the obvious, pained look that surfaced on his face that was followed by a loud *sniff*.

When Mrs. Carter went back to the kitchen, Joseph's mother sat in one of the dining chairs and pulled her son close to her. She took his distraught face in her hands and kissed each of his cheeks. As she looked straight into his eyes, she said softly, "I know, Joseph. You miss your daddy, especially now that it's Christmas. I miss him every hour of every day, but I can just feel it in my heart that he will be joining us soon. We will find a place to live, and you can go back to being my little boy, and your daddy will go back to being the man of our house." As she smiled at Joseph, she took her thumbs and wiped the tears that had just started to fall from his eyes. "Now, Joseph… and John," she said as it just seemed to register that I had witnessed this intimate moment, "the both of you need to get to work. We've all got a lot to do."

Joseph soon joined me as we cleaned the windows in the dining room with vinegar and water before hanging holly leaves with red berries from the draperies. Mrs. Carter brought out bone china with gold rims and hand-painted Christmas scenes. Joseph was fascinated by the pictures of the shepherds, wise men, and the baby Jesus in the manger. "Mr. Rossiter would decorate his mansion for Christmas," he exclaimed, "but it was nothing like this!"

Seemingly revived from his momentary grief, Joseph told me everything he knew about Christmas as we polished the silver candlesticks, platters and bowls, and a confusing variety of knives, forks, and spoons. "Father Matthew taught me about the birth of the baby Jesus in Bethlehem. His mommy and daddy couldn't find room in the inn, so Jesus ended up being born in a manger behind the inn, sort of like the stables out behind *this* inn. He was visited by shepherds and three wise men who brought gifts. Now that I think of it, sort of like the three wise men—Mr. Dickens, Mr. Darwin, and Mr. Marx—have come to visit President Lincoln here at the inn.

"I've noticed in town," I added, "that everyone has been collecting gifts for the soldiers out in the field. They do things for Christmas here *way* different than they did in Mississippi."

"I don't understand about Santa Claus, though," Joseph said out of the blue. "I saw his picture on a poster on a lamppost in town. He looks a lot like Mr. Marx."

I laughed. "I was taught that Santa Claus is this 'jolly old elf' who supposedly brings presents to all the good kids in the world on Christmas morning."

"Either I've been bad," Joseph replied, "or Black kids don't count, because Santa's never brought me anything."

Miss Estelle carried in an ivory, starched-linen tablecloth that bore the letters *CH* in gold script in each corner. We spread the linen on the long table until it was as smooth as a snowy field. Mrs. Carter showed us how to set each place setting for the eight chairs at the table. We went out to the porch and brought in Mr. Early's fir tree, which we placed on the cherry sideboard beneath the portrait of the late Major Carter that hung in the dining room. There was a note tied to a branch of the tree which Mrs. Carter read with an increasing blush on her face.

Mrs. Carter had placed bowls of dried fruit, popcorn, and roasted chestnuts on the sideboard. She helped us string this odd assortment of foods on a thin piece of twine which we wrapped around the tree. When we had finished, Mrs. Carter placed bits of brightly colored paper and small spun-glass ornaments on the tree which sparkled in the late afternoon sun.

As I was laying a fir bough across the fireplace mantle, a charred piece of paper lying beside one of the andirons caught my eye. I plucked it out of the fireplace and tried to read it as I showed it to Joseph. He held it up to the light of the window and said, "I have an idea I read about one time." He took one of our cleaning rags and dipped it into the vinegar and water.

He soaked one of the windowpanes with the solution and stuck the charred paper to the glass. Almost immediately, the vinegar began blanching out the ink against the blackened background. In block letters, we could now read very clearly: *DELAY. OBSTRUCT. DECEIVE.*

* * *

"What are you boys doing?"

Joseph's mother's head poked through the swinging door from the kitchen, allowing all the smells to drift into the dining room. She was cooking President Lincoln's favorite meal: stewed scallops, roasted pheasant, and a succotash of turnips, rutabagas and carrots, and my favorite food as well—apple pie.

"Still cleaning the windows," Joseph answered guiltily as he slid in front of me while I peeled the strange message off the glass.

"I need some bacon from the smokehouse," Miss Estelle said, seemingly oblivious to our subterfuge. "The succotash just needs a little something else. Would y'all go get me some?"

The smokehouse was located on the opposite side of the stables from the servants' quarters. It was a small, white, brick cylinder with a cone-shaped roof. At the peak of the roof was a narrow metal smokestack. I hid the charred paper in my pocket as we walked through the kitchen and out the back door. I opened the heavy timber door to the smokehouse and left it open so we could see all the different meats and fish hanging from hooks on the wall. To my left were salted slabs of beef, pork, and venison, while to my right was an assortment of bass and bluefish—the bounty of our successful fishing trip to Sesachacha Pond last spring.

Joseph started coughing as soon as he entered, as the air was thick with salty hickory smoke. He croaked, "Only been in a smokehouse… ugh… ugh… one other time. Mr. Rossiter had one behind the kitchen at Raw Cedar, but he guarded its contents like it was gold. I watched one slave get whipped within an inch of his life for daring to take a sliver of ham from the floor of the smokehouse to feed his starving children." *I almost feel guilty for the pinch of venison that I just tasted after pulling it off that hanging carcass.*

After Joseph had found the bacon his mother needed, I pulled the note out of my pocket. *DELAY. OBSTRUCT. DECEIVE.*

"We have no idea why our three guests are here at the request of President Lincoln," I whispered.

"Yeah. What *do* we know?" Joseph whispered back.

"We have to assume they are all going to meet together. Mr. Dickens is a writer, Mr. Darwin is a scientist, and Mr. Marx is an economist. Why *these* three men?"

"It seems like if President Lincoln wanted to talk about the war, he would have invited a bunch of generals to meet with him," Joseph reasoned.

"So maybe they are not going to talk about the war itself," I countered, "but instead discuss the causes of the war."

DELAY. "So," Joseph began as I could just barely see the thoughtfulness in his eyes in the darkness of the smokehouse, "you have to figure the 'bad guys'—whoever that may be—are going to try and delay President Lincoln's meeting with his three guests."

"That's not going to be easy to do," I said, "because they're all here at the inn now."

OBSTRUCT. "Then," Joseph continued, "if they cannot delay the meeting, they will obstruct—try to throw roadblocks—in the way."

"Yeah, that's what we need to keep our eyes and ears open for."

DECEIVE. "Well," Joseph concluded, "that could mean anything."

"I also think we know," I said, "that our three main guests certainly seem to be who they are supposed to be, but we know next to nothing about Mr. Pinkerton and his *detective agency.*"

"Yeah," Joseph agreed. "Shouldn't they be a *protective* agency? Aren't they here to protect the president? Maybe *we* need to be the detectives right now."

I knew that we had been gone too long—finding some bacon is not that hard—so we cut short our speculations and closed the door to the smokehouse. After we secured the lock, however, we heard the *clopping* of hooves in the gravel drive of the inn. Joseph and I ducked for cover behind a pile of bags on the back side of the smokehouse. As we peeked over the top of the pile, we saw a closed carriage turn the corner around the rear of the inn and stop in front of the stables. Shades were pulled down across the windows, making it impossible to see the occupants of the carriage. Mr. Pinkerton's colleague Rifleman climbed down from the driver's box and did a quick three-hundred-sixty turn to be sure that he wasn't being watched. *He was.*

He opened the door of the carriage and extended his elbow up to a woman who began easing out of her seat. She was pretty but not in a girlish way. Her hair was graying, and she was dressed in a simple, dark dress with a shawl thrown around her shoulders. As Rifleman briskly escorted the woman to the rear of the inn, I could see the kitchen door open, and Mr. Pinkerton's face appeared. He helped hustle the woman inside as he also checked to make sure he had been successful in keeping her entrance unobserved. *He wasn't.*

Joseph and I waited a few moments for the coast to clear, and we were met by an irate Mrs. Carter as we entered through that same kitchen door. "Well, I've never been made to feel that I was an intruder in my *own* house," Mrs. Carter blurted to us, "but Mr. Pinkerton just ordered me and Estelle out of the kitchen so that he could sneak *some woman* into *my* inn. I don't know what's going on, but I'm pretty sure they went straight up to the president's room. That is *not* the kind of establishment that I run here!"

Miss Estelle took Mrs. Carter by the arm, eased her into a chair, and poured her a cup of tea. "I'm sure there's an innocent explanation for this," she reassured her employer.

What if I have this all wrong? What if it's the president who is not who he pretends to be?

Chapter 21

By seven-thirty that night, all the guests except President Lincoln had assembled in the dining room. Mr. Darwin and Mr. Dickens were dressed in expensive-looking three-piece suits with silk ties. The latter was checking the time on a beautiful gold pocket watch which hung from a chain attached to his vest. Mr. Marx still looked a bit out of place in the same ill-fitting black suit he had been wearing that afternoon, but the drinks being served during the "social time" had helped make him feel most comfortable with the other guests.

In the kitchen, Joseph's mother adjusted the jacket and bowtie which Mrs. Carter had given Joseph to wear and tried to mold his hair into some sort of order. Every time she pushed in one direction, however, his hair would pop out in the other direction. "Joseph," she said with exasperation, "the good Lord sure did bless you with an abundance of hair. Now, son, remember you always serve from the left and take away from the right. You are to be seen and not heard, except to say, 'Yes, sir' or 'No, sir.'" She hugged him tightly and then moved on to inspect me.

"John," she said with a crooked grin, "you look like a polecat caught in a wire trap—like if you twist an inch, you might lose a body part. *Just relax.*" She stuck a finger inside the collar of my shirt and loosened it a bit and rearranged my bowtie so that I could almost breathe. She looked ill at ease herself in a pressed black smock with a starched white collar that poked out from under a stiff linen apron. She smelled like cinnamon and cloves and had a patch of flour on the side of her nose. She smiled and looked Joseph and me in the eyes as she said, "*Both* your fathers would be *so* proud to hear that you are serving our president." *Maybe one of them would.*

I heard the jingle of Mrs. Carter's bell from the dining room, and Miss Estelle pushed us through the door just as Mr. Pinkerton was announcing in a solemn voice to the gathering of guests, "Ladies and gentlemen, the President of the United States."

President Lincoln walked into the room unsteadily, as if the floor were shifting under him. He towered over everyone else, though there was a hunch in his shoulders as if his height had become a burden. His face looked drawn and ashen, and his deep-set eyes were dark and sad. I had seen portraits of him when he took office less than two years ago, and he now looked ten years older. The sleeves of his black suit rode up his wrists as he nervously tugged at his scraggly beard with his long, thin fingers. He stared blankly at Mrs. Carter as she took him by the arm. She seemed to have forgotten that afternoon's misgivings about her guest of honor, as she spoke up loudly drawing everyone's attention: "Mr. President, it is my honor to introduce you to our guests from London—Mr. Charles Dickens, Mr. Karl Marx, and Mr. Charles Darwin."

President Lincoln smiled thinly and shook each man's hand. "It is my honor to meet you," he said in a shrill, trembling voice. "I appreciate the sacrifice you have made to your families to come here during Christmas time at my humble request."

Mrs. Carter next led the president to Joseph and me as we stood at some odd form of military attention. Joseph tried to push his hair down, but it kept popping up like a rooster's comb. "Mr. President," Mrs. Carter continued, "you have met Estelle. I would like you to meet her son, Joseph, who will be one of our servers tonight."

A new warmth came into President Lincoln's eyes as he bent down to shake the hand of the suddenly tongue-tied Joseph. "Hello, Joseph. I have heard so much about you from Estelle. Your mother and her wonderful cooking have brought me back to life—like Lazarus from the grave. I believe you and I share a passion for horses."

Joseph remembered his mother's instructions and struggled to say, "Yes, sir."

President Lincoln turned his wrinkled face to me and asked, "Who is this young man?"

Joseph finally found his voice saying, "This is my friend John."

President Lincoln smiled initially as he shook my hand and said, "John, you remind me so much of my son Willie," but suddenly the warmth in his eyes was extinguished like a candle flame blown out by an unexpected wind. "My poor boy, he was too good for this earth. God has called him home. His mother and I lost Willie this February to typhoid."

Mrs. Carter divined a downturn in the president's mood and deflected the conversation. She directed Joseph and me to serve the two trays of small foods that Miss Estelle had laid on the sideboard. "Mr. President, you must try Estelle's salmon canapes." Seamlessly, she segued back to the previous conversation. "You and the First Lady have several children, don't you?"

The president's blank eyes re-engaged with the question. "We do, indeed, Mrs. Carter. You are very kind to ask. Our oldest son, Robert, is in his second year at Harvard College. My wife and I are very proud of him—as we also are of our younger son—though we have to keep reminding Robert that his days are better spent in the classroom than on the battlefield."

Mr. Darwin joined the conversation as he picked a canape from the tray I extended to him. He inquired of the president, "Your son wants to enlist?"

"He does," President Lincoln answered, "but luckily his younger brother Tad—he's nine years old—seems to carry more sway than his parents. Robert does not want to miss out on hunting with Tad on all the grounds that we now have at the White House. Last week they shot a bobcat near the stables just outside the Oval Office." President Lincoln caught himself as he chuckled inwardly. "Enough about me, Charles. You have children as well?"

"My wife Emma and I are blessed to have had ten children—but we have also shared your pain of losing three of our precious young ones. William, our oldest—like yours—is now in college. Are you aware, Mr. President, of what else we have in common?" President Lincoln looked back at him with curiosity. "We were born on the same day: February 12, 1809."

* * *

Mr. Darwin turned to me and said, "My oldest son is studying for a career in banking. Joseph tells me that you handle some of the money matters here at the inn. Can you see yourself becoming a banker?" Before I could answer, Mrs. Carter rang her bell and bid everybody to take their seats at the dining table. She and President Lincoln were at opposite ends of the long table, while Messrs. Dickens, Marx, and Darwin sat down one side, and Mr. Pinkerton and Rifleman sat down the other with an empty chair between them. I saw Mr. Pinkerton signal with a nod of the head to Red Scarf, who proceeded to position himself by the front door.

The chandelier above the dining table with its festive green and red candles made the silver, china, and crystal sparkle atop the ivory tablecloth, and a warm fire crackled on the hearth. Mrs. Carter circled the table pouring a deep-red wine for the guests as Joseph and I went back into the kitchen to retrieve two trays with steaming bowls of stewed scallops ready to serve.

As I returned to the dining room with a tray, President Lincoln began to speak: "Dear guests, I regret that we must be here under such trying circumstances during what should be a joyous time of year. However, our devastating defeat at Fredericksburg has convinced me that the Union cannot win the war. I have decided to end it and try to reunite our fractured nation."

As the president spoke, all the guests at the table stared intently at his face. Just as he was getting ready to resume speaking, there came a loud knocking at the front door. Mr. Pinkerton got up from the table and went to the front hall where low voices could be heard. When Mr. Pinkerton came back into the dining room, he whispered into President Lincoln's ear and handed him what appeared to be a telegram. I was standing by Joseph as everyone waited anxiously for the president's explanation. Whatever he had been told caused the president's face to assume the hardness and chill of a mask. Joseph whispered to me, "He looks haunted."

"I'm afraid I have some terrible news," the president began. "I have been informed by Secretary of War Stanton that he just personally delivered the news to our friend Henry Longfellow at his home in Cambridge that his son was killed at Fredericksburg. I have also been given a copy of a rather disturbing telegram that Mr. Longfellow received from England."

The guests were shocked by the president's announcement. Mrs. Carter—ever the cheerful hostess in her gold and burgundy Christmas gown—tried to steer the talk away from war, and nervous conversation percolated among the guests as they ate. I heard Mr. Darwin ask Mr. Marx, "Karl, have you ever tasted such heavenly scallops before?"

"Never," he replied, "and this cabernet is utterly delightful." Despite the guests' awkward attempts at social banter, an uneasiness hung over the room like a silent fog. After a concerned glance at the president, Mr. Pinkerton abruptly left the table, and we could hear the solid steps of his boots as he climbed the stairs of the inn. When he came back, he was accompanied by the woman that I had seen clandestinely arrive in the carriage that afternoon.

Without any introduction, the woman immediately walked over to the stricken president. Kneeling by his chair, she spoke quietly but reassuringly to President Lincoln. I could only hear snatches of the whispered conversation: "Mr. President, these men are here to help you... The burden is not yours to bear alone... You cannot hold yourself responsible for every soldier's death... It's Christmas time, Mr. President—you are here with friends."

Gradually the president's composure began to return. He looked around the table and realized that an introduction was in order. "Gentlemen…" he said and then paused uncertainly. "Guests…" he tried again as he looked at the woman. She nodded subtly. "Friends… I would like to introduce my physician, Mrs. Elizabeth Blackwell."

I now understand why she is here. Something is wrong with the president.

Miss Estelle next filled a tray with plates full of roasted pheasant and root-vegetable succotash and held the door open as we returned to the dining room. All talk stopped as the aroma from the tray greeted the guests like a welcome companion. The president looked noticeably better and spoke to his dinner guests again: "I apologize for the previous interruption, and I will try not to talk politics again. We will leave that for tomorrow. For now, it's Christmas Eve, and Miss Estelle's cooking deserves our full attention."

Mrs. Blackwell was seated at the empty chair between Mr. Pinkerton and Rifleman. She was introduced to the three famous guests seated across from her and was immediately accepted by them when she declared that she was a fellow Brit: "I was born in Bristol, England, but my family moved to America when I was eleven after my father lost his business in a fire. When we settled in New York, my parents became active in the abolitionist and women's rights movements. I grew up in a political household, so I guess that's why the president feels comfortable with me as his physician. We have some rousing discussions!" For now, however, all talk of politics disappeared as the guests cut into the dark, rich pheasant, and holiday cheer truly began to spread around the table as Mrs. Carter again circled with another bottle of wine.

Mr. Marx patted Mrs. Carter's arm as she refilled his glass, making sure he received a healthy pour. After sipping the new wine, Mr. Marx waxed poetic, "As the Bard so eloquently wrote, 'The wine-cup is the little silver well, where truth, if truth there be, doth dwell.'" With his cheeks becoming a bright, flushed red, he really did resemble the pictures of Santa Claus which I had seen in the holiday issues of the *Saturday Evening Post* lying in the sitting room.

As Joseph replenished Mr. Darwin's plate with pheasant, I could tell that Mr. Darwin was again talking to him about birds because he was flapping his arms like they were wings. "*Caw, Caw!*" he screeched loudly as everyone laughed at the table.

* * *

President Lincoln summoned Joseph to his side and motioned to his empty plate. "Joseph, please give my compliments to your mother on another delicious meal. Where in the world did she learn to cook like that?"

"She was born in New Or-lins, sir. She says the cooking is just mixed into her blood."

"Did you ever live in New Orleans, Joseph?" the president asked.

"No, sir," he replied. "Mamma and I passed through—along with John—after we were emancipated. She showed us the slave market where she was sold on Christmas Day to a man in Jackson, Mississippi when she was nine years old."

I could see President Lincoln flinch when Joseph said this, and he lost his train of thought. Mrs. Blackwell noticed this as well and came to the rescue: "Mr. President, what were you going to ask Joseph about New Orleans?"

President Lincoln shook his head slightly as if to clear the cobwebs from his mind. "Did you get to ride on a riverboat when y'all passed through?" he asked us as he noticed me standing beside Joseph.

"No, sir," I answered, "but we have a good friend, Sam, who is a riverboat pilot."

"Would you believe me, boys, if I were to tell you that I invented something that is used on every riverboat now?" I glanced at Mr. Pinkerton—and I'm sure that he didn't mean to—but he rolled his eyes slightly. President Lincoln caught this too.

"Now, Allan," the president said chuckling, "I know you've heard this story before, but I'm sure our guests haven't. Humor me, just this once." As he said this, all the other guests at the table stopped their conversations and listened to the president. He obviously enjoyed telling this story, and all attention fell on him.

"When I was about twenty-two, I canoed down the Sanga-mon River where I took up residence in New Salem, Illinois. I got a job delivering goods down the river to New Orleans on flatboats. Well, one time my friends and I had a load to deliver but no boat, so we decided to build our own." *Do I dare interrupt the President of the United States to tell everyone about the raft that Jim and I built?* I looked around the table, and everyone was entranced by the president's story as they sipped their wine and listened to his every word. *No, of course I don't.*

"My father was a carpenter," the president continued comfortably, "so I knew the basics of building, and we cut down a bunch of trees and built ourselves a flatboat. When we loaded it and put it in the river, it wasn't thirty minutes before we had it stuck on Rutledge's Dam. The bow of the boat was sticking up in the air, and the stern was down in the river, but we couldn't budge it because it had taken on so much water. All the locals had come out of their houses to make fun of us for grounding our boat, but I had an idea. I took a knife and cut a hole in the stern of the boat, just above the waterline. We lifted the bow enough for the water to drain out, and then I stuck a plug back in the hole. That boat floated true all the way to New Orleans. Now every riverboat on the Mississippi River has a plug in the stern for draining water."

As he finished talking, he took a long sip of water. "Just thinking about all that good honest work," the president laughed, "has given me a renewed appetite. Joseph, could you ask your mother if she might have a little more pheasant in the kitchen?" As Joseph left, President Lincoln turned to Mr. Pinkerton and teased, "Now, Allan, that wasn't *too* painful of a story, was it?" Mr. Pinkerton smiled in quiet deference to his boss.

Another bottle of wine emerged and made its way around the table as talk gave way to drink. Mrs. Blackwell broke the lull in the conversation: "Mr. President, you need to tell your guests how Mr. Pinkerton came to be in charge of your protection. It is a fascinating story."

"Well, if you insist," the president guffawed. *He is really enjoying himself now. He is a born storyteller.* "I first met Allan when he was hired by the Illinois Central Railroad to investigate a series of train robberies that the company had suffered. I was just a country lawyer doing some legal work for the railroad when I was introduced to Allan by the railroad's chief engineer, George McClellan. I have nothing else to say about *that* man." The president paused for another sip of water and a moment—I believe—for his temper to subside. "Allan, the story of how you came to be a detective is much more interesting. You need to tell that…"

Mr. Pinkerton was obviously uncomfortable to be thrown into the spotlight, but as he began to speak, I noticed a slight accent that I had not heard before. Out of the corner of my eye, I also saw Red Scarf slip out the front door of the inn. "I'm not sure how interesting it is, but I—like our guests at this table—was born across the pond. In my case, my childhood and early years were spent in Glasgow, Scotland. When I was twenty-three, I immigrated to America and settled near Chicago. I opened a small cooperage that kept food on the table."

"Allan," the president interrupted, "you're being too humble. Tell them about Chicago."

"I guess you mean that I was a conductor on the Underground Railroad in Chicago. It gave me the honor of getting to meet people like John Brown and Frederick Douglass." Suddenly, his intense gaze fell on Joseph and me. "According to reconnaissance we did for the president's trip to Nantucket, we discovered John and Joseph's involvement with the Railroad."

All the guests' faces turned towards Joseph and me as we stood frozen in the shifted spotlight. Before we could offer any defense, however, Red Scarf peeked through the door from the kitchen. Mr. Pinkerton again got up to investigate. As he returned, President Lincoln asked with great frustration, "Allan, surely not another interruption of this fine meal?"

Mr. Pinkerton replied firmly, "Mr. President, the stables are on fire."

Chapter 22

r. Pinkerton took the president by the arm and tried to lead him towards the stairs. "No," President Lincoln resisted, "we need every able-bodied man to save Mrs. Carter's stables."

Mr. Pinkerton insisted, "Sir, the Nantucket Fire Brigade will see the smoke and come. Isn't that right, Mrs. Carter?"

She answered in near panic: "They're all off fighting in the war!"

"It's up to us then," said President Lincoln as he started for the kitchen.

Joseph ran ahead of him and out the back door. I was right behind Joseph, and I heard his mother yell, "Joseph! Wait!" *There is no time to wait.* As I sprinted towards the stables, the black smoke was already billowing from the double doors. Somehow, the president's carriage was already out, and Red Scarf was calming the horses. Caddy and Quentin, two of the inn's riding horses, were in the first two stalls, and I could hear Quentin's nervous neighing. The fire seemed to have started in the back right corner under the loft where I had placed the unused Christmas tree near some hay bales. Joseph started with Caddy while I went to Quentin's stall. Joseph had been teaching me everything he had learned about riding from his father, and Quentin was the horse I most often rode. She impatiently pawed at the metal door while Caddy, an old mare, stood seemingly oblivious to the commotion. She let Joseph lead her out. After coaxing Quentin out of her stall with the bribe of a carrot, we soon had both of them safely tied to a rail out in the yard.

Luster, the dray horse, was next, but he would not be nearly as easy. As I ran back in, he was standing on his rear legs and thrashing violently, his wild eyes showing sheer terror. His hooves pounded at the stall door at the same level as my head. From out of nowhere, Joseph scampered up the door and jumped on Luster's back. I swung the door open and beckoned, "Come on, Joseph! The fire is still spreading." I wrestled Luster through the door as Joseph clung to his back. President Lincoln was there in the yard to grab the reins from Joseph.

As the president led him to the rail, Joseph jumped off and headed back to the stables. Benjy, the youngest riding horse, was not standing at his door. Instead, he was hunkered down in the back of his stall shivering like he was freezing. As I watched, Joseph eased into the stall and bent down, taking Benjy's bridle into his hand. He pulled… and pulled… and pulled. It was no use—Benjy was not moving.

I joined Joseph in the stall and sat on the floor pleading with the terrified gelding: "Come on, Benjy! You've got to move!" The smoke drifted into the stall, floating to the ceiling. Like a flash, Joseph ran out of the stall and out the doors of the stables. I didn't know what he was doing, but it seemed like he was gone an eternity. As I looked back over my shoulder, I could see President Lincoln peering around the corner of the door with Mr. Pinkerton protectively at his side. Just as suddenly,

I heard Joseph's muffled footsteps in the straw as he flashed back into the stall. He threw something from his pocket onto the floor by Benjy's head. The horse's eyes widened in frantic fright, and he bolted up and out of the smoky stall as a blue crab scuttled across the floor. The president grabbed Benjy's reins as he trotted out the stable door to safety.

"How did you know that would work?" I shouted to Joseph as we double-checked the four, now-empty stalls.

"I didn't," Joseph said, "but I had that crab in a bucket on the back porch, and it scared the bejesus out of me when I almost stepped on it at the beach yesterday."

The smoke kept getting thicker in the main aisle of the stables as Joseph and I made our way out the doors. I breathed for what felt like the first time in the last ten minutes as I watched the horses standing innocently with their tails swishing back and forth. They were Mrs. Carter's horses, but I almost felt as if they were mine. *I know that Joseph feels the same way.* Even though the horses were safe, we still faced the dilemma of saving the stables from the fire.

I heard President Lincoln shouting orders as the unlikeliest-bucket-brigade-ever-assembled took shape at the back right corner of the stables. Mr. Darwin, Mr. Marx, and Mr. Dickens had all shed their coats and were passing buckets of water up the line to throw onto the fire fed by the blazing Christmas tree. Joseph's mother pumped furiously on the crank of the well as the doctor caught the splashing cold water in the buckets. I could see the mist of their breaths as they worked in the frigid air. President Lincoln ran up and down the line shouting encouragement and imploring his Pinkerton guards to join in: "Come on! We can do this!"

The buckets of water were holding the fire at bay, but we

were not making any progress in actually putting it out. As I stared at the fire, I thought back to our disastrous Christmas two years ago in Ripley. *Deja vu, General Beauregard had called it. What could I do to help? Of course!* I ran to Mrs. Carter and asked her what was in the bags behind the smokehouse. I grabbed the bucket off the back porch that had held the blue crab and ran around to the back.

"John!" Joseph yelled trying to catch up with me. Once he saw me filling the bucket from a bag I had ripped open, he asked, "How do you know that will work?"

"It's a trick I learned from the Ghost of Christmas Past," I yelled back as I glanced across the yard at Mr. Dickens tossing a bucket of water onto the fire. Joseph looked at me like I was crazy, but he set about searching for another container. Not seeing any alternatives, he pulled off his servant's jacket, turned it inside out, and began loading it from the bag after I had filled the bucket. "Mrs. Carter is going to kill you!" I said as I ran back to the stables. When I got inside, I threw the contents of the bucket onto the smoldering tree, the hay bales, and an area of fire that had spread out of the back corner. Joseph was right behind me as he shook out his jacket onto the flames. It blazed a bright orange before extinguishing immediately.

"It worked!" Joseph cried in triumph as the president and the bucket brigade crowded around in disbelief to see our sudden success.

"It's salt," Mrs. Carter declared to her soot-faced guests. "John is a genius!"

* * *

I joined Joseph in a newly generated salt-bucket brigade with Mrs. Carter. Between the water and the salt, we just about had the fire out. Just then, a horse-drawn fire engine labeled *Nantucket Fire Department* pulled into the yard carrying two old men and a young boy at the reins. They were met by the improbable sight of seven men, three women, and two boys completely covered in black soot all hugging and slapping each other on the back. "We did it! We saved the stables!" President Lincoln said with pure joy as he shook everyone's hand.

One of the old men hopped down from the wagon and walked over to Mrs. Carter. As he came out of the darkness, Mrs. Carter called out in surprise, "Mr. Early?"

"Yes, ma'am. I'm sorry we couldn't get here any quicker. We had loaned out the fire engine for the Christmas parade in town, and it took us awhile to find who had it."

Mrs. Carter stared at the fire engine. Something was tied on to the red metal panels on the side of the wagon. She asked, "Are those..."

"Yes, ma'am," Mr. Early said, "those are antlers. Our fire engine was Santa's sleigh in the parade, and those are the reindeer's antlers. We didn't have time to take them off when we saw the smoke coming from the inn." He looked towards the stables and said, "It looks like y'all got the fire out without us, though. I would be happy to come back up here after Christmas and help you repair the damage."

Miss Estelle was standing by Mrs. Carter, and she gave her a nudge on the arm. Mrs. Carter replied with a girlish lilt to her voice: "That is very nice of you to offer, Mr. Early. I would be most obliged for your help."

Mr. Early glanced around at the men standing near the

stables, moving towards them as he asked, "Say, is that…?"

Mr. Pinkerton quickly intercepted Mr. Early and said, "No, whatever you think you see… you don't." Even in the midst of this chaos, after hearing those words, I couldn't help but wonder, *Where is General Beauregard on this Christmas Eve?*

Mr. Pinkerton took Mr. Early by the crook of the elbow and steered him back to the fire engine. "We have this under control now," said Mr. Pinkerton as he practically lifted Mr. Early into the driver's seat. "Thank you for coming." As the wagon passed, I could see my blackened face reflected in the aluminum water tank mounted on the side. *I am again "el negro."*

When the wagon was out of earshot, Joseph's mother took her son aside and began fussing at him: "Joseph, you could have been killed! You are as reckless and foolhardy as your father! *Together*, you and John go rushing headlong in without thinking of anybody else."

Before she could really get going, however, President Lincoln walked up and patted her on the back. "Estelle, you have a brave son here. We all have him to thank for saving the horses." The president continued, "And we have John to thank for saving the stables. That was mighty quick thinking with that salt." He looked at me again, as if he was seeing me for the first time. "John," President Lincoln said looking deadly serious, "you look like you're ready for one of those god-awful minstrel shows." He roared with laughter at his own joke as he threw his arms around Mr. Marx and Mr. Darwin. "Let's go finish that dinner, boys."

Miss Estelle whispered to Joseph that they would continue their talk in her room that night, but for now she had to resume dinner. I went back into the stables to check if any fire remained. The only trouble spots were the scattered piles of manure in the stalls that flamed up now and then. The smell was horrible and made my eyes water. When I walked back to the corner where the fire started, something red caught my eye at the base of the skeletal remains of the Christmas tree. Tucked underneath the trunk, I discovered a piece of red fabric. I sniffed it, and it reeked of a sickly sweet, familiar scent. On his way to his mother's room, I whispered to Joseph to meet me in the hayloft at daybreak. "I've found something."

Joseph held up the telegram that had been delivered to the president. "So have I."

Excerpt from Joseph's journal dated December 25, 1862:

I slept fitfully last night, but right before I woke up, I had a dream. My father was riding on the track at the Hinds County Fairgrounds. Each year, the owners would allow slaves to come to the fair on the Tuesday afternoon before the fair opened on Wednesday. I was standing by my mother behind a fence on the backstretch of the track. She was wearing the same blue-floral cotton dress that she wore to the fair every year. She always wore her hair very simply, but today she had a blue hyacinth tucked behind her ear because it brought my father good luck.

My father wore green silks and was riding a huge chestnut mare. As he rounded the final turn and was heading down the long straightaway, he was in the lead by half a length. I took my mother's hand as we cheered him on. The jockey on the second-place horse wore a black bowler hat and a bright-red jersey. As they passed us, I could see smoke coming from the jockey's back. As he got closer to my father, he would reach out and strike my father's back with his whip. I could see the whip cut through my father's green shirt, but each time my father would slide further up the saddle until finally his head was down between the horse's ears. I closed my eyes to wish him on harder.

When I opened my eyes, it was me riding the horse, just like my father taught me. Leaning forward in the stirrups, I became a part of the horse. I closed my eyes as the dirt flew up and hit me in the face as I raced along the track. When I opened them again, I was rising into the air—the oval of the track receding further and further beneath me. I dipped my wings into an eastward glide and my eyes flickered open and shut as I sailed into the sun.

Then, I was back behind the fence holding my mother's hand. If my father won this race, he would have enough money to buy his own freedom. At the finish line, my father leaned forward as they crossed the line—a quarter of a length ahead of the man in the bowler hat. As my father approached the grandstand, his master stood in the shadows. He was tall and thin with a scraggly beard and wore an ill-fitting black suit. He looked at my father with those sad, dark eyes and said, "You're a free man." I woke up.

* * *

When I climbed up the chain to the hayloft, a thin sliver of sunlight was just shining through a crack in the stable wall. The light focused on the dandelion hair of my friend Joseph who was sitting on a hay bale in the middle of the loft writing in his journal. The smell of burned hay hung in the air like a veil. "I just had the most amazing dream," Joseph said.

Joseph let me read his journal entry, and he asked me, "What do you think it means?"

"I think it means you miss your father very much."

I took the tattered piece of red fabric out of my pocket and handed it to Joseph. "Smell this and see if you recognize it."

When Joseph held what was obviously a piece of a red scarf to his face, I thought he was going to pass out. His eyes rolled up and his jaw went slack. He stammered, "I could never forget this… It's the last thing I remember before I woke up in the tunnel."

"I saw Red Scarf slip out the front door of the inn when Mr. Pinkerton was distracted," I said, "and he must have taken the carriage out right before he started the fire with this piece of his scarf that he dipped in this "knockout" drug that must be highly flammable. All this time I thought it must be one of the guests from London—or even the president himself—who was *not who he pretends to be*. But it's one of President Lincoln's own men! Why is he doing this?"

Joseph took out the telegram and said, "This may help explain it:"

LONDON 24 DECEMBER 1862 15:32

I HAVE BEEN INDISCREET *STOP* *HF* KNOWS LIN-COLN WANTS TO END WAR *STOP* ALSO KNOWS ABOUT NANTUCKET *STOP* WILL DO ANYTHING TO KEEP LINCOLN FROM RECONSIDERING *STOP* *HF* IN CAHOOTS WITH *JD* *STOP* LINCOLN'S GUARDS COM-PROMISED *STOP*

GODSPEED,

NATHANIEL HAWTHORNE

"Who is *HF*?" I asked. "Wait a minute! How did you get the telegram?"

"When the fire started," Joseph said, "the president left it on the table. I do not think he even got the chance to finish reading it, but I did not want it to fall into the wrong hands."

"We don't know whose hands are right and whose are wrong. I want to ask Mrs. Blackwell about this chemical," I said, "but first, we need to go straight to President Lincoln."

When we walked into the kitchen, Miss Estelle was busy making breakfast for the guests. She began, "Merry Christmas, boys!" Then she got down to business: "Joseph, Mr. Darwin is looking for you. He said y'all were going to the beach—on Christmas Day of all days! I don't know what you two boys have been up to, but I know you've been in the stables. I can smell the smoke on you."

She pulled a sheet of biscuits out of the oven and laid them on the table to cool. The smell of the biscuits was making my mouth water. She saw us longing for them, but she said sharply, "Y'all's breakfast time has come and gone. Joseph, I need firewood—now. This food is not going to cook itself."

Joseph ran out the back door and began loading firewood into his arms. I quickly joined him *because we are a team.* When we went back in the kitchen with our arms full, Joseph's mother softened a bit. She seemed to have forgotten about being upset with Joseph last night.

"That's plenty of wood. Now you boys stay out of trouble," she said with a nod and a wink. *If she only knew.*

When we were out of the kitchen, Joseph asked me, "Is it all right if I go to the beach with Mr. Darwin?" He was already headed up the stairs to Mr. Darwin's room.

"Of course, I think you should. We need to play this as close to the vest as possible so we don't draw attention to ourselves. I will try and talk to President Lincoln."

As I walked through the entrance foyer, I looked out the front door and saw Mr. Dickens and Mr. Marx sitting side-by-side in rockers on the front porch. Perhaps wanting to postpone divulging our conspiracy ideas to the president, I stepped out to the front porch to ask our two guests if they needed anything.

Mr. Dickens looked up from the writing he was doing in a leather-bound journal and smiled. "Merry Christmas and thank you for the offer, John, but I'm happy as a clam sitting here with my new friend on this beautiful morning."

"It *is* a beautiful Christmas morning," laughed Mr. Marx as he looked up from the newspaper he was reading, "even if I choose not to acknowledge this peculiar holiday." As he talked, I could read the main headline of the *Boston Daily Journal* that lay in his lap: "What Will Be Economic Impact of Loss of Slavery in the South?"

The front door opened behind me, and Joseph and Mr. Darwin stepped out. "Good morning to you all," said Mr. Darwin, "and Merry Christmas! Joseph and I are first headed for a holiday exploration to an inland wildlife sanctuary where my late friend John James Audubon was inspired to create some of his most beautiful paintings in his *Birds of America*." They waved goodbye as they walked down the front porch steps towards the street. *The writer, the economist, and the scientist*, I thought. *Can these three men change the president's mind about the war?*

Mr. Pinkerton was standing outside the library, and through the slightly parted doors, I could see the president sitting behind the desk of the library. He was signing papers with his reading glasses precariously perched on his long nose. As I approached, Mr. Pinkerton—the ever-present watchdog—said formally, "Good morning, John. I hope you are well this fine Christmas morning."

I can't wait. "Yes, sir. I need to talk to President Lincoln."

Chapter 23

Mr. Pinkerton smiled patiently and replied, "The president is extremely busy this morning. I am sure he could see you later today—"

But before he could finish, President Lincoln called out through the doors: "Nonsense, Allan. Send John in."

Mr. Pinkerton closed the doors behind me as I entered the library, and the president motioned for me to sit down. There was a soft, red leather armchair across from the desk, and when I sat, my feet no longer touched the floor. "That was quite an adventure last night, John," President Lincoln said. "I was so exhausted afterwards, I fell asleep with my boots on. I haven't slept that well in years. And I woke up this morning thinking about Miss Estelle's biscuits." There was a plate full of biscuits and honey and a pot of coffee sitting on the desk. My mouth started watering again. As the president poured himself a cup of coffee, I couldn't help but read a letter that was right in front of me on the desktop.

Executive Mansion-December 23, 1862

Dear Fanny,

It is with deep grief that I learn of the death of your kind and brave Father; and, especially, that it is affecting your young heart beyond what is common in such cases. In this sad world of ours, sorrow comes to all; and, to the young, it comes with bitterest agony, because it takes them unawares. The older have learned to ever expect it. I am anxious to afford some alleviation of your present distress. Perfect relief is not possible, except with time. You can not now realize that you will ever feel better. Is not this so?

Before I could finish reading, Mr. Pinkerton picked up the letter and addressed the president: "Is this the letter you began the other day?"

"Mmm… Yes, Allan," President Lincoln answered as he laid his cup down after a long, moaning sip of coffee. "I just finished it. Would you see that it gets posted promptly?"

"Of course, Mr. President. I'll step outside and leave you with John, unless you need anything else."

"Thank you, Allan. I'm good for now." After Mr. Pinkerton left, President Lincoln resumed our conversation: "I'm just glad no one got hurt last night, and all the horses made it out. John, you were mighty brave in last night's accident. Now what can I help you with?"

"That's why I'm here, sir. It wasn't an accident."

"What do you mean, John?"

I took out the letter that had fallen off the porch, the charred paper I had found in the fireplace, the telegram, and the piece of burned red scarf and laid them on the desk. When President Lincoln saw the scarf, he immediately got up and went to the door of the library, summoning Mr. Pinkerton back into the room.

I didn't know how to say this—I was a fourteen-year-old runaway talking to the President of the United States—but I had to try: "Uh, Mr. President, can I talk to you alone?"

President Lincoln smiled and said, "John, I trust Mr. Pinkerton with my life every day. In fact, he has saved it more than once."

As Mr. Pinkerton came into the room, he too saw the red scarf and asked sharply, "Where did you find that?"

I told them about finding the scarf under the burnt Christmas tree and the suspicions I had when I saw the president's carriage already out of the burning stables.

President Lincoln nodded to Mr. Pinkerton to respond: "When we woke up this morning," Mr. Pinkerton began, "Jack Burton—the man who was wearing the red scarf—was nowhere to be found. Our rifle is missing also, but luckily, I had the ammo locked up. He tried to blame the fire on Joseph last night. He said that Black stable boy probably left a lantern burning." Mr. Pinkerton then saw the letter and the telegram, and all remaining friendliness left his voice: "How did you get those?"

"Now wait a minute, Allan," President Lincoln interrupted. "There's no need in using that tone of voice. John has come to *us*. Now start at the beginning and tell us how you got all of this." President Lincoln took off his reading glasses and looked directly into my eyes. There was definite concern on his face, but his eyes were not cold and dark like when I met him last night. They were alert and alive.

So I began with the letter that Mr. Longfellow had given Mr. Pinkerton—*One of the men is not who he pretends to be*—and how it had dropped from his pocket off the porch. "I have been searching for that everywhere!" Mr. Pinkerton said with exasperation. I next explained how I had found the charred paper in the fireplace and how Joseph had made the cryptic message visible: *DELAY. OBSTRUCT. DECEIVE.*

Finally, I got to the telegram that Joseph had taken when the fire began—*LINCOLN'S GUARDS COMPROMISED.*

President Lincoln looked perplexed as he said, "I understand why you wanted to talk to me alone, but I can assure you with all my being that this doesn't refer to Allan."

"Who are *HF* and *JD?*" I asked.

"We don't know, John," Mr. Pinkerton said quietly as if someone else might be listening. "Mr. Longfellow was so distraught after hearing of his son's death that he couldn't help us at all. I didn't know what to think when the telegram disappeared last night."

President Lincoln shook his head as if to clear his mind. "John," he said, "we again have you to thank for bringing us this information. But I'm beginning to understand what Joseph's mother was talking about last night. Y'all do tend to rush into things, and you're going to find yourself in over your head sometime if you're not careful. You and Joseph need to forget about all of this amateur sleuthing and leave it to the professionals. Mr. Pinkerton has been a detective for twenty years. He will get to the bottom of this. And I'm sure we've seen the last of Jack Burton. He was probably on the first ferry off the island this morning." President Lincoln reached his hand across the desk and took mine. "Thank you again for coming to us, John. Now go spend Christmas with your friends like a boy your age is supposed to do."

When I walked out of the library and back out to the front porch, Joseph and Mr. Darwin were already back from their inland exploration. Now Joseph was grabbing the buckets and hand shovels from his seashell collection and loading them into his orange and white fannah basket. Joseph called out, "John, would you like to come with us to the beach?"

Mr. Darwin echoed Joseph: "Please, John. We would love to have you along. I have been telling Joseph that I have a new theory that seeds can survive a flight across the ocean in the gut of a seagull, explaining how the same plants show up in England and America." So, I ran back to the kitchen and asked Miss Estelle if it was okay for me to also go to the beach on Christmas.

"Sure, John," Miss Estelle answered. "Why should Joseph have all the fun?" I grabbed my overcoat from the hook in the foyer and ran to join my friends like *I'm supposed to do*.

* * *

We walked down the drive of the inn just as a soft snow began to fall. We continued on North Water Street until we turned onto Easton Street which ran towards the harbor. On the corner of Easton and North Beach Street stood a small one-story post-and-beam building with weathered, gray-shingled walls and white trim. "This is where my mother and I go to church," Joseph told Mr. Darwin. "It's called the African Meeting House."

"Do you attend school here as well?" Mr. Darwin asked.

"No, sir. John and I go to the same school at the Quaker Meeting House."

"What do you like to study?" the ever-curious scientist inquired.

"I like math and science," answered Joseph, "but I especially like to write."

"I like to read more than anything," I answered. "I love to read about history and geography and exotic places. Sorry, but I'm not very good at science."

"Nonsense," said Mr. Darwin. "Your idea to use the salt last night was brilliant. And besides," Mr. Darwin said as he winked at both of us, "you just haven't had the right teacher yet." We continued walking along the cobblestones of North Beach Street, which was lined with brick-and-shingle shops, taverns, and Victorian homes all the way down to Jetties Beach. Red ribbons were tied to the gas lampposts along with boughs of holly and mistletoe.

Mr. Darwin was particularly interested in the storefront window displays featuring the nativity scene in different sizes and styles. "I've never seen the birth of Jesus commercialized in such a way," he observed. Though it was Christmas morning, there were still quite a few people out strolling in the increasing snow. A block ahead of us, a group of carolers was singing, "Hark the Herald Angels Sing" to a gathering of people. One man, however, walked right past them with his head down and his hands in his pockets. He wore a black bowler hat. *Jack Burton.*

I did not have time to explain, and I didn't want to alarm Mr. Darwin, so I whispered to Joseph that I would meet them back at the inn. I quickly crossed the street so that I would have a better angle to follow Jack Burton. I think that Joseph then saw him, too, because he suddenly stopped and began an animated discussion with Mr. Darwin about the contents of a butcher shop storefront window. As Jack Burton moved along the street, I stayed in the shadows about a half block behind. He stopped several times to nervously check his pocket watch, so I assumed he had an appointment to meet someone. Maybe it was *HF* and *JD.*

As the snowfall grew thicker, I became bolder in my pursuit. I was only about thirty yards behind him when he turned into Coal Alley behind the Nantucket Playhouse. There was a carriage parked at the rear stage door with the stationary driver and horses suddenly finding themselves covered in snow. I entered the dark alley and hid behind a seedy tavern's garbage cans. The smell of rotting fish made me want to gag, but I forgot about that as something furry brushed across my leg. I pictured a huge rat like the ones you always see on Whaler's Wharf, but it was just a scrawny tabby cat looking for dinner. It reminded me of the empty feeling I felt in my stomach—I didn't know whether it was fear or that I hadn't eaten anything all day.

The cat jumped on top of one of the cans, knocking a bottle onto the alley cobblestones. Jack Burton turned around and began walking back towards the mouth of the alley where I was hiding. I pushed myself against the damp and grimy brick wall of the tavern and got as low behind the cans as I could. Still, he kept approaching. I clicked my tongue at the cat, only causing him to look back at me with bored, hungry eyes. As quietly as I could, I hissed *Shooo* at the cat, and he sprung off the can into the middle of the alley. Jack Burton jumped, but he stopped walking. He reached into his pocket to check the time again as I held my breath in the shadows. Finally, he retreated back into the alley as a sound came from the rear of the theater.

A well-dressed man with dark hair and a mustache came out the stage door and started gesturing dramatically to Jack Burton. Though I couldn't hear what they were saying, their conversation quickly turned into a heated argument with the well-dressed man pushing Jack Burton into the carriage by the stage door. They started down the end of the alley and turned on South Water Street. Despite my previous "tailing" success in New Orleans, there was no way I could keep up with the carriage on foot, so I just had to take the chance that they were heading for the ferry which left from the end of Broad Street.

I ran through every back alley and shortcut I knew. The cold air was burning my lungs, but I kept pushing as hard as I could. Once, as I sprinted around a wagon full of flowers and baskets of fruit, I thought I caught a glimpse of the carriage at the end of another alley. The streets began to turn slushy with snow and ice as I scuttled under a tall tree turned on its side that two men were carrying into a church on Easy Street. Finally, when I emerged onto Broad Street, I saw the well-dressed man jump out of the carriage as it came to a halt at the ferry dock.

I stayed low behind a wall and got up right behind the carriage, waiting for Jack Burton to step out. As I waited, I watched the well-dressed man run up the wide gangway and jump onto the ferry. The ferry stationmaster was ringing the bell loudly to let everyone know that the ferry was leaving. I looked at the clock by the bell and it was ten o'clock. There was a chalkboard beneath the bell with a handwritten notice that the ferry would only be having two crossings on Christmas Day: ten o'clock and four o'clock.

Still no sign of Jack Burton. I climbed over the wall and crept up to the carriage door. I felt another sense of *déjà vu* as I thought back to inching my way to the toolshed at the house on Flood Street. *Please, God, on Christmas, do not make me relive that disappointment again.* Rising up, inch by inch, I peeked into the window.

Oh, no! The carriage was empty.

* * *

While the carriage driver was distracted talking to a woman who had just arrived on the ferry, I opened the door and climbed into the carriage. The only thing left in it was a long, cheap sheet of paper lying on one of the leather seats. It was a playbill from the Boston Museum Theatre for a play called *The Apostate.* The lead actor was pictured in the center of the playbill as playing the villain, *Duke Pescara.* It was definitely the same well-dressed man I had seen arguing with Jack Burton before they got into the carriage. I looked down the cast of characters, and the part of the villain was played by John Wilkes Booth.

As I walked alone back to the inn, I thought about all the clues which Joseph and I had found in the last two days. *I wish Joseph was here right now. I have so many ideas I would like to bounce off him.* These weren't just hypothetical clues that might be the products of two teenage boys' overactive imaginations. *DELAY. OBSTRUCT. DECEIVE* had already been put into action. There was no other way to interpret the fire in the stables last night. None of the clues fit together, however. It was like a jigsaw puzzle that was missing pieces. It seemed obvious that Jack Burton worked for or with John Wilkes Booth, but there was no *HF* or *JD* in Booth's name. Nevertheless, something gnawed at me the more and more I thought about it. Nathaniel Hawthorne sent an urgent telegram to Henry Wadsworth Longfellow warning him that *HF* would do *anything to keep Lincoln from reconsidering* his decision to stop the war. Hawthorne and Longfellow and *HF.* They had to have all known each other.

I knew of Nathaniel Hawthorne from Mr. Herman's satchel

of books. I had read *The Scarlet Letter*, but I had no idea that Hawthorne was also a diplomat until we had found the note beneath the porch. I had never read anything by Longfellow other than listening to my teacher recite "Paul Revere's Ride" in our Ripley school house. *Is it possible that HF is another writer?*

When I walked into the inn, Christmas Day was continuing on as if nothing unusual had happened. Mrs. Carter was dusting in the sitting room outside the library where President Lincoln continued to work. I had cleaned everything the day before, so I suspected that Mrs. Carter was snooping, a skill at which she was most accomplished. She said that Joseph and Mr. Darwin had not come back from the beach yet, even though it continued to snow outside. I walked back to the kitchen to see if Miss Estelle needed any help, but she shooed me away like an unwanted alley cat.

There was a wall in the sitting room that featured many paintings, lithographs, and photographs of the Carter House Inn. I passed by this wall ten times a day, but I had stopped paying any attention to the pictures long ago. *But not today.* In an arrangement of signed testimonials hung a daguerreotype of three men standing in front of the parlor fireplace. In the ghostly, silver-tinted picture, the man on the left had a long full beard and looked vaguely familiar. In the center, stood a thin, delicate man with a neatly trimmed mustache. The man on the right had a head full of dark hair and smiled broadly as he held up his wine glass to the camera. The hand-signed inscription at the bottom read, "Mrs. Carter, thank you for a lovely week. Best wishes from the Bowdoin Boys—*HWL, NH, and HF*" It was dated March 13, 1857.

"Mrs. Carter," I asked. "Who are the people in this picture?"

She took the picture off the wall so that she could hold it in the light of a wall lantern. She thought a minute before she replied. "Why that's Mr. Longfellow, who you met the other day, Mr. Hawthorne, and President Pierce. They came here together about five years ago."

"What do they mean by the *Bowdoin Boys?*" I asked.

"They were all classmates at Bowdoin College in Maine in the 20s, and they've stayed close friends ever since," she answered.

I looked at the daguerreotype closely again before asking, "I understand that Henry Wadsworth Longfellow is *HWL*, and Nathaniel Hawthorne is *NH*, but who is *HF?*" I remembered learning in school about President Pierce, and his name was *Franklin Pierce. FP?*

Mrs. Carter closed her eyes as she thought about this, and a broad smile came to her face. She leaned her head in towards me and spoke in hushed tones so that no one would overhear: "To be honest, John, President Pierce seemed to like his wine very much. If I remember right, he was still upset about not being re-nominated by his party for president, and he was drowning his sorrows with alcohol." She gave a girlish giggle as she continued, "But he was a really happy drunk. And the vainest man I have ever met. He got Flora, one of my housemaids at the time, to brush his hair before bed each night. So, Mr. Longfellow and Mr. Hawthorne started calling him 'Handsome Frank,' and I think President Pierce liked it." *HF—Handsome Frank.*

Is it possible that an ex-President of the United States is responsible for a conspiracy against the current president? I had already imposed on the president once this morning, and I felt guilty asking again. *But this can't wait!*

I entreated Mrs. Carter to approach President Lincoln and Mr. Pinkerton to see if I might talk to them again immediately. "Is it that important?" she asked.

"It *can't wait.* I think it may be a matter of life and death."

I heard her *knock* on the door of the library and saw her stick her head in before asking in her typically loud voice, "Mr. President, I am so sorry to interrupt you, but John says he needs to speak to you urgently."

"Send him in, Mrs. Carter. Mr. Pinkerton and I were finishing up anyway."

I walked into the library carrying the picture from the wall as Mrs. Carter retreated from the door. Again, I thought, *There isn't a minute to waste.* "I think I know who *HF* is."

Chapter 24

As I related my story of following Jack Burton through town to his meeting with John Wilkes Booth and what Mrs. Carter told me about the picture, President Lincoln's eyes grew wide. Mr. Pinkerton nodded slowly as he listened. When I finished with my theory about *HF*, the president looked at Mr. Pinkerton and asked, "Do you think this is possible?"

"Yes, Mr. President," said Mr. Pinkerton, "I think that John has done an extraordinary job of doing what I am supposed to do. When I first read the telegram from Hawthorne to Longfellow, I thought of Pierce because he was the one that appointed Hawthorne to his post as consul. However, *HF* threw me off course, and Longfellow was in no condition to help me with it. But now a lot of the pieces of the puzzle start to fit. I think that Hawthorne still feels a strong loyalty to his friend Pierce, so he used a code—*HF*—that only Longfellow would understand. I think he also was hoping that his suspicions were wrong."

President Lincoln asked, "What do we know about what the esteemed ex-President Pierce has been up to lately?" His voice dripped with irony.

"Not much," replied Mr. Pinkerton, "but as you know, Jefferson Davis was his Secretary of War when he was president, and the telegram must mean that Pierce is in cahoots with Davis, or *JD*. Pierce is from Vermont, but everyone called him a 'doughface,' a Northerner with Southern sympathies. I'm afraid he may be conspiring with the Confederates against you."

"Is there anything more concrete tying him to this?" asked President Lincoln.

Mr. Pinkerton pondered this for a second and a startled look appeared in his eye. "I just realized, sir, that it was Pierce's ex-chief of staff who recommended Jack Burton to me. He said Burton had served in President Pierce's security detail and had done an excellent job."

I was reluctant to speak up, but I added, "If President Pierce had been here five years ago, he would know everything about the inn. He could have told Jack Burton all about the stables."

President Lincoln asked Mr. Pinkerton, "What do we know about this Booth character?"

Mr. Pinkerton answered, "I have heard of him—he is a well-known Southern sympathizer—but he has never been seen as a threat before. We have heard rumors of a clandestine meeting earlier this year in Montreal among sympathizers, and Booth may have been there. Supposedly this group has been trying to recruit ex-slaves to infiltrate the Underground Railroad, but Harriet Tubman has outsmarted them so far. I need to telegraph my friends in Vermont to see if Pierce is in with this bunch."

"Speaking of the Underground Railroad, John," the president said, "what did Allan mean when he said they had discovered yours and Joseph's involvement with the Railroad?"

I began by recounting the meeting we were summoned to

at the Quaker Meeting House where we were questioned by Deborah's parents, the Quaker elders, and more importantly, Mr. Thoreau and Harriet Tubman.

"John," President Lincoln interrupted with a laugh, "I'm beginning to think I need to hire you as my social director. Is there anybody important that you *don't* know? And, by the way, did Mrs. Tubman happen to share her opinion of me to you? It is *not* kind at all."

I blushed as I thought of an appropriate answer to ribbing from the President of the United States. This good-natured conversation veered suddenly darker when I told President Lincoln about Joseph's and my encounters with the Reverse Underground Railroad.

"I've always thought rumors of that were just devious ways to scare Black people into further submission," the president said as he shook his head. "It is impossible to underestimate the evil that exists in this country under the guise of commerce."

There was a soft knock on the door, and Mrs. Blackwell stuck her head in. "Mr. President, I apologize for the interruption, but it's time for your medicine."

"No need to apologize, Elizabeth. You've saved John from having to endure another one of my sermons." The president sat passively down at the desk and swallowed the blue pills that his physician handed to him.

While I had the opportunity, I retrieved the piece of the red scarf from the desk and handed it to the surprised doctor. "Excuse me, ma'am," I said, "but you are the only person I know that could help. Do you recognize the smell in this?"

"Of course, I can," she said. "I noticed it the second I walked into the library, but I couldn't imagine what the source of the smell was… It's ether. It's the most common anesthetic used by doctors now prior to surgery."

"So, it knocks you out?" I asked crudely.

"Oh, yes. It brings on a state of deep unconsciousness almost instantaneously."

"Is it also flammable?"

"Highly," she replied. "The safe storage of ether is always a concern because of the danger of fire. Doctors are using chloroform more and more to avoid this risk."

"Well, Allan," said the president, "What do we do about Jack Burton for now?"

Mr. Pinkerton replied, "I stake my entire reputation on the integrity of my other man, Paul." *Rifleman—but now without his rifle.* "I will have him make rounds about the inn property. But it's Christmas Day, and we are on an island thirty miles from the mainland, so reinforcements are out of the question. For now—we keep our eyes and ears open."

We heard a disturbance outside the door, and I recognized Joseph's imploring voice: "Mrs. Carter, I *have* to talk to John."

* * *

Joseph and Mr. Darwin came through the library doors, stopping dead in their tracks when they saw who else was in the room. "I'm so sorry to interrupt, Mr. President," apologized Mr. Darwin, "but we've just seen the man who started the fire." I looked at Joseph—he was supposed to keep what we knew a secret—but he threw his hands up in the air. Mr. Darwin's face crinkled as he sniffed loudly. "Why am I smelling ether?"

Mrs. Blackwell showed him the piece of the red scarf and

explained how Jack Burton had dipped it in ether to start the fire in the stables. "How do you know the smell of ether?" she asked Mr. Darwin.

"I've used it for a long time with my specimen jars when collecting insects. I've searched for a more humane method—if *humane* is even the right word in reference to bugs—but I haven't found one yet. Where would Jack Burton have been able to get it?"

"Unfortunately," said Mrs. Blackwell, "the war is making ether and chloroform essential commodities on the battlefield, so the Union Army has been contracting with big private labs, like Squibb's, to manufacture it in bulk."

"Also, unfortunately," added President Lincoln, "I have been making too frequent visits to these same battlefields to visit our wounded, and I've been accompanied by Allan, Paul, and Jack Burton. He could have grabbed the ether anywhere along the way."

With a twinkle in his eye, it was obvious that Mr. Darwin was now intrigued: "Doctor Blackwell, how is it that you are so knowledgeable about the Union's drug ordering?"

The president abruptly intervened. "This is strictly classified, Mr. Darwin, but Mrs. Blackwell, along with her sister Emily, and Clara Barton, have been spearheading my administration's efforts to create a functioning nursing corps for the battlefields."

"I'm so sorry, Mr. President," apologized Mr. Darwin. "I didn't mean to stick my nose where it doesn't belong."

"That's quite all right, Charles," reassured the president. "Now tell us more about what you and Joseph saw."

"I originally saw Jack Burton right after John did, but we agreed not to alarm anyone until later on," Joseph explained.

"While Mr. Darwin and I were on our way to the beach, however, we both saw Jack Burton slide out the side door of a carriage. It was obvious he was trying to avoid detection by someone."

"That would be me," I answered sheepishly, "and he was successful. I continued following the carriage—thinking he was in it—all the way to the ferry dock. When the other man got out of the carriage to board the ferry, I snuck up to look in the window, only to find that the carriage was now empty."

"Do *we* know who the other man in the carriage was?" asked Mr. Darwin, obviously wanting to be included on our detective team.

"Yes," answered Mr. Pinkerton, the only *true* detective in the room. "He appears to be John Wilkes Booth, an actor with known Confederate leanings. We know this because of John's stellar detective work." I couldn't help blushing again.

"*Booth*, you say?" inquired Mr. Darwin as he scrunched his face again in deep thought. "I once saw a *Junius Brutus Booth*—who could ever forget that name—perform *Richard III* in Covent Garden. He was famous at the time in his Mother England, but I believe the bottle got the best of him, and he ended up moving to America. I wonder if John Wilkes Booth might be his son?" Joseph looked at me with subtle bemusement as he tried to get Mr. Darwin's tangential narrative back on track.

"John," Joseph interjected, "Jack Burton's method of escaping the carriage reminded me so much of how we snuck out of the police wagon when we were trying to leave New Orleans. Instead of a trap door in the floor, however, he waited until the carriage was pulled up right beside a wagon that was unloading sacks of flour at a bakery. He opened the side door of the carriage just enough to slither out, then dropped to the road and rolled under the wagon. If you were on the opposite side of the carriage, it would have been impossible to see him leave."

I was, and I didn't.

"After he rolled out the other side of the wagon," Joseph continued, "we followed him until he turned down an alley."

Mr. Darwin jumped back into the narrative: "Mr. Burton *was* kind enough to keep his bowler hat on, so he had a very distinctive silhouette. He ignored the most basic rule of survival in the wild—like a chameleon, you must adapt your appearance to your environment. But I don't think he was thinking clearly, because fear was literally written all over Burton's face."

"How so?" asked Mr. Pinkerton with growing interest.

"Ever since prehistoric times," answered Mr. Darwin in professorial tones, "humans have responded to being scared with an open mouth. I believe that this allows a person to breathe more freely in preparation for fight or flight. Mr. Burton was definitely in *flight* mode this morning as he seemed to be constantly gasping for air, but..."

"But *what?*" asked the detective.

"We think he's getting ready to fight," answered Joseph. "After we watched Red Scarf—I mean Mr. Burton—turn down that dark alley, we heard glass break, and we found a box pulled up to a broken window on the back of the building. We went around front to see what kind of shop it was. You're not going to like this... It was a gun shop."

* * *

There was another gentle tap on the doors, and Mrs. Carter stuck her head in to announce, "Mr. President, all the other guests are in the dining room. Christmas lunch is served." I suddenly remembered who was supposed to be serving it, and Joseph and I rushed back to the kitchen. We started apologizing as soon as we passed through the kitchen door, but Joseph's mother was too busy to have any of it.

"I'm sure you've been off saving the world from all those bad people you like to read about, but for now I need the both of you to wash your hands and put on aprons." We did as we were told. I filled eight bowls with Miss Estelle's version of New England clam chowder. It was hot and thick and creamy, and that empty feeling came back into my stomach as I took the soup out to the guests. Mr. Pinkerton was not at the table, however, so I returned one bowl to the kitchen. Miss Estelle had cooled off, and she asked me, "John, have you had anything to eat today?"

"No, ma'am."

"Well, I have things under control just now," she said, "so sit down and eat your soup."

Joseph joined me at the table, and his mother ladled another bowl for him. As we sat there, Joseph's mother told us about the first Christmas that she could remember: "I must have been about five years old, and me and my mamma were owned by a mean old coot who ran a boarding house down by the river in New Or-lins. Mamma and I used to cook for the sailors who stayed in the house, and Lord, what a melting pot of people we had. There were Creoles, Chinamen, Spanish, French, Indians, and Africans. That first Christmas that I can remember, all these sailors had been lying around drinking all day—feeling sad because they were away from their families on Christmas—when they decided they were going to see the new steamboat that had just begun running into New Orlins. Our master had been drinking with them and had long since passed out, so we walked down to the Pontchartrain docks with the sailors, who sang ragged Christmas carols in all different languages."

"It was nighttime when we got there, and we could just see the boat coming down the river. It had brightly colored streamers hanging from all the rails and bunches of large, burning candles inside red-and-green glass hurricane globes sitting on the decks. It looked like a wild celebration going on board the boat—there was loud music and people dancing on deck.

"As my mother and I watched it, I still remember thinking that Christmas was part of a world I would never know. As the boat was passing right in front of us, someone must have kicked a candle over, and a fire started at the rear of the boat. The streamers on the rails caught, and the fire raced to the front of the boat. The sailors from the boarding house were all so drunk that they just whooped and hollered as the blazing boat passed—like it was all part of the Christmas show.

"Then the fire must have gotten into the engine room because the boat exploded into a thousand pieces. Some of the sailors jumped in the water to help, but I don't think they got anybody out alive. Looking back, it was all very sad… just tragic." Miss Estelle smiled at us with a far-off look in her eye. "That was a Christmas to remember."

Joseph had obviously been as hungry as me as he listened to his mother's story in silence. When he reached the bottom of the bowl, however, his eyes perked up like they did when he had a fresh thought. "That reminds me of when John and I were leaving the harbor in Charleston on that whaling ship," he said. "We had waited around on deck for the longest time for our ship to get permission to leave, so I was only half awake when I felt us move in the water. Suddenly, the night sky lit up, and I thought the ship had exploded, but it was Fort Sumter getting shelled."

I had just finished my second bowl of chowder when we heard the bell ring from the dining room. Joseph's mother had prepared a traditional holiday dinner of Cornish hens with a sausage and chestnut stuffing, sweet potatoes, and mustard greens.

The Cornish hens resembled miniature turkeys with their glossy, golden skins and tiny, splayed drumsticks. Bubbling droplets of butter twinkled in the candlelight as they sizzled out of the birds that had just come out of the oven. The stuffing, which Joseph and I had helped mix, smelled of the smokehouse and of the verdancy of a rainy forest in the fall. The redolent orange of the sweet potatoes was speckled with a dusting of cinnamon and brown sugar that Miss Estelle applied from her palm with precise circular motions of her thumb and forefinger. All this sweetness contrasted with the vinegar and pepper sauce that she had drizzled over the mustard greens. As we carried Miss Estelle's food out, I thought, *This is a meal prepared with love.*

Joseph and I served each of the plates to the assembled guests and were heading back into the kitchen when President Lincoln spoke: "Joseph, please ask your mother to come out here."

We told her that the president wanted to see her, and she nervously checked her hair on the bottom of a shiny pot hanging on the wall. She said, "I'm not at all dressed for this…"

but Mrs. Carter came back and convinced her to join everyone in the dining room.

"Miss Estelle," the president said, "it would be our honor to have you and Joseph and John join us for this feast. Let us all stand and join hands to give thanks for this meal we are about to receive." As we stood around the table, I felt Mrs. Carter's warm hand take my left hand into hers, while Mrs. Blackwell took my right. I looked across the table where President Lincoln's long, thin fingers wrapped around Miss Estelle's hand. She grasped Joseph's left hand and held it tightly like a lifeline. Even though it had been two years, I saw Joseph instinctively lift his right hand. He held it in the air for a single, hopeful moment, then let it drop to his side.

PART SIX: The Christmas Meeting
(December 25, 1862)

Interlude: Oxford, Mississippi (1922)

T he old man sat up in bed and reached for the water glass on his bedside table. He had been talking nonstop for the last hour, and his throat was parched. A cool breeze blew in through the open French door that looked out onto Courthouse Square. He could hear a radio outside broadcasting the play-by-play of the Giants-Yankees World Series game. *My vision may be about gone, but I can still hear.*

"Mr. Falkner, let me help you with that," said Betty, the young, brunette-bobbed stenographer that his grandson had hired to take down the details of his *humdinger* of a story.

"I can get it just fine, Betty, and as I tell you every time, my name is *John*."

She sat back down in the chair beside the bed and situated her steno pad in her lap with her pencil ready.

After a long sip of water, the old man cleared his throat and asked, "Where did I leave off?"

"Y'all had all just given thanks for your Christmas lunch."

He remembered back for a moment, but he was not ready to continue. Instead, he looked across the bed at Betty poised to write and asked, "Do you use shorthand to write down what I'm saying?"

"I do, Mr. Fal— I mean, John," she stumbled. "Then I go home and transcribe my shorthand into regular text."

"Where did you learn shorthand?" he asked.

"I went to secretarial school in Tupelo during the war."

"Did you know that Charles Dickens wrote in shorthand?"

"No, sir. How do you know that?"

"He gave me notes that he had taken of the meeting on Christmas afternoon with the president as he was leaving Nantucket. He said that 'ocean voyages are always risky,' and he wanted someone to have a record of what was discussed. When I looked at the notes with him, it looked like chicken scratch to me. He laughed and called it *the devil's handwriting*, but he assured me I could figure it out 'if it ever became necessary.'"

"Did it? I mean, did you ever figure it out?" asked Betty.

"I did. I never told Billy this, but this story I'm dictating to you is not the first time I ever wrote about the Christmas meeting. When I still had illusions of being a writer, I started college in Boston after the Civil War and took an English class my first year. The professor assigned us the task of writing an autobiographical piece about a pivotal moment in our life. I had kept the story of President Lincoln's meeting with Charles Dickens, Charles Darwin, and Karl Marx a secret for over five years, but I felt like it was a story that now ought to be told. I retrieved Mr. Dickens's notes from the trunk under my bed in my dormitory room and holed up in the university library for an entire weekend until I had broken the 'Dickens Code.'"

"How did you do that?"

"His shorthand method was actually an existing system called *brachygraphy*, and once I located a book on that in the library, I was able to translate his notes. I had recently seen a three-act stage adaptation of *Uncle Tom's Cabin* on campus, and it was just god-awful. I half expected the Professor and O'Malley to walk out on stage in blackface at any time. Harriet Beecher Stowe was in the audience, and she looked like she wanted to hide under her seat. I decided I could write a better play than that, so my autobiographical piece became a three-act play called *The Christmas Meeting* in which each act featured one of President Lincoln's guests. With Mr. Dickens's notes, it wasn't that hard to write, and I turned it in to my professor that Monday."

"And?"

"When the professor returned our graded writings, he had given me a *C+*. He said that the basic premise of the play was *preposterous*. The idea that these men would have ever gotten together was 'not even remotely believable,' and besides—the assignment was to write about a pivotal moment in *our* life. He said I wasn't even a character in the play."

"What did you say to the professor?"

"I told him that this was not just a pivotal moment in *my* life, but it was pivotal for everyone who calls themself an American."

"Did that change your professor's mind?"

"He told me I should give up on the idea of being a writer, so I switched to law school instead. That eventually led me to come back to Oxford to start that bank across the square. So, my secret remained intact for another fifty years."

"Did you save your play?" Betty asked.

"It's in the trunk under this bed."

Chapter 25

ACT I: *It is one o'clock in the afternoon on Christmas Day, 1862, in the parlor of the Carter House Inn. Charles Darwin and Karl Marx are seated on a sofa, while Abraham Lincoln and Charles Dickens are seated in armchairs flanking a fireplace. There is no one else in the room.*

LINCOLN: Now that we have shared that splendid Christmas meal prepared by Miss Estelle, it is time for us to get down to business. To put it bluntly, the Union war effort is going poorly. I replaced that idiot McClellan with General Burnside, but we have yet to see an improvement. The calamity at Antietam three months ago was just repeated at Fredericksburg where we suffered more than 13,000 casualties. In the Mexican War, the total number of American deaths on the battlefield was 1,733. As commander-in-chief, I have to ask myself, how many more brave men am I willing to sacrifice in a futile effort to end slavery? When I arrived here, I had reached the conclusion that our splintered nation had sacrificed enough.

Some things have changed since we arrived here in Nantucket, however. We have learned that the fire in the stables last night was deliberately set. There are people who will do anything to keep us from having this meeting that you have so graciously consented to attend at my request. These people think that I am now committed to ending the war, and they are trying to prevent me from changing my mind. In this sense, however, their plan has backfired. I am more determined than ever to seek out your thoughts and ideas about the future of this war and this country. You are the smartest people in the world that I know, and you have been very outspoken on your beliefs about slavery, so before I decide anything, I want to hear from *my* "three wise men."

It is my firm belief that it is slavery that has torn our nation apart, and the issue of slavery must be resolved once and for all if we are again to have peace. Though I issued a preliminary proclamation of emancipation of the slaves in September, I am fully prepared to rescind that executive order if it will bring peace. America is at a crossroads, and unfortunately, so is my presidency. Maybe together, we can decide on a path to restoring this fractured nation to its inherent greatness. Who would like to begin?

DARWIN: If I may, sir, I would like to begin with a story about the human race. Even as we speak, there are Confederate agents in Britain spreading pro-slavery propaganda, under the guise of science, about pluralist human species. In other words, they are trying to convince Brits that Blacks are a different species than whites. White slave masters consider their slaves to be subhuman, thus not entitled to even the basics of human dignity. However, it is my scientific conclusion—based on *real* science and research—that there is only one species of the human race, despite differences in skin color, facial features, and size. These are environmental factors, not characteristics of separate species. We all spring from a common ancestor, like branches of a tree from a central trunk.

LINCOLN: Charles, I can appreciate your scientific argument. It's why I wanted you to be here, but there are many other factors to consider in the question of slavery: politics, economics, and social welfare.

DARWIN: Yes, Mr. President—

LINCOLN: Please, Charles, call me Abraham.

DARWIN: Well, uh, Abraham—all these factors are still predicated on the belief that slaves are less than human. Even going back to your Constitution—a marvelous document of democracy—a slave is only counted as three-fifths of a person—in other words, less than human. I believe that Mr. Marx can best speak to the economic status of a slave. As for me, I am a naturalist, and my mind is ruled by what I can observe and touch and feel. And you gentlemen cannot honestly tell me that when Joseph and Estelle were slaves two years ago, they were in any way less human than you or me; and to follow the South's twisted logic, that they suddenly became *real* human beings at the moment they were emancipated. *(There is a nodding of heads and voiced agreement among the occupants of the parlor.)*

LINCOLN: Excellent point, Charles. I am so glad that you are here today.

DARWIN: Abraham, Charles, and Karl. It is an honor to sit with such an intelligent and thoughtful group of men. When I wrote *The Voyage of the Beagle* thirty years ago, I stated unequivocally, "I thank God, I shall never again visit a slave-country." I could act all *high and mighty* that England abolished slavery in 1833, but the whole truth is that the British government paid *millions* to slave owners to end it, but not one farthing to the slaves that suffered for centuries under this abomination. Following the slaves' supposed *freedom*, most of them were required to do long, unpaid apprenticeships. My grandchildren—should I be blessed enough to have some—will be paying off this government debt to slave owners for the rest of their lives.

So, I have come to America this week because I believe I have an opportunity to help right a terrible wrong. My family— going back to my grandfather Lord Wedgeworth—has been dedicated to ending slavery; indeed, this strong sentiment has been the air that I have breathed my entire life. I hope to not just convince you, Abraham, that slavery must be ended, but it must be ended in the *right* way. We cannot sit idly by and see families such as Joseph and Estelle's being torn apart by this terrible institution. Who knows if Joseph will ever see his father again?

(END OF ACT I)

***

While the president met with his guests in the parlor, Joseph and I helped Miss Estelle and Mrs. Carter clear the dining table and wash dishes in the kitchen. Though I had so much I wanted to talk with Joseph about, I knew it needed to wait until we had some time alone. For now, it was enough just to be with my friends—and what was now my family—on Christmas with a chance to laugh and relax in the kitchen. The threat of danger was still present, however. Every ten minutes like clockwork—I checked the old brass clock on the mantle of the kitchen fireplace—I would see Mr. Pinkerton's remaining guard, Paul, make his rounds at the rear of the house and around the stables. Each time he walked by, I could hear the horses stir. We had been able to put Quentin and Caddy in their stalls, but Luster and Benjy were still too skittish to go back into the smoke-infested stables; therefore, they stayed tied up to a rail in the rear yard. Although we had saved the stables as a whole from the fire, there remained a good bit of repair to be done at the damaged back-right corner of the building.

"Estelle," Mrs. Carter said as she dried a stack of wet plates on the counter, "I can't thank you enough for that delicious lunch. After all the interruptions during last night's dinner, I'm glad we all got to enjoy your cooking in peace. And that's really the way it ought to be on Christmas Day—*in peace.*"

"I can't believe," replied Miss Estelle, "that I just ate lunch with the President of the United States. Joseph, your father is not going to believe it when we tell him *this* story."

Joseph remained quiet as he conscientiously worked his way through drying the mountain of knives, forks, and spoons on the kitchen table.

"And he is going to be so proud," Joseph's mother continued cheerfully as she kept her eyes locked on her son, "when he hears how you two boys saved the horses and the stables."

We all turned around to the rear wall of the kitchen when the door opened. "I'm sorry to intrude," apologized Paul as he held his bowler hat in his hand, "but there's a gentleman in the rear yard that wants to speak with you, Mrs. Carter."

Mrs. Carter's eyes crinkled in puzzlement. "Do you know who it is?"

"He says his name is *Early,*" answered the detective. "I apologize because it *is your* inn, but if you don't mind, could you talk to him outside? I'm under orders to not allow anyone inside the inn while the president is having his meeting."

"No need to apologize, Paul. I understand completely," Mrs. Carter said. "After everything that's happened, I don't really want any extra people inside either." Paul doffed his hat to her in appreciation as she passed him walking out the door.

Miss Estelle had tried her best to be a subtle matchmaker for this couple, so she could just not help herself as she watched—and listened—out the rear kitchen window which had been left slightly open to help the smoke and the heat of the kitchen dissipate. Joseph and I eased over where we could surreptitiously peer through the foggy glass panes in the upper half of the door. Mrs. Carter walked down the steps of the rear porch and greeted Mr. Early, gently touching his arm as she spoke. I looked over at Miss Estelle as she unconsciously nodded her head.

We could only catch snippets of their conversation through the window: "So kind... been *so* busy... can't really discuss." Finally, Mrs. Carter turned and motioned to Joseph and me with her flittering hand, making it very clear that she knew that we had all been eavesdropping.

Miss Estelle, Joseph, and I all walked out the door, trying to act like we innocently did not know what was going on. "Good afternoon, Mr. Early," Miss Estelle said as we approached. "Merry Christmas!"

Mr. Early paused before awkwardly reciprocating, "Err... Merry... Christmas."

An odd look passed between Mrs. Carter and Miss Estelle. Using her considerable talents as a host, Mrs. Carter tried to smooth over the bumpiness of the current conversation. "For all these years," she began, "I've assumed that Mr. Early was a Methodist or an Episcopalian, like some of us churchgoing folk on the island, because he has delivered a fresh-cut fir tree to me every Christmas." As she said this, Mr. Early shyly looked down at his boots. "Well," she continued as she tried to make eye contact with her visitor, "it turns out that I had made a foolish assumption."

"Aww, Mrs. Carter," Mr. Early interrupted as he came to her defense. "Anyone would have thought the same thing…"

"That's kind of you, Mr. Early," she responded back, "but I should have asked you a long time ago. Anyway," she said as she turned to face Miss Estelle, Joseph, and me, "it turns out that Mr. Early is a Quaker—as many are on this island, and he has come to offer his help with the stables."

I began to understand Mr. Early's earlier awkwardness about Christmas as I thought back to a conversation I had had with my schoolmate Deborah at the beginning of the holiday season. When I had noticed decorations going up on streetlamps around the town, I asked Deborah if the Quaker Meeting House—our school—was usually decorated for Christmas.

"Quakers don't really single out Christmas as a holiday," she had explained. "We believe that *every* day is a holy day, so we like to think we treat every day like it is Christmas Day."

"It's not just me," said Mr. Early as I saw a flicker of disappointment pass across Mrs. Carter's eyes. "I let the Quaker elders know what happened last night, and there was unanimous agreement that we would like to help you with repairs. Even though we do not celebrate Christmas in the same way, *stables* have a very special meaning to all of us on Jesus' birthday."

* * *

Mrs. Carter motioned for Rifleman—*or Paul, I should say*—as he passed by, making his rounds. After she explained the situation privately to him, we heard him say, "I will need to check with Mr. Pinkerton on that, but I'm sure, regardless, that everyone would need to stay out of the house."

After Paul entered the door into the kitchen, Mr. Early suggested that we walk around to the front of the house where the Quaker elders were waiting. As we rounded the front corner, I could see Deborah and her parents standing alongside the elders that I had met with in the summer. They had brought a small mule-drawn wagon that was loaded with hay bales and planks of wooden siding. "Hey, John and Joseph! Merry Christmas!" Deborah called out as we approached. They were all dressed in work clothes, like it was any other day, while we were dressed for serving a holiday lunch.

"I hope we are not interrupting," said Mr. Hussey, "but when Travis told us about the fire last night, we could not think of a better way to spend Christmas Day than in service to a member of our community in need."

We heard the front door above us on the porch open, and Mr. Pinkerton, Paul, and Mrs. Blackwell stepped out. As they walked down the front steps to the gravel drive where everyone had gathered, a uniformed man on horseback sauntered up the drive from the street. "Good afternoon, Constable Clark," said Mr. Pinkerton guardedly. "To what do we owe this pleasure?"

"I heard about the excitement last night, Mr. Pinkerton," replied the jovial policeman, "and I just wanted to make sure that everything was okay at the inn."

"We're doing fine, thank you. Now..." Mr. Pinkerton reassured him dismissively.

"Mr. Pinkerton," interrupted Mrs. Hussey.

"And you are?" inquired Mr. Pinkerton as his right eyebrow arched.

"Elizabeth Hussey," she answered with a stiffening of her spine as if she had been challenged. "I'm one of the Quaker elders here in Nantucket. As well as helping with the repair of the stables, we were hoping…"

Her husband stepped forward and touched her forearm as he interjected, "Darling, I'm not sure this is—"

But his wife was not to be deterred from her mission. "As I was saying, we were hoping that we might have a word with…" She paused as if she suddenly doubted her own resolve. She quickly regained her footing, however, as her husband stepped back in line. "With the *president*, sir. We want to express our support for what he has done for this country. Our Quaker community has been torn during the war between abolitionists and supporters of non-violence. Those of us against slavery were hoping that President Lincoln would join us in a prayer."

Mr. Pinkerton let out a sigh of exasperation. "Constable Clark, I thought we had an agreement that all of this was to remain confidential."

"It was until last night," the policeman replied. "But…" Mr. Early's face suddenly turned as red as a beet.

"Without confirming *anything*," Mr. Pinkerton uttered with steely resolve, "*that* would not be possible."

"I'm afraid *that* cat is already out of the bag," said Mrs. Hussey. "We *know* that President Lincoln is at the inn. All we ask is a second of his time."

Mr. Pinkerton looked imploringly to Mrs. Blackwell for reinforcement. She complied, unequivocally saying, "I'm sorry, Mrs. Hussey, but Mr. Pinkerton is correct."

"And you are?" asked Mrs. Hussey with her own arched eyebrow.

Mrs. Carter tried to intervene to relieve the tension. "Elizabeth, I'm *so* sorry. I'm not being a very good hostess. Mr. and Mrs. Hussey, let me introduce you to Mrs. Elizabeth Blackwell, the president's ph—

Mrs. Blackwell raised her right hand as she abruptly silenced Mrs. Carter. "Secretary," she said loudly. "I repeat, without confirming anything, I am the president's secretary."

It was Mrs. Carter's turn to blush as she realized the grievous error she had almost made. With barely a pause in motion, Mrs. Blackwell took Mrs. Hussey's hand in hers in an introductory shake. "One *Elizabeth* to another," she smiled, "I'm hoping we can have a private word together." She led her off to the side in an act that did seem to defuse the situation.

With another available watchful eye in Constable Clark, Mr. Pinkerton allowed the group to move to the rear of the house to work on repairing the damaged back corner of the stables. The constable stayed at the rear while Paul continued his rounds about the inn. Mr. Pinkerton had a whispered word with Mrs. Blackwell after her animated discussion with Mrs. Hussey, and he walked back up to the porch and disappeared inside.

"I need to work off some of that holiday feast," Mrs. Blackwell announced as she rolled up her sleeves and joined the others in their Christmas community service.

Soon, the rear yard echoed with the *buzz* of handsaws and the *rat-tat-tat* of hammer hitting nail. Charred pieces of siding from the rear wall of the stables were pulled off and replaced with new planks. The hay bales that had caught fire and still reeked of smoke were removed and replaced with fresh bales. As everyone worked, stories of past Christmases and past traditions were swapped back and forth. "I'm all for treating every day like Christmas," Joseph said as we admired our work. By the time Miss Estelle brought out pitchers of spiced cider, the gulf between the Quakers and the rest of us had narrowed significantly.

Chapter 26

ACT II: *After a brief period of small talk about family and friends, the room again grows quiet except for the crackling of the fire and sporadic, faint banging coming from the rear yard.*

LINCOLN: Thank you, Charles, for your eloquent discussion. Who wishes to proceed? *(After a short silence, Karl Marx softly clears his throat and sits forward on the sofa.)* Karl, please go ahead. And don't mind the banging out back. Allan swears that no one is shooting at us. *(The president smiles.)* He told me that some of the neighbors in town have come out to help repair the stables. I wish more of our fractured nation shared the spirit of community that inhabits this island.

MARX: Thank you, sir. I want to second Charles's statement. I am very honored to be here with you. Though I have not always agreed with everything each of you has done or written, I have only the highest respect for everyone in this room.

LINCOLN: Thank you, Karl. I can assure you that I have not agreed with everything *you* have written. *(All the men laugh, including Karl Marx.)* But if I had just wanted people to agree with me, I would have had another cabinet meeting. Karl, I want you to speak straight. Tell us what you believe.

MARX: As I was talking to Estelle and Joseph yesterday, I confided to them that I felt I had spent half my life sitting in the British Museum reading about economics. To me, slavery—as wrong as I believe it to be—has always been just an economic category. Slavery, like different machines such as the cotton gin, was just a natural development in the cycle of capitalism. Things that seemed so clear to me sitting at that table at the museum surrounded by books don't seem so clear right now.

LINCOLN: In what way, Karl?

MARX: Years ago, Mr. Horace Greeley hired me to be a European correspondent for his *New York Herald Tribune.* My comrade Frederick Engels and I have written many articles about America, slavery, and most recently about your Civil War. It was not particularly difficult because it is easy to keep your objectivity from a distance. However, actually being here in America makes it not so easy. Again, I have always viewed slavery as an economic issue, and its abolition is a necessary first step towards workers gaining control of their own destiny.

LINCOLN: Karl, you and I share a friend in Horace Greeley as well as his partner at the *Tribune,* Charles Dana. I have eagerly followed your writings in the *Tribune,* and I hope you don't mind, but I borrowed some of your ideas for my first "annual message" to Congress.

MARX: I'm flattered, Abraham. Which ideas were those?

LINCOLN: In fact, I brought a copy of that message with me. *(President Lincoln shuffles through some papers before locating a particular one. He dons his reading glasses as he recites aloud.)* "Labor is prior to and independent of capital. Capital is only the fruit of labor and could never have existed if labor had not first existed. Labor is the superior of capital and deserves much the higher consideration." Does that ring a bell?

MARX: Of course. I was telling my colleague Engels just last year that the two biggest things happening in the world were, on the one hand, the movement of the slaves in America started by the death of John Brown, and on the other, the movement of the serfs in Russia. Caught in the middle of these two struggles are the workers in England that I see every day.

DICKENS: Pardon my interruption, Karl, but this is an issue in which we have much in common. I know that each of us has written in our own way about the social problems we see in England. Two of my most popular books, *Oliver Twist* and *David Copperfield*, focus on the growing divide between the wealthy and the poor in England. I believe that my readers— in England and around the world, if you will indulge my brief pomposity—enjoy my books because they see their own social struggles in my words. Do you see the same in America?

MARX: Even worse, Charles. There exists here a competition between Northern workers and Southern slaves which undermines the chances of prosperity for both, and this spills over to textile workers in England. It is only when there is a common interest between these three groups that real change will come. That is why I am so appreciative of your efforts, Mr. President, to inform the British workers and the unions through your letters which appear in our newspapers.

LINCOLN: Do you think my letters are having a positive effect on the image of our Union in England?

MARX: Yes, sir, but it is an uphill struggle. The Confederates may be winning the propaganda war with the British press right now. The British textile industry is so dependent on cheap Southern cotton, that its leaders act as if the Union started the Civil War, rather than the Confederates firing on Fort Sumter. British industrialists believe that without slavery you have no cotton. In the past, I have seen slavery as a necessary evil on the way to a classless society, but now I just see it as evil.

LINCOLN: Why have your attitudes changed being here?

MARX: Because my theoretical concepts about slavery now have a face and a name and a history. I see a boy and his mother who have lost their father and husband through an evil institution that destroys families and degrades human beings. In a recent article, Mr. President, I called you "the single-minded son of the working class," and I firmly believe that you are the person to lead your country and the world into a new era of civilization. However, the first step must be the abolition of slavery in America, and if it takes a war to do that—so be it.

(END OF ACT II)

* * *

With everyone working shoulder to shoulder, the repairs were finished by mid-afternoon. Mrs. Carter sent Mr. Early and the other Quakers home with grateful holiday hugs and tasty leftovers from Miss Estelle's lunch. While Mrs. Blackwell and Miss Estelle finished putting up the dishes and silverware. Mrs. Carter flitted back and forth between the kitchen and the dining room, trying to eavesdrop on the meeting in the parlor. One time, when the door swung open as she returned, I could see Mr. Pinkerton pacing in the front hall. There was a sense of nervous readiness in the way he moved, like he knew something was going to happen. As I looked out back, I could see the guard coming around from behind the stables. Mrs. Blackwell yawned loudly as she said, "Mrs. Carter, you have been a most gracious host, but I think I need to retire upstairs now for some rest."

"Of course, Elizabeth," said Mrs. Carter. "I need to go upstairs as well and check on our guests' rooms." After a look from his mother, Joseph held the door open for the two women, and he accompanied Mrs. Carter upstairs.

Miss Estelle began preparing a fresh pot of coffee. She said, "John, please go get me some firewood. The fire's getting a little low." I went out the back door, looking at the clock as I walked by. It was time for the guard to make his round. I scanned the rear yard and the stables as I gathered the firewood in my arms, but I saw no sign of Paul. As I returned to the kitchen and put the wood into the stove, Joseph's mother and I both heard Mrs. Carter's silver bell ring from the parlor. "Go check on the president," said Miss Estelle. "They're probably ready for some fresh coffee. I need to get some water from the well." As she walked out the door with bucket in hand, I could hear the horses rustle.

I glimpsed Mr. Pinkerton exiting the front door as I entered the hallway. I peeked around the corner into the parlor, drawing President Lincoln's attention. "John, we would like some more coffee. And Mr. Marx was hoping there might be some of Miss Estelle's apple pie left over from last night." Mr. Marx nodded, looking slightly embarrassed.

"I will be right back, sir. I do believe we have some pie left." I returned to the kitchen, but Joseph's mother wasn't there. "Miss Estelle?" I called out. I looked out the back door but did not see her. I walked down the porch stairs and looked towards the well. *My heart stopped.*

Jack Burton—still wearing his bowler hat—stood behind Miss Estelle with his hand in his pocket pushing into her side. Joseph's words echoed in my brain: *You're not going to like this... It was a gun shop.* "Okay, kid, this is what we're gonna do, and no one gets hurt," Jack Burton said. He wrenched Miss Estelle's arm behind her back when she tried to speak.

"We're all gonna walk slowly to the stables right now," Jack Burton said as he began backing away from the well while gripping Joseph's mother. The rear yard was now blanketed with white snow, and our footsteps fell silently as we slowly moved towards the stables. As we got near the giant elm, I could see a flash of red on the far side of the trunk. Two more steps and I could see that it was Paul sitting with his back against the base of the tree, his arms tied around the trunk and a piece of a red scarf stuffed in his mouth to keep him quiet. "See, John?" said Jack Burton. "It's just us out here now. Nobody to save you."

As Jack Burton and Joseph's mother passed under the tree, I saw another glimpse of red—no, orange—flash across my vision up in the tree. I was too scared to look up. I kept my eyes locked on Miss Estelle's face. She looked so calm, even as Jack Burton continued to force her arm behind her back. In the time it took me to blink, the flash of orange fell straight from the tree, striking Jack Burton a glancing blow on his back and shoulder. *Boom!* His gun fired down into the snow as he fell. Joseph lay beside him in a drift, trying to get back to his feet after jumping from the tree—his fannah basket with its bright-orange straps slung over his shoulder like a quiver. Jack Burton stood shakily and tried to pull the gun out, but his coat pocket was on fire from the gunshot. He screamed in pain as he threw the red-hot gun down into the snow.

Just as he was bending down to pick it up, Miss Estelle recovered from the shock of Joseph's jump and began a long swing upward with the bucket in her hand. In what seemed like slow motion, I watched as the bucket began its arc upward towards Jack Burton's face. *Wham!* A metallic ring shattered the snowy silence as the bucket caught him under the chin. All I could see next was the bottom of his black boots as he sailed backwards into the snow.

Unbelievably, as he landed on his back, he continued in a backwards roll ending up on his feet again. His eyes looked glazed as he struggled to gain his bearings. He staggered across the side yard to where the horses stood. He untied Benjy's reins from the rail and threw himself over the top of the horse. They started galloping down the drive. I looked at Joseph and his mother as I sprinted to the stables. "No, John!" she cried. "This has nothing to do with us!"

After making sure his mother was not hurt, Joseph started towards the front of the house to look for help. He almost collided with Mr. Pinkerton as he rounded the corner of the front porch. "Is anyone hurt?" I heard Mr. Pinkerton yell as I untied the reins of my favorite horse, Quentin. I jumped on and began trotting down the gravel drive. Before I picked up any speed, however, I felt Quentin twist and dip. Joseph magically appeared in front of me after jumping off the front porch onto the horse's back. His bow and arrows poked out of the fannah basket on his back.

Miss Estelle screamed, "No, Joseph!" but it was too late. *Together*—a bareback-riding tandem team—we took off after Jack Burton who was now far ahead. *We can't wait for anyone else to help!* I dug my heels into Quentin's side while wrapping my arms around Joseph's waist. It was easy to follow Jack

Burton's trail, however, as his horse's hoofprints were the only disturbances in the fresh snow. As we turned onto North Water Street, I could see him heading towards the harbor. The last time I looked at the brass clock in the kitchen it had been ten minutes to four. *He's trying to make the ferry,* I thought as the chase began.

* * *

Joseph leaned forward into the horse's neck, riding just like his father taught him, while I clung to him for dear life. As we got closer, I could see Jack Burton look back at us. At first, I thought he had pulled another red scarf over his face, but I realized that it was a sheet of blood pouring from the wound in his chin that had been delivered by Miss Estelle's bucket. As the ground raced by beneath me, I could see Jack Burton's trail flecked with bright red.

We were within a few lengths of him as we turned onto Broad Street with its long, flat straightaway ending at the ferry dock. Looking at Burton, I could see his pocket still smoking from the gunshot, and I thought of Joseph's dream: *The jockey on the second-place horse wore a black bowler hat and a bright-red jersey. As they passed us, I could see smoke coming from the jockey's back.* Quentin was deep into her long, natural stride. She liked racing Benjy, so we had to do little more than hang on. We were just about even with Benjy's tail when I heard the ferry bell start to ring up ahead. Jack Burton started striking Benjy's side violently with his flat, bare hand in a final push to stay ahead. As we pulled even, he lashed out with his boot catching me right above the knee. A searing pain shot up my leg, and I almost fell off.

The streets of Nantucket seemed to be empty now as we raced for the ferry. After the kick, Jack Burton pulled ahead. He skidded as he jerked back on the reins, leapt off the still-sliding Benjy, and ran to the ferry ramp. Joseph and I stayed on Quentin, and we jumped up onto the boardwalk cutting Jack Burton off before he could reach the ticket window. I had no idea what we were going to do—I just knew we had to stop him from getting on the ferry. I jumped down from Quentin, but my leg buckled where he had kicked me, and I hit the ground hard.

As I lay helpless, Jack Burton, now without his gun, grabbed a gas lantern from a post by the boardwalk and heaved it at Quentin and Joseph. The lantern shattered as it hit the hard planks, and flames erupted at the feet of the panicked horse. Quentin reared up on her hind legs, but one of her hooves hit a slick spot in the snow, and the horse toppled heavily, trapping Joseph beneath. I felt rough hands grab me by the collar, and Jack Burton began dragging me towards the water. He hissed under his breath, "No one even cares what I do with you, kid. You're just a worthless little runaway who's gonna drown on Christmas Day."

I tried to scream, but he backhanded me across the mouth. As he dragged me along the ground, images flashed by like I had fallen through the ice of a frozen lake, and I was being carried along by the current. There seemed to be a barrier between me and the world around me—as if I could see everything, but no one could see me. I looked up the ramp and people were starting to get off the ferry, but no one seemed to see what was happening. The ferry master looked on—doing nothing—as I neared the edge of the pier. "Stop!" I tried to yell, but I just tasted blood as a weak cry escaped my lips.

"That's right, kid. Nobody cares. You've gotten in my way one too many times today." I tried to grab on to the base of a lamppost as I slid closer and closer to the side of the pier, but it was icy and slick, and I lost my grip. As Jack Burton pulled my body over the edge, I locked my legs around the lamppost. He held my collar leaving my torso dangling into the dark void.

I looked over his shoulder and saw movement behind him. Quentin appeared, sidling closer to us with careful lateral steps. Jack Burton looked back and sneered, "Ya think the horse is going to save you now?"

Quentin began a slow rotation, and I saw a hand clutching her mane from the side hidden from us. Two more circular steps, and I could see Joseph hanging off her with his feet held up into the air. *He really did learn all of his father's riding tricks,* I thought as Joseph let go of her mane and dropped silently into the snow.

"I'm going to throw you into the water," Jack Burton hissed, "unless you tell me everything you know about us." He loosened his hold on my collar causing me to drop further over the edge. Looking under Jack Burton's arm, I watched Joseph reach over his shoulder and draw an arrow out of his fannah basket. He nocked the arrow and raised the bow into shooting position.

The ferry bell began ringing again. "Nevermind, kid. No time." Jack Burton said. "I gotta get on that ferry." I looked up into death's face just before he let go of me. As I was tumbling off, I saw the point of the arrow punch out under Jack Burton's collarbone. I fell through the air and waited for the water… the cold… the darkness. Instead, I landed on something hard and flat that knocked the air out of my lungs.

I had dropped into the bottom of a small wooden fishing boat tied up to the pier. I lay there stunned, unable to move as I gasped for breath. In a haunting echo of my fall, I looked up to the pier and saw Joseph dangling over the edge. The now one-armed Jack Burton held onto the scruff of Joseph's neck. In a moonlit silhouette, the arrow poking out of Jack Burton's back looked like a new sinister appendage. Joseph's arms and legs were flailing in the air like a discarded rag doll buffeted by the wind. He dropped…

I'm sure I was delirious from hitting my head on the floor of the boat, but my first thought was back to that morning when Joseph was talking to Mr. Darwin on the front porch of the inn: *Sometimes I dream that I am flying myself.*

Joseph hit the water hard beside the boat. My disjointed thoughts shifted to Joseph's confession to Mr. Herman: *I can't swim.*

The fogginess left my head instantly, as my most basic instincts kicked in, telling me I needed to act. *Joseph's going to drown.*

I thrashed around in the bottom of the boat, latching my hand onto a paddle. I lifted it over the gunnel of the boat to where Joseph's splash still reverberated. Moving the blade of the paddle in ever-larger circles, I felt a tug like I had when I had lowered the sounding line into the tunnel. In the moonlight glow of the water, I could see Joseph's hand latched onto the end of the paddle. For the second time in our brief history together, our hands reached through the darkness and locked.

Chapter 27

ACT III: *Mrs. Carter brings in a fresh pot of coffee. President Lincoln thanks her as he stands to stretch his long legs, then sits and motions to Mr. Dickens.*

DICKENS: Charles, Karl, and Abraham. I am not a scientist or an economist. I am a writer, a compulsive note-taker (*he scribbles in a journal in his lap*), and a not-very-successful newspaperman. Regardless of my own ineptitude, Karl, I also always found your *Herald Tribune* articles to be well written and well-conceived.

DARWIN: As did I, Karl.

DICKENS: But unlike Karl and Charles, this is not my first trip to America. I sailed to America twenty years ago on the steamship *Brittania*—a trip that I thought would be the last I would see of this earth. Our voyage was so violent that all my wife and I could do most of the time was huddle at one end of a sofa in our cabin and drink thimblefuls of brandy. It's a wonder I can remember any of it.

MARX: That sounds much like our voyage this week.

DICKENS: Yes, Karl, but this week I was drinking out of choice and not necessity.

MARX: There's a difference? (*Everyone laughs heartily.*)

DICKENS: My previous trip to America had wonderful

things which I remember fondly to this day, and many other things which I would like to forget. I met my poor friend Henry Longfellow on this trip, and he showed me both the highlights of Boston, such as the house where George Washington was quartered during the Revolutionary War, as well as the seedy waterfront areas of Boston. Henry came to visit me in London later that year, and I returned the favor, showing him some of London's most illustrious slums. Evidently, it's the social downtrodden that attracts writers like us.

I shall never forget my visit to Baltimore prior to our railroad trip out west to St. Louis. I happened to run into Washington Irving at the railroad station as he was preparing to leave the country. We had a most pleasant chat about a variety of things, and I told him how much I enjoyed his tales of Old English Christmas traditions. Some of my friends have suggested I must have had this meeting in mind when I wrote *A Christmas Carol*, but whoever knows where inspiration comes? Later, I returned to my hotel to find an odd little man with a black mustache waiting for me in the lobby with a book in his hand. It was a book of his poetry which was just published here, and he wanted my help in getting it published in England. I was unsuccessful, and I had forgotten about him until several years later when I saw his new poem "The Raven" had been published to much acclaim. I never got to meet with Edgar Allan Poe again, and I regret that very much. But I digress too long.

During my trip to America in 1842, I toured New York, Philadelphia, and Washington, giving readings from my books and lectures against slavery. Both were well received in these Northern cities, but I did not feel I could really understand slavery without witnessing it firsthand. So, I traveled to Richmond, Virginia, which was in most regards a truly beautiful city. However, I was absolutely appalled by both the physical treatment of the slaves that I could see on the city streets as well as the cruel and condescending attitudes which the white Richmond citizens had towards the Black people, both slaves and freedmen. I returned home to England with such profound disgust that I sat down in my study for two solid weeks and immediately wrote a book of my experiences entitled *American Notes.*

DARWIN: One of your finest writings, Charles.

DICKENS: Thank you so much, but as a portrait of Black people's plight in America, it pales in comparison to the *Narrative of the Life of Frederick Douglass, An American Slave.* The beauty and the savagery of Mr. Douglass's writing never fails to reduce me to tears.

LINCOLN: Charles, it's funny that you've brought up Frederick Douglass. He is a friend of mine, though oddly enough, we haven't met in person yet. We exchange frequent letters, and I honor his advice, though he is sometimes very critical of me. He was supposed to join us today in our meeting, but something came up, and he had to cancel. Now, Charles, you were saying...

DICKENS: Yes, in my *American Notes,* I ended the chapter called "Slavery" with a catalogue of atrocities which I had heard were inflicted upon supposed runaway slaves by their white masters. This included brandings, amputations, whippings, and broken bones. This was *not* the America that immigrants risked their lives coming to, trying to escape persecution in Europe. This was *not* the America that was founded on the "self-evident truths" of the Declaration of

Independence. Now, twenty years later, this indefensible institution of slavery has torn your country apart. Abraham, it is your unenviable task to put this fractured nation back together again, but keeping slavery cannot be the solution. For all the obvious reasons: political, economic, scientific, and just common decency, slaves must be freed and recognized as equal human beings, just like you and me. Your plan to reunite this country must end slavery, where families such as Joseph and Estelle's that have been torn apart can be brought back together again—for good.

DARWIN AND MARX *(in unison):* Hear! Hear! Mr. President.

LINCOLN: I have heard you. Thank you all, gentlemen. You have provided my brain with ample food for thought. *(President Lincoln stands, arches his back, and unsubtly rubs his belly.)* Now, I want to see what Miss Estelle has to offer my soul.

(END OF ACT III)

* * *

I pulled Joseph into the boat, but it listed violently to one side as Jack Burton pounced, shoving Joseph down hard. I could hear Joseph's head hit the bottom of the boat with a sickening *thump*. Burton dropped on top of me with all his weight. I tried to fight back, but my hands were tangled up in a fishing net lying in a wad around me that smelled of rotting fish, oil, and old wet rope.

Burton sneered at the dazed Joseph who lay beside me: "You did me a favor there, kid. Now nobody's gonna see what happens to either of you." For a second time, I looked into the face of the man who was stealing my life. The bloody gash on his chin where Miss Estelle had hit him with the bucket had dried, and he looked like some monster with two mouths. His face was scarlet red, and his dark eyes narrowed under the brim of the bowler hat to cold, black slits as he exerted himself even more on top of me. He put his hands on my throat and started to squeeze. I looked up at the moon past his evil face, and I had a last sad, doomed thought: *Joseph's mother was right. We jump into things without thinking. Now... it has killed me.*

The boat rocked again as Joseph stirred beside me whispering deliriously, *Daddy?* The grip loosened on my throat as I looked up and saw strong fingers wrapped around Jack Burton's neck. His face went from scarlet to purple as his eyes rolled back into his head. He crumpled off of me and went over the side of the boat into the water.

"Is it really you?" Joseph asked weakly as he tried to sit up. A small Black man kneeled down next to Joseph in the bottom of the boat and hugged him hard.

"I told you I would come home to you and your mamma."

He gently helped untangle my arms from the fishing net as he held his son's bleeding head propped in the crook of his arm. Joseph reached up to touch his father's cheek to be sure he wasn't dreaming—or worse. He looked over at me and said, "John, this is my father. Daddy, this is my best friend, John. He's now saved my life twice."

Joseph's father reached out to shake my hand but thought twice about it; instead, he wrapped me up in a big hug with his free arm. "Thank you, John. My name is Nathan."

"Joseph saved my life in Mississippi," I replied. Then I pictured the arrowhead popping through Jack Burton's shirt. "And today. We've wiped that slate clean." I looked into the kind face of Joseph's father as he released me from his hug: "But now you've saved both of our lives."

"Our slates are clean," smiled Nathan as he squeezed us. "This is what fathers are supposed to do." *Some fathers.*

"How did you see us?" Joseph asked.

"It was your hair, Joseph—your mamma's *shadow of a dandelion.* When I watched that vermin drop John off the pier, I saw your hair in the moonlight as you charged at him. Even though it's been two long years, I knew it was you. My heart stopped when he dropped you."

He helped me stand just as Mr. Pinkerton ran onto the pier with his gun drawn. "Boys, are y'all all right?" Mr. Pinkerton yelled as he looked down at us in the boat. "Who is this man?"

Joseph looked up again to make sure he wasn't dreaming. He wasn't. "This is my daddy."

His father nodded at the startled Mr. Pinkerton and said, "Glad to meet you, sir. My name is Nathan. You better pull that man out of the water before he drowns."

Jack Burton thrashed around in the icy water trying to stay afloat. "Yeah," said Mr. Pinkerton, "we've got other plans for him." He and a couple of men from the ferry roughly fished Jack Burton out of the water and handcuffed him shivering to a light post.

A tall, distinguished-looking Black man leaned over the edge of the pier and helped pull Joseph and his father out of the boat. "Boys," said Joseph's father, "I want you to meet a new friend of mine who helped me to get home to you. This is Mr. Frederick Douglass. Mr. Douglass, this is my son Joseph and his best friend John."

"Joseph, I feel like I already know you," said Mr. Douglass as he shook his hand.

Joseph's father looked his son in the eye standing beside him and laughed out loud. "Joseph, you're as tall as I am! You've up and become a man while I've been gone!"

After Jack Burton was taken away to the Nantucket jail by Constable Clark, who had just arrived on his horse, Mr. Pinkerton walked back over to us. He was surprised yet again. "Mr. Douglass? The president thought you weren't coming."

"I wasn't," said Mr. Douglass. "But I have a new friend whose story I wanted President Lincoln to hear." He smiled. "And I think this humdinger of a story just got better."

"President Lincoln knows nothing about what's happened this afternoon, and I want it to stay that way until after he has finished his meeting," Mr. Pinkerton warned all of us. "My other man, Paul, was a little shaken up, but I left him patrolling around the inn until I get back." Mr. Pinkerton had ridden Caddy from the inn, and she was tied up in front of the ferry office. He pointed to her and said, "Mr. Douglass, would you like to ride back with me?"

"Yes, of course, Mr. Pinkerton. But how will my friends get back?"

I looked up Broad Street and saw Benjy standing in front of the telegraph office, chewing on a Christmas tree. Miraculously, Quentin was not hurt in her fall and stood beside Benjy.

"We'll be fine, Mr. Douglass," I said as I pointed to the horses. "There's our ride home."

Joseph and Nathan rode together on Benjy. Joseph sat with his arms wrapped around his father's shoulders as Nathan's strong fingers gently held the reins. "I dreamed about you last night," Joseph said. "You won a race, and it gave you the money to buy your own freedom. Is that how it happened?"

We rode slowly as he started to tell us about his long journey from Jackson to Nantucket. "Not exactly, Joseph. The only blessing I felt after you and your mamma left was knowing that you really did make it out just in time. After the war started, things got so bad on the farm that I didn't think I would live long enough to buy my freedom. The Mississippi militia took all of Mr. Rossiter's horses for the army, so we had no way to harvest our crops or take them to market. The crops we had planted just rotted in the field. All us slaves had to eat was what we could grow ourselves in secret, but the soldiers usually found it and stole it from us. And without the horses, I lost my chance to win enough races to buy my own freedom."

"Mr. Rossiter was so desperate for money," Nathan continued, "that he rented out all his slaves to the Mobile and Ohio Railroad that was building a line north, just east of Jackson. It's a long story that I will wait and share with you and your mamma, but the short of it is that I worked on and rode a lot of railroads over the past year to get here."

Joseph and I took turns telling his father the story of our last three days: the visit from the men in the bowler hats two days ago, the late-night arrival of the president, yesterday's Christmas Eve dinner, the fire in the stables, and today. As we walked up the drive to the rear yard and the stables, I felt exhausted. Today seemed to be the day I would die; however, I didn't. *And from now on—until the day I do die—I will never forget the look of pure, shining joy that came over Miss Estelle's face when Joseph led his father into the back door of the kitchen.*

* * *

After Joseph's father had been introduced to Mrs. Carter—who immediately offered him a job at the inn—and he was safely ensconced at the kitchen table. With his left hand wrapped in Miss Estelle's and his right hand holding a soup spoon for his steaming hot clam chowder, he resumed the narrative of *his* incredible odyssey.

"We had worked our way north laying track up to Corinth where the Mobile and Ohio intersected with the Memphis and Charleston Railroad. The rebels were pushing us like dogs to lay track so they could supply their troops in Tennessee, but in April of this year, they got routed at Shiloh by Grant and retreated all their troops to Corinth. From then on, the Union controlled the railroad to the North."

He paused his story as Miss Estelle brought him a cup of cider, and Mrs. Carter checked on the meeting in the parlor. "Mr. Douglass has joined them in there," she informed us.

Joseph's father continued, "A small Confederate general who talked real funny and had dark skin and a black beard told all the slaves that were working on the railroad that we were free to do whatever we had to do to survive."

My ears perked up with his description. I asked, "Do you remember his name?"

"Yeah," Nathan answered. "It was *Bo-re-gard*, or something like that. He may have said we were free, but they didn't give us any freedom papers. Before long, it felt like we were just slaves again with different masters when we worked on the same railroad lines for the Union Army. I got pretty good at hopping railroad cars in the dark of night, and I made it up to Salem, Ohio, where I was given the name of a white family that hid and helped out runaway slaves in the basement of their house."

"From there I made it to Baltimore on a different kind of railroad. It was called the *Underground Railroad*."

"One of the other men that I traveled with to Baltimore had heard of a woman named Moses who helped runaway slaves. We hid out in a boarding house in Baltimore until Moses showed up about three weeks ago. It turns out her real name is Harriet—Harriet Tubman, and she helped us get to Boston where I met Mr. Douglass. That was three days ago."

"We know Harriet Tubman!" Joseph and I cried out together.

"Well," Nathan said, "I owe Moses and Mr. Douglass my life."

Just as quickly as the nor'easter had blown into Nantucket that Christmas morning with its snow and frigid gales, the winds shifted in the late afternoon bringing warm, balmy breezes from the south. As the stories of the strange occurrences at the ferry dock spread across the island, the residents of Nantucket began to learn of the Christmas meeting at the Carter House Inn. Mr. and Mrs. Lester, owners of a tapestry shop on Broad Street, walked up to the inn with a basket of flowers and a note to the president. Mr. Pinkerton intercepted them in the front yard, but they cheerfully told him they did not want to disturb the president, but could they "please just leave the flowers on the front porch?" Just as they were leaving, Dr. Brown and his wife Matilda brought a bushel of corn and quietly laid it on the front porch by the flowers. Within the hour, the steady illuminated parade of residents carrying candles of hope had left buckets of clams, oysters, and shrimp; and baskets of bread, ham, and potatoes— each accompanied by a thank you note or a letter of support and holiday wishes to the president.

At five o'clock that afternoon, President Lincoln rang the bell and announced to Mrs. Carter that he and his guests were "done for the day and tired of being cooped up in the house." She led the president out to the front porch to show him all the gifts that had been left. After an afternoon full of talking and listening—he was truly speechless. Mrs. Carter took Joseph's mother out to the porch. "I know it's short notice, Estelle, but what can you do with all this?"

Miss Estelle's eyes—already glowing from her husband's return—lit up even brighter. "Why, Mrs. Carter, haven't you ever heard of a Lowcountry boil?" When Nathan came back to the kitchen wearing a clean pair of Joseph's overalls, Mrs. Carter got us to load up the wagon with the food, firewood, blankets, pots, and dishes. I sat in the back with the supplies while Joseph rode between his mamma and daddy, and they drove the wagon to Jetties Beach. Nathan and I built a huge bonfire while Miss Estelle and Joseph prepared the large pot for the boil.

Just as the moon re-emerged from behind the clouds, the president's carriage drew up to the beach with President Lincoln and his guests. All formalities were dropped as Joseph chased birds up and down the beach with Mr. Darwin. As the fire shot flickering sparks up into the dark sky, Mr. Dickens, Mr. Marx, and Mrs. Blackwell could be heard trading verses to an Old English Christmas hymn as a bottle was passed around. Joseph's father hung back shyly tending the fire until Mrs. Carter and Mr. Douglass came up to him. "Nathan, it's time you met the president," announced Mr. Douglass.

President Lincoln stood back from the fire in the darkness, watching the activity swirl around him. He stepped forward into the light of the fire as he shook Nathan's hand. The president looked like a different man than the person I had met in the dining room just yesterday. He stood tall, and there was a relaxed posture to his shoulders as if he had regained a purpose. His eyes were bright, and there was a genuine smile on his face as he talked to Joseph's father: "Nathan, Frederick has told me about your journey from the South to rejoin your family."

The president put his arm around Nathan's shoulders and guided him away to the far side of the fire. As they talked, Nathan became less guarded and began to gesture with his hands like Joseph had described by the campfire the night we met. At one point, Nathan bent over at the waist with his hands holding imaginary reins in front of him. They were talking about horses.

Epilogue: Nantucket (December 26, 1862-January 31,1863)

The next day, we all gathered in the rear yard to say goodbye to the president and his guests before they climbed into the carriage. As we had done before lunch the day before, we formed a big circle and took each other's hands. The guests—Charles Dickens, Charles Darwin, and Karl Marx—again dressed in their traveling clothes, stood side-by-side comfortably clasping each other's hands. Mrs. Blackwell and Mr. Pinkerton flanked the president protectively. Joseph's mother guided her son's left hand into hers. Joseph again lifted his right hand into the air expectantly and, this time, felt it grasped by his father's warm, calloused hand.

President Lincoln spoke to us: "This Christmas meeting with our extraordinary guests has brought a clarity to my mind that I haven't known in ages. I do not know what all lies ahead for our nation, but I do know this: *We will continue to fight for what is right.* And I can promise this to you and your family," President Lincoln said as he turned and looked down at Joseph with kind but determined eyes, "This time next week, Joseph, your father is going to be a free man."

* * *

Excerpt from the prologue of the 1898 best-selling cookbook *Recipes for Food and Freedom* by Joseph Freeman:

On January 1, 1863, President Abraham Lincoln signed the Emancipation Proclamation freeing the slaves in the ten Confederate states not already under Federal control, including Mississippi. A new year and a new life had begun. My dream—and my daddy's dream—had come true... Freedom.

* * *

Excerpt from John's new journal (a Christmas gift from Joseph) dated January 31, 1863:

Mr. Douglass visited the inn again today and brought a note from Mrs. Tubman to Joseph and me. The note read, "The President's Emancipation Proclamation is a good—but incomplete—step. At this point, it's just words on a page without any real enforcement. You boys want to head back South with me? I'm leading a band of scouts down to the Combahee River, and I could use your help. We have some Gullahs to save."

Can't wait.